A JEWEL IN THE CROWN

A JEWEL IN THE CROWN

DAVID LEWIS

JOHN SCOGNAMIGLIO BOOKS
KENSINGTON PUBLISHING CORP.
www.kensingtonbooks.com

KENSINGTON BOOKS are published by

Kensington Publishing Corp.
900 Third Ave.
New York, NY 10022

All Kensington titles, imprints and distributed lines are available at special quantity discounts for bulk purchases for sales promotion, premiums, fund-raising, educational or institutional use. Special book excerpts or customized printings can also be created to fit specific needs. For details, write or phone the office of the Kensington Special Sales Manager: Kensington Publishing Corp., 900 Third Ave., New York, NY, 10022. Attn. Special Sales Department. Phone: 1-800-221-2647.

The JS and John Scognamiglio Books logo is a trademark of Kensington Publishing Corp.

Library of Congress Control Number: 2024934897

ISBN: 978-1-4967-4909-3

First Kensington Hardcover Edition: August 2024

ISBN: 978-1-4967-4911-6 (ebook)

10 9 8 7 6 5 4 3 2 1

Printed in the United States of America

For Gwen & Stan

ACKNOWLEDGMENTS

First, my gratitude to the friends who encouraged me for so long. Without their support there would be no book: John Callas, Vince Cefalu, Don Potter, and Jake Warga. Next, my agent, the tireless Marlene Stringer, aka M, who heard me banging on the door and opened it, if only to stop the noise. And finally, Kensington Publishing's editor, John Scognamiglio, whose patient guidance was invaluable.

1

London, 1939. Police Constable Caitrin Colline did not like walking the beat along Ryers Road on Friday nights, and neither did her partner, Florence Simmonds. Florence, with her shambling gait and apologetic face, was a worrier by nature and would perhaps have been much happier as an undertaker than a policewoman. Apart from her unease at being on Ryers Road, Florence was concerned because Hannah, her Czechoslovakian pen pal, had recently stopped writing. Months earlier, Magrit, her pen pal in Vienna, had stopped writing too. Magrit's last word was *Anschluss*. Florence did not understand German—they usually wrote in English—and only learned what *Anschluss* meant when she read about the Nazi annexation of Austria in the *Daily Mail*. It did not sound good.

Ryers Road, like all the other slum streets in London's Docklands, was narrow, with rows of pinched houses on either side. There was no color, even on the brightest of days, and sanitation was rudimentary. Smoke from innumerable coal fires made the air sulfurous, and soot coated the walls and windows. The street gaslights cast disheartening, bilious puddles on the pavement that only made the shadows deeper.

Each house, with two rooms up and two down, was just big enough for a small family, as long as no one tried to be expressive or gained too much weight. There were few fat people on Ryers Road, and how the fecund Irish with their restless, swelling broods managed to fit into such confined spaces was a refutation of the laws of physics.

Only poor people lived on Ryers Road, along with their poor diseases and stunted horizons. And although Caitrin was not as uneasy as her partner, Florence, about being there, it was still not the best place for a woman, even a policewoman, to be, especially on a Friday night.

A rat skittering toward a drain made Florence gasp; a baby cried upstairs in number 14; the door to number 16 crashed open, and a middle-aged woman in a torn nightdress and with blood streaking her face stumbled past them to sprawl face down in the street. An instant later, a man—broad, shirtless, braces flapping around his knees—roared out of the house, pushed between the police officers, and stood over the woman.

Florence shrank back into the shadows as Caitrin approached him and shouted, "Stop that!"

He swatted her to the ground with King Kong ease and swore at the woman lying at his feet. Stunned, Caitrin rolled and cracked her truncheon hard against the man's shin. He shrieked in pain, and she struck at his other shin, sending him to his knees as she rose to her feet.

"Don't move." She pinned his arm behind his back to hold him down. "Simmonds!"

"What?"

"What?" Caitrin glared at her. "Handcuffs."

Florence edged out of the shadows and at arm's length offered Caitrin her handcuffs. Caitrin shot her an astonished look and said, "You can see I'm perhaps a little busy here, no? A little help, maybe?"

Florence handcuffed the man's wrists as if she were stroking a cobra and jumped back.

"There's a call box at the end of Jubilee Terrace," Caitrin said. "Get someone to come and pick him up."

Florence hurried away. The woman sat up, swiped blood from her cheek, pulled her nightdress around her, stared at Caitrin as if she were some demonic apparition, and said, "What the hell are you doing to my poor Cyril?"

"If this is your poor Cyril, I'm arresting him."

"Arresting him? What for? What's he done?"

"For impersonating King George VI?" Caitrin stared in amazement at the woman's bloodied face. "For assault and battery. On you."

The woman sniffed and waved away her answer. "Oh, that's just my Cyril. He's had a hard week, he has, and it wasn't him, it was the drink what did it. When it gets into him like that, it takes over. Changes his character, it does."

"He also assaulted me."

"Probably thought you was one of the Beezer Boys. They're always hanging around here causing trouble, doing a bit of thieving like, scuffling with the men. Let him go; he's all right. It's my fault. I answered back when I shouldn't have and forgot to stay out of his way."

Caitrin could not believe what she was hearing. "You're not pressing charges?"

"On my poor old Cyril? No, never, not in a month of Sundays. Let him go. With a good cuppa tea inside him he'll be fine in the morning, and he's got to go to the docks early. I hope you haven't hurt him too much; we can't afford for him to miss work. C'mon, missus, let him go. He'll be all right."

Caitrin freed Cyril from the handcuffs, and the woman helped him hobble back into the house. The front door closed with a bang, leaving Caitrin standing alone in the middle of the street. She stifled her frustration, dusted herself off, and hurried away to catch Florence before she could call for the Maria. And stopped.

A man stood underneath the street lamp just a few feet away, watching her. He wore a long greatcoat and a trilby that cast a deep shadow over his face.

"Miss Colline," he said in a dry, accent-less voice.

"It's *Constable* Colline."

"We have been watching you."

"We?"

In reply, he thrust out a hand and offered her a pasteboard card. "I was asked to give you this. Call first thing tomorrow morning."

Caitrin took the card and half-turned away from the man to catch the light. On it was a handwritten telephone number and a name: *Goodman*.

"Who is this Goodman?" Caitrin said as she looked back, but the man had vanished. It was another Friday night on Ryers Road. But this one was just a bit different.

2

The next morning, Caitrin called the number from the police station. It was answered on the first ring by a woman's soothing voice. "Good morning, this is Bethany Goodman."

"Why have you been watching me?"

"Thank you for calling so promptly, Caitrin."

"How did you know it was me calling?"

"Shall we have tea?"

"Tea?"

"Why not? It's a civilized way to get to know each other."

"You can be civilized by leaving me alone, and if I see your amateur detective skulking around again doing his bad American gumshoe act, I will arrest him. Then I will come and arrest you. No tea."

She slammed down the receiver, left the room, and was almost through the front door when the phone rang again. The duty sergeant answered and called after her, "It's for you, Caitrin."

She returned and put the receiver to her ear to hear Bethany say, "Coffee, then?"

"You are persistent."

"I have to be to keep things running smoothly, but I am also quite harmless, I can assure you. Shall we say ten tomorrow morning at the ABC Tea Shop on Rathbone Place? It was a favorite tea shop for Bernard Shaw and his Fabian lectures—which were often enlightening, sometimes pretentious—and we won't be noticed because it's always busy."

"Why should I meet you?"

"Because we desperately need you, Caitrin."

"Who's we?"

"England."

The ABC Tea Shop was crowded, as Bethany said it would be, but Caitrin arrived early and found a table in a far corner. From there, with her back to the wall, she could survey the whole room and watch who entered. She had no idea what Bethany Goodman looked like but sensed she would know her. And she would see Goodman first.

Sitting alone at a table away to her left was a young vicar—ascetically slender, curved, already balding, and wearing a new dog collar a few sizes too large for him—who blushed whenever he caught Caitrin's eye. She imagined that by controlling the length of eye contact it would be possible to make him blush in Morse Code: short short short, long long long, short short short. SOS. *I wonder how long it would take to make him blush out "Jesus Wants Me for a Sunbeam"?*

"George Orwell has become rather grumpy since he was shot in Spain," a woman said, sitting directly across the table from Caitrin. One moment the chair was empty, the next she was sitting there, and Caitrin had not seen her enter. She was a neat, middle-aged woman, dressed in a dark tweed suit; someone who could easily be overlooked at first glance. She continued, "It was not unexpected. After all, George is six feet two, and standing in a trench dug for shorter Spanish soldiers he must have stuck up a bit. I'm surprised he wasn't shot to smithereens much sooner. I am Bethany Goodman. Good morning, Caitrin, I am so pleased to meet you."

A little confused and struggling to catch up, Caitrin took her offered hand. "Good morning."

"George loathed this place." Bethany leaned forward, her voice adopting a masculine tone as she puffed out her cheeks and growled, "The Aerated Bread Company Tea Shops are a sinister strand in English catering, the relentless industrialization in which everything comes out of a carton or a tin or is squirted from a tap or squeezed out of a tube."

She sat back and grinned, her head making a little rocking motion. "Poor George. Born into a well-off family and forever yearning in vain for the pious virtue of poverty."

"Some have poverty thrust upon them. But we're not here to drink tea and talk about poor George Orwell, are we? That's not why we're here," Caitrin said. She had caught up.

"No, we surely are not. Would you like tea or coffee?"

"Tea, please."

Bethany waved to a waitress, ordered, and inspected Caitrin as she stirred her tea. First there was the hair; a mass of glowing red, shining wild curls, completely at odds with the current fashion of obedient waves. Beneath the hair was a pair of fiercely blue eyes, a generous, relaxed mouth, and a precise nose graced with a spattering of freckles. And hidden under that appealing exterior lay a keen intellect and a steely determination.

"All right, here goes the background information," Bethany said. "The Germans will invade Poland, we are bound by treaty with France to defend them, and a war spreads across Europe. That means we women have to fight."

"The armed services don't want us, unless it's to be jolly good sports and whip off our knickers on request."

"That's not for us. We have to fight a different enemy, one

that lives among us. Germany has for years infiltrated England with agents and saboteurs who will do great harm if they are not checked."

"And how do you intend we stop them?"

"We women have had the vote for over ten years but are still considered the weaker sex. Outside our traditional roles we are invisible to most men. We can use that disdain and invisibility to our advantage. Join us, Caitrin, and you will be taught the skills needed to combat Nazi infiltrators."

"What kind of skills?"

"Everything we know about the enemy and everything necessary for your survival, under all conditions. I guarantee it will not be safe or easy. Will you join us?"

"Who exactly is us?"

"We are 512, an all and only female counterespionage unit."

"Why 512?"

"We had to be called something, and I didn't want a *glorious* or masculine name," Bethany said and looked a little embarrassed. "And 512 happens to be the birthday of my Dandie Dinmont."

"Do you have a cute Dandie Dinmont?"

"I do."

Caitrin sat back in her chair, sipped her tea, noticed the young vicar leaving with a parting radiant blush, and said, "In that case, how could I possibly refuse?"

"Splendid. Then you can take the Duchess."

"The Duchess?"

Caitrin, along with nineteen other young women, stood waiting at the corner of Marloes Road and Lexham Gardens in London's West Kensington. A sharp-eyed woman with eye-watering mint breath and a black coat that smelled of mothballs sidled up to Caitrin and asked, "Are you here for the Duchess?"

"Yes, I am."

"Me too." The woman, impatient, glanced at her watch. "Then where the bloody hell is she?"

"That would be her over there, don't you think?" Caitrin said as she pointed to a Bedford pantechnicon that had pulled up on Marloes Road. It was battered and dirty, with the faded words DUCHESS REMOVALS stenciled across the side. She saw the address was from the East End, didn't recognize it, and guessed it was probably fictitious. She also noticed there was no telephone number.

The driver—a middle-aged man with a tooth-challenged smile, a flat cap, and a shabby suit—leaped from the cab, scurried to the rear of the pantechnicon, threw the doors open wide, bowed, and grandly announced, "Trevor's the name, ladies, and your carriage awaits."

"What! You expect us to go in there?" the mothballed and mint-breathed woman said as they clustered around the doors. "It's a lorry."

"Technically speaking, it's a pantechnicon, Miss. There are boxes inside to sit on, and the drive won't take long."

"There are no windows."

"That's the point," Caitrin said. "They don't want us to see where we're going." She did not know Trevor's face but recognized the voice. He was the man who had given her Bethany Goodman's card on Ryers Road.

"Hello, we've got ourselves a real bright one here. And I'll take your watches, if you please. Promise I won't flog them, but I might keep the prettiest one for the trouble and strife."

"Watches?" Mint-breath asked.

"He wants the watches to stop us from timing the journey," Caitrin said before anyone could question why he needed them.

"We'll definitely have to keep the old mince pies on you, I can tell," Trevor said to her as he collected the watches, ushered the women inside, and drove away.

Caitrin had mentally counted thirty-five minutes before the pantechnicon stopped and reversed. The doors opened to reveal it was parked hard against a doorway. They were briskly herded through the building and into a classroom. Outside the windows was an anonymous landscape of fields; they could have been anywhere in the southeast of England. They had barely settled into the desks when the room door opened, and Bethany Goodman entered. Her appearance came as no surprise, but what she wore did. Bethany was dressed as a nun, a Mother Superior. She stood at the blackboard, spread her arms wide, and grinned as she said, "Bless you, my children, but fret not; this is only a disguise. I am not a professional nun."

There was relieved laughter as she continued, "This was once a girls' school, until the headmaster disappeared one day with the gardener, took all the funds, and left the hollyhocks. Now it belongs to us."

"Why the nun's costume?" a woman asked.

"Because, as a cover, this place will now be known as Langland Priory, a church-run home for unwed mothers. For the first months of training, those still with us will be confined to the building and grounds. Later, you may go to the village, but only as either a nun or an unwed mother with a cushion tucked under your skirt."

"What about an unwed nun?" someone said to laughter.

Bethany did not falter. "As a nun is assumed to be a *virgo intacta*, her, um, condition would obviously attract a great deal of unwanted attention. So no, certainly no pregnant nuns."

"You said, those still with us," a woman said. "What does that mean?"

"I'll explain. There are twenty of you here, but I would be surprised if more than five complete training. You will learn about the Wehrmacht command, the SS, the Gestapo, and the Abwehr. You will be instructed in survival skills and taught how to shoot and kill. That is the hardest part for many." She paused, her eyes sweeping the room. "The first test. Does anyone know where we are? If you do, write it down on the paper you will find in your desk, and tell me how you discovered it."

No one moved, except Caitrin. She raised her desk lid, took out a sheet of paper, and scribbled her answer. Bethany read it and waved for everyone to leave. She waited until the door closed and said, "You wrote somewhere near Gerrards Cross. You are right, and I want to know how you worked out our location."

"We had no watches, so I mentally counted the minutes as we drove west. Trevor should have made a few turns or driven in a circle to disorient us. I heard several aeroplanes to our left and guessed it was the Great West Aerodrome at Heath Row. I flew there a few times with my brother Dafydd. We turned right and headed north. After a few minutes I smelled a brewery. Would it be Waterston's? It's only a guess. And if you don't mind, I don't want to be a nun. I'd much rather be thought a wicked and fallen woman who at least had some fun on the way down."

Bethany laughed. "I hope you make it through."

"I hope so too."

The women were assembled outside the priory to meet their trainer. None of them was at all impressed with him; neither was he particularly awed by them. Chopper Jones, so-named because of his habit of punctuating his speech with abrupt chopping gestures, was a little man of intense character and glaring eyes. Chopper never stayed still as he issued instructions. "A moving target is hard to hit, ladies, so always move. Never remain at rest." He stuck out his hand as a gun. "Move, so I can't shoot you. Come on, move."

Feeling more than a little silly, the women moved, a step here, a step back, a little lean to the right and back again as he closed an eye and aimed his hand at them and muttered *bang!*

They bumped into each other, apologized and giggled, and went silent as Chopper cleaved the air, bellowing, "Laugh if you want, but giggles and guffaws will bring the Hun down on your pretty necks. They will hear you. It is a known fact that Germans have bigger ears than the British."

"Are they bigger anywhere else?" asked a brave lass, anonymous in the group.

Her remark had no effect on Chopper, who was a married man with six daughters and eight sisters and knew some, but not all, of the intricate ways of women. He chopped the air, this time with both hands, and said, "The invading Hun slaughtered innocent vicars, raped nuns, and killed their poor babies in Belgium."

"That was the Great War," Hermione Richards, a solicitor's well-educated daughter, said with a barely concealed trace of condescension. Unlike the rest of the women, she had been to Belgium and had no recollection of ever seeing a pregnant nun there. "I don't wish to appear contrary, but when I was in Knokke le Zoute—"

A stabbing chop cut her off, and he answered, "That war was nothing but practice for this one. The Jerries are cunning blighters who passed their evil knowledge down from father to son, and so they're even better at it now. Line up—tallest on the left, shortest on the right."

They did as instructed, although it took some awkward measuring and there were questions about three women who seemed to be the same height. Chopper solved it by arranging them alphabetically, according to their first names.

Satisfied, or at least accepting their attempt to sort themselves out, Chopper strode up and down the line. "Your body, your person, is sacrosanct, and yes, I do know what that means."

He stopped, facing Caitrin. "Step forward."

She did as she was ordered.

"In combat you must decide where the border of your person is, and if it is trespassed, you must strike instantly. Once the enemy has a grip on you, all surprise is lost, and it becomes a battle, which you, being the weaker sex, will lose, or at least be damaged. And a wounded soldier is of no more use than a dead one. Worse, because he needs looking after. Name?"

"Caitrin Colline."

"Reach for me, Caitrin."

She put out her hand, he bellowed at her, and she shrank back. "Not like you want my smashing body for your physical pleasure. As if you want to attack and maim me."

Her hand shot out to grasp his sleeve, but before she could touch him, his right hand whistled past her ear. She froze.

"My sacrosanct border is three inches away from my body. If this had been actual combat, Miss Colline would have a broken and bloody nose before she touched me. But it wouldn't hurt for long because I would have killed her before she fell to the ground." He wagged his finger. "Decide what's sacrosanct, and act immediately to defend it."

"What if it was a mistake and he was just being friendly?" Hermione said.

"Then, if you haven't already killed him, you apologize, buy him a pint, and tell him a broken nose looks appealing on a man. Adds a wicked air of danger. Back into line."

As Caitrin stepped back into line, Chopper pointed to a low hill in the distance. "Even with me war wounds, I can walk there and back, double-time, in twenty minutes. I expect you to do so in fifteen."

"Why?" Hermione asked.

"Why? Because I said so."

"When?"

"Now."

"Shouldn't we change into our gym clothes first?" Hermione said. Caitrin stayed silent because Chopper was the man in charge who knew things that they did not, which meant there were times, like this one, when anonymity was a good and wise thing to practice.

"Step forward if you will, please, Miss," Chopper said, and Hermione took a reluctant step out of line. He inspected her with his glaring eyes—front, back, and both sides. "Do you speak French?"

"*Oui.*"

"Speak it well, do you?"

"*Naturellement.*"

"I don't speak a bloody word of it," he said. "Why not? Because it's foreign."

"It's beautiful."

He faced her, rocking on his heels. "So's my beloved Phyllis, a beautiful woman who is the *pomme* of me eye and the light of me life. But she'd never survive being dropped into France. And do you know why?"

"She'd bounce?" Hermione said and by his reaction instantly saw she had made a grievous mistake.

"Because she's never been outside Wapping is why, and wouldn't go to France, or any other foreign country, even if the king said pretty please Phyllis, just for me. But if she had to go abroad, say to save her beloved hubby's life, she'd be smart enough not to worry about her gym clothes. Now, Miss, you, with your perfect French. Let's imagine you've been dropped into France at night, and as luck would have it, land a hundred yards away from a whole German battalion. Right next to all those Huns with their big ears and other supposed large things. Not the place to display your French language skills. Instead, you run and run and run—and with the Hun on your heels would do it in your civilian clothes, the ones you are wearing to blend in with all the other Frenchies. No time to change into gym togs."

Hermione nodded, indicating she understood.

"Off you go, then, up the hill, and do it in ten minutes, or less."

"And if I don't do it in time?" Hermione said, determined to go down with at least some guns firing.

"If you don't do it in time?" The question baffled Chopper, so he repeated it. "If you don't do it in time? Then you do it again and again until you *can* run it in ten minutes. Go! The Germans are after you!"

He gave Hermione a head start and sent the rest of the women after her.

Hermione tried and failed three times to run there and back in less than twenty minutes and left the priory the next morning. Two more followed her, after failing a series of grueling exercises. After living through the austere Thirties, many of them were ill-nourished and physically incapable of meeting 512's demands. But although Caitrin had grown up in a filthy coal-mining town, it was at the bottom of a narrow valley and the steep slopes above were physically challenging playgrounds with cleaner air, and that made her strong and resilient.

After surviving Chopper, those still remaining met their weapons instructor in the shooting range beneath the priory. Billy "The Brick" Donnelly, 512's weapons instructor, was a Liverpool-Irish lad with a compact body and low center of gravity. Regardless of weapon caliber, recoil, or blast, when Billy pulled the trigger, only his finger moved. He didn't even blink. Billy was a stone-cold marksman.

An assortment of weapons was laid out on a table, and Billy went through them, explaining their vices and virtues. "This is your Lee Enfield Number Four rifle, the mainstay of the British Army. The Thompson submachine gun, which you have all seen from American gangster films. The Bren, a fine weapon, and the Sten submachine gun, mass-produced and used by overseas partisans and resistance fighters. Next, pistols. The Enfield Number Two Mark One, standard British Army issue; the American Colt; the Browning Hi-Power; and this odd, somewhat obsolete creature, the Webley-Fosbery automatic revolver. This one is a .38, and not, as many think, a .455, and holds eight rounds, not six. An unusual weapon and heavy. The cylinder and barrel assembly slide back after each shot. A man, or especially a woman, would have to be capable of using it properly to gain any level of accuracy. It's easily recognizable by the diagonal grooves on the cylinder."

He weighed the pistol in his hand. "You might like a particular weapon and grow quite proficient with it, and that is good, but you have to be adept with more than one. You never know where you'll be and in what circumstances. There will be no time to learn; you will have to pick up any gun at hand and shoot to kill. That being said, find the one that suits you best, the one that will make you an expert."

He stood in front of Caitrin. "Redheaded lassies usually have a temper to match."

"I have been known to have my moments," Caitrin replied.

"And in one of those moments, did you perchance fire a gun?"

"No. Well, a shotgun, twice."

"Which one would you like to try?"

"That one," she said, pointing to the revolver in his hand.

"Do you think you can be an expert with this monster?"

"I can try."

"Step forward to that mark," he said, pointing to a white line on the floor, and loaded the cylinder.

She did, and he gave her the pistol. It was heavy in her hand.

"You will never point a weapon at anyone, or put your finger on the trigger, unless you intend to kill what or who you're aiming at," Billy said and gestured to a paper target, a silhouette of a Wehrmacht soldier. "You are thirty feet away from that German, who is intent on killing you. In the heat of battle, when your life could end in an instant, there is no time to be a thinker. You shoot to kill. First shot in the heart, the next in the head, and you keep shooting until the enemy is no longer a threat. And then you shoot him one last time to make sure. Understand?"

"Yes."

"Repeat: shot in the heart, next in the head."

"Shot in the heart, next in the head."

"Good. Off you go, lass. When ready, there's your enemy; kill him before he kills you." Billy stood to one side.

Caitrin brought up the revolver, sighted, and fired until the gun was empty. The target was hidden in smoke, her hand tingled from the recoil, and her ears rang from the shots.

Billy stared at her for what seemed like an eternity and did not move or speak. Finally, he said, "You have never fired a gun before?"

"Just the shotgun."

Billy went to the target, unclipped it, and gave it to her. Seven of the eight shots, all grouped, were shared between the head and heart of the target. The eighth was just below the heart. "You're quite sure you have never fired a gun before?"

"Sure."

"Are you trying to fool me?"

"No, not at all, but I really didn't want that nasty German with the big ears and whatnot to get me."

"Big ears and whatnot?"

The women chuckled, and Billy, being the only man in a crowd of women, knew well enough not to embarrass himself by asking further questions. He gestured to the revolver in her hand. "That is now your weapon. Take good care of it, and it will look after you."

Three of the women failed weapons training; one of them pulled a revolver trigger, winced at the recoil, put it down, and left without saying a word. Two more dropped out when, as part of their endurance testing, they were left alone at night in the woods and scared each other silly. Only two survived the full course. One was the sharp-eyed woman with the mint breath and black coat, who then mysteriously vanished one night, taking with her the priory office petty cash. The other one was Caitrin Colline.

3

A year later, Winston Churchill had been the British prime minister for only a few troubled months when he wedged himself behind a small desk and set to work. He wore a sky-blue velvet siren suit, modeled on a workingman's one-piece boiler suit, although with a long zip instead of buttons. Turnbull & Asser, who supplied his bespoke shirts, had made several such suits for him, including one in gray pinstripe for more formal occasions.

Churchill was not an early riser, preferring to begin work at midday, and then while in bed or from one of his twice daily baths. But this was not a usual day, and this was not his usual office. He was hidden away in a junior secretary's room upstairs at the end of a long corridor in 10 Downing Street. It had no window and little furniture, apart from the tiny desk, a few chairs, and a painting of ducks in flight at dawn with a tear in the corner. This obscure place had been chosen to give him some anonymity for the task in hand.

One of the chairs was pushed into a corner and sitting in it was Walter Thompson, Churchill's bodyguard, a man with a splendid nose, assessing eyes, and, although tall, the uncanny ability to be inconspicuous. Thompson had placed the chair so he would be hidden from view behind the office door when anyone entered.

A hard rap on the door was answered by a response from Churchill. The door swung open. A young woman appeared and said, in a strong, clear voice, "I was supposed to say I am Number Nine, but I do actually have a name."

The previous eight women had been much of a muchness, polite and somewhat overawed at his presence, but this one, Number Nine, was different. She stood confidently erect and wore well-tailored slacks, a white shirt, and a short tweed jacket. Number Nine was her own unexpected presence.

Flustered, Churchill flicked open a file and ran a finger down a list. "Number Nine. You are—"

"I am Caitrin Colline."

"Sit down, please, Miss Colline," Churchill said, a little more in command. He leaned back in his chair and fiddled with a cigar. He did not approve of women wearing trousers. "You, young lady, in that trousers getup, look rather like a keen cavalry subaltern."

"And you, Sir, with that blue velvet romper suit, look rather like Winnie the Pooh."

"I *am* Winnie the PM," Churchill answered, startled by her bold reply.

"Yes, Sir, that you most surely are." Caitrin sat upright, her back not touching the chair. She met his gaze, and he saw no insolence or bravado in her expression, only confidence. This young woman had a simple grace. She made no unnecessary movements, did not fidget or make nervous gestures of habit. Also, she seemed not at all awed by his presence, and apparently was not much impressed by him either.

"Halifax called me that once. Do you know why you are here?"

"No."

"You volunteered."

"I was encouraged."

"Very well. A gentleman should never ask a young lady this—"

"I am twenty-six."

"Unmarried?"

"Oh goodness, yes."

Churchill focused his attention on the file. "Policewoman. You're not in uniform."

"It being such a mysterious meeting, I thought it better to come in mufti."

Churchill smiled to himself. She was toying with him and enjoying it. So was he. "Your accent. Welsh?"

"Yes, Sir. Abertillery, Monmouthshire, South Wales. Coal-mining town."

"Then you will know of Tonypandy?"

"It was a bit before my time, but yes, I certainly do."

In 1910, miners in Tonypandy, South Wales, had gone on strike for better wages and conditions. Churchill, as home secretary, sent soldiers in to support the police and mine owners. There was violence, and several miners were killed. Understandably, he was remembered and not much liked in South Wales.

"In my defense, I did not do what they say I did."

"Perhaps not, Sir, but the Welsh have long memories. My grandfather has never forgiven Edward I for building his castles in Wales."

Churchill's eyes widened. "That was over six hundred years ago."

"True, but my grandfather says he knew a man who knew a man who knew Edward and said he was not a kind person. Always complaining about the weather or lazy brickies, and spoke terrible Welsh," she said and laughed at his expression.

"But, in fairness, my grandad was known to tell a wild tale or two after a few pints of Webb's finest pale ale."

Churchill held back his own laughter. This was, after all, meant to be a serious meeting.

"I do have a question, before we go any farther. Why am I being interviewed by the prime minister?" Caitrin asked. "And why in a cupboard, of all places?"

"I will come to that in due course, but only if I consider you the right candidate. I have more questions."

Caitrin raised a graceful hand and, without looking around, pointed behind her. "Before you start, Prime Minister, would you ask the gentleman in the corner to move to at least the edge of my vision? I feel uncomfortable having someone staring at the back of my head."

Churchill nodded at Thompson, who was surprised she had noticed him and shifted his seat so he could be seen.

"Now, young lady, let's begin the interview," Churchill said. "Who are your heroes?"

"That's easy." Her answer was immediate. "My father and my mother."

"Why?"

"Because to take care of his family my dad went down the pit every day and cut coal. Then he came home, coughed, and spat up black filth. And when he died from black lung, my mother looked after us, without a penny of pension or compensation."

The laughter was gone.

He asked, "And who else? Think hard. One more."

"Easy again." Caitrin's chin tilted. "Keir Hardie is another, for caring about the working man and woman enough to create the Labour Party. Who is your hero?"

The question was unexpected.

"That would be John Churchill, first duke of Marlborough. A self-made man and a general who never lost a battle."

"I read your biography of him, all four volumes."

"And?"

"I could have done it just as well in three."

And now Churchill did laugh. This young woman was a cleansing, boisterous wind in a dark time. "With your background and admiration for Keir Hardie, I assume you are a socialist?"

"Fervent."

"Which means what, exactly?"

"It means that after the war, the aristocracy should be, will be, dismantled and the country estates divided up for the people. We will bring an end to centuries of inbred titled parasites doing nothing to validate their existence but feed off the people."

"Bold steps. And what will you do with royalty?"

"They will have to work for a living. And we turn Buckingham Palace into a retirement home for old miners." She was not laughing or smiling.

Churchill grunted and bit the end of his cigar. "Perhaps you are not the right candidate."

"Fair enough. Come in Number Ten?"

"Your Britain is different from mine, Miss Colline. I believe in the accrued wisdom and guidance of tradition," Churchill said and lit the cigar, taking his time so he could arrange his thoughts. "Just weeks ago we rescued three hundred and thirty thousand men from the beaches of Dunkirk. Partly at my behest, the press and the BBC hailed it as a mighty achievement."

"It was."

"Of a kind, but an evacuation is by no means a victory. We got most of the men back but left behind their equipment, stores, and weapons: one hundred and twenty thousand vehicles, two thousand three hundred artillery pieces, eight thousand Bren guns, ninety thousand rifles, and seven thousand tons of ammunition. It will take many months to re-equip and train them. Meanwhile, the Luftwaffe is bombing England daily, while the Germans are only a few miles away from Dover, waiting for the right time to invade. The British people will be brave and deny it, but they are scared."

"Should they be?"

"Yes. Our survival is fragile. I'm afraid if the Germans come, we'll have to fight them with beer bottles."

"Empty ones, I hope."

"Our code name for the German invasion is Cromwell."

"An odd choice for a royalist, no?"

"Not really, although he did overthrow the king and install a republic. Don't you dare smile that socialist smile at me, young lady," Churchill said and disappeared behind a cloud of cigar smoke. "What I say next is an official secret, so I could hang you if it gets out."

Caitrin's fingertips brushed her neck in the most graceful of gestures. "Never a word."

Churchill waved a hole in the cigar smoke to see her. "Just a few weeks ago, a convoy of British ships left these shores, braved German U-boats, and crossed the Atlantic, carrying all of our country's gold and wealth. In that month, the U-boats sank fifty-seven of our ships, and the loss of just one gold vessel would have been disastrous. We all remember the *Laurentic*."

"I don't."

"No? In 1917, she was carrying gold to Canada and hit a mine off Malin Head on the coast of Northern Ireland. Three hundred and fifty-four of the crew successfully abandoned ship but then unfortunately died from exposure in their lifeboats."

"I was three years old, and that was the year my brother Evan was killed in France."

"My sympathies. We lost so many good men. Fortunately, our ships all crossed the Atlantic without harm, and the nation's treasure, billions of pounds in gold, is now locked safely away in a Montreal bank vault."

Caitrin was silent. Her eyes met his and held, and Churchill was aware that he had been intently listened to. She had heard and absorbed every word. It was an unusual feeling, and he sensed that, if asked, she could have repeated everything he had said verbatim.

"I did it, alone. I took the gamble and accepted the responsibility to save England and the British Empire," he said. "The loss of only a few ships with their gold would have brought the country to its knees. It was solely my idea and a perilous one."

She leaned toward him. "And your next perilous idea, Sir? The one that involves *me* saving my country? *Our* country."

And with that reply the decision was clear to him. The search was over. Caitrin Colline was the one.

4

Churchill gestured to Walter Thompson, who rose to his feet, slipped out of the room, and closed the door behind him. Once the sound of the bodyguard's footsteps had faded away, Churchill repeated Caitrin's words to her. "You said, our country."

"Our country," Caitrin echoed. "I do not get teary-eyed at hearing 'Land of Hope and Glory,' will never wag a flag at the king or queen, and the sooner the House of Lords is abolished, the better. We have different backgrounds and aims, Prime Minister. That does not make us different. In my way, I am just as British as you are in yours."

"And I believe as a member of the constabulary your job is to protect, regardless of rank or prejudice."

"Yes. Royalty, gentry, or even a dog."

"Even a *King* Charles spaniel?"

She grinned. "Even him."

"Good. Operation Fish—"

"Fish?"

"That was the name given to the transport of Britain's treasure to Canada. It required hundreds of people to make it a success and keeping it secret was a minor miracle. But word has now gotten out, and the Germans will be ready for a second attempt. That means our next operation—"

"It has no name?"

"Not so far. However, it must be different and will require the services of just two."

"Me and?"

"Your husband."

"I am not married."

"Not at this moment, but for this operation you will need to be." He put up a hand to stay the conversation as footsteps grew louder outside. The door opened, and Thompson ushered in a young man. He was about Caitrin's age, had a ruddy outdoors complexion, a shock of unruly blond hair, and wore a tailored yet threadbare Norfolk jacket.

Churchill stood, as did Caitrin, and said, "Caitrin Colline, let me introduce you to your new husband, Hector, Lord Neville-Percy of Marlton."

Caitrin stared in amazement at Hector while Churchill continued, "Hector, meet your new wife, Caitrin Colline, Welsh firebrand, antiroyalist, and future destroyer of England's aristocracy. That would be all of them, including you."

"How do you do?" Hector said in a clipped English accent and put out his hand.

"How do I do what?" Caitrin laughed. "Hector, Lord Neville-Percy of Marlton? Couldn't you have taken just one name and shared the rest with your chums? What does your mum call you: Hecky?"

"What does your mum call you?" Hector replied, once he had recovered from her taunting question. "Cat-ty?"

"Operation Cat," Churchill said with a finger snap. "That's a splendid name. Now both of you sit down and behave. We'll deal with this first issue and have ourselves a bloody class war later."

They all sat, Caitrin shooting sly glances at Hector, who was staring fixedly ahead at the duck painting.

"As husband and wife—"

"If we are supposedly to be married, can it be as Mr. and Mrs. Colline?" Caitrin said. "I could never be Mrs. Neville-Percy."

"That's quite certain," Hector muttered.

"What!" Caitrin glared at him.

Churchill compressed his lips to hold back a smile. *This poor man has no idea what a whirlwind he's about to encounter.* "As I explain the task further, Miss Colline, you will come to understand it would be best for the success of the operation if we use the Neville-Percy name."

Caitrin shrugged a reluctant acceptance but seemed not at all convinced.

"Our country's treasure is now safe in Canada, but there is one other thing that is still in grave danger: the Crown Jewels. They are the priceless icons of our race, and with the nation worried about an imminent German invasion, if they were to be destroyed—bombs are dropping closer daily—or, worse, captured and paraded in Berlin, I believe the country would lose heart and capitulate."

"They're going to be sent to Canada too?" Caitrin asked.

"Yes, but now the Germans have learned what we did to move the gold, they will be looking for us to repeat the operation. If we use the same heavily guarded routine again, they will attack the shipment on its way to the docks, and at sea the alerted U-boats will be waiting."

"So what are we going to do with them?" Caitrin asked.

"Lord Hector—"

"Please just call me Hector, Sir," Hector said, half-turned to Caitrin, and winced what might have been considered a smile. "Or Hecky, if you must."

Caitrin patted his hand in a temporary truce, gifted him a nose-wrinkling smile in return, and whispered, "Hecky."

"Catty." Hector returned his version of her nose-wrinkle smile and whispered, "I beg your pardon, Prime Minister, but I was under the impression this was to be a solo operation."

"You were given the wrong impression. No, it is not."

"Sir, forgive me, I don't wish to be troublesome, but I was trained to operate alone and have never worked with—"

"A woman?" Caitrin finished his sentence for him.

"Yes, a woman, but also as part of a team. I really must protest."

"Methinks the gentleman doth protest too much," Caitrin said with stiletto grace.

"I do not! And I am just not trained to work as part of a team."

"Well, you are now, and I shall explain to you exactly why," Churchill said and soldiered bravely on. "There are no doubt spies watching the Tower, who if they see a strong military presence will assume the Jewels are being moved. Once out of the vaults and in the open they are prey to a German fifth column, or perhaps even a surprise bombing attack. Therefore they need to be removed without fuss. Lord . . . Hecky has driven a horse box down from his family estate in the North. He—with you, Miss Colline—will go to the Tower, where the Jewels will be safely loaded and covered with hay bales. Once ready, you will be nothing more out of the ordinary than an anonymous rural couple driving home, perhaps from a stable or a gymkhana. The Jewels will have vanished into the safely anonymous bosom of England."

"They won't fit," Caitrin said. "You'll need a bigger box."

"I am well aware of the magnitude of the Crown Jewels collection," Churchill said, his feathers ruffled by her fearless candor. "But the general public, and certainly the Germans, think only of crowns and orbs and scepters, when they think of the Jewels at all. That is what you will be carrying. The rest of the collection—gold plate, goblets and caddinets, and such—will be scattered and hidden in places around England."

"Surely there are vaults here where everything could be safely stored?" Caitrin said.

"There are indeed," Churchill answered. *This young woman is relentless.* "But someone will necessarily know the location, and if the Germans do invade, Admiral Canaris's Abwehr, Heydrich's SD, or Himmler's Gestapo will be thorough with its investigations. Sooner or later, they will force out the information."

"They are a most unpleasant people," Hector said.

"There's some good old spiffing English understatement for you," Caitrin said.

Churchill growled to bring their attention back to him.

"You will keep to side roads as much as possible, drive only in daylight because of the blackout, and spend each night at a country estate until you reach Scotland."

"Why a country estate?" Caitrin asked, as Churchill knew she would. He wanted to say *Because they are the backbone of the nation* but did not, to avoid an instant Welsh socialist insurrection. Instead, he slid a sheet of paper across the desktop toward them and said, "Because they are usually secluded, somewhat removed from towns, and strangers would easily be noticed at a distance. That makes them safe and secure. This is a list of the homes."

"I know some of these," Hector said as he scanned the list.

"Of course you do," Caitrin said. Hector ignored her.

"In eight days, *HMS Talisman*, our fastest long-distance submarine, will arrive at Greenock, leave the following day with the Jewels, and speed alone across the Atlantic. It is too small to carry the bullion but can easily handle the Jewels. You have plenty of time to get there."

"When do we go to the Tower?" Caitrin asked.

"Today is Saturday. They will be ready by Tuesday, three days from now, and that gives you five days to reach Greenock."

"Seems straightforward enough," Hector said.

"I wish it were so," Churchill said. "There is one problem." As he settled back in his chair, for the first time Caitrin was aware of the weight bearing down on him. He was not a young man and looked weary. The lives and futures of millions of people, and countries even, depended on the decisions he made.

"Not only do we have the Wehrmacht massed at the French coast waiting to invade, we also have enemies within."

His remark silenced the room. Off in the distance somewhere a telephone rang, and high above an aeroplane's engines grumbled as it struggled for altitude.

Churchill lit a cigar. "There are fools like Lindbergh and Joe Kennedy who prophesy our downfall, and inevitably the impossible, buzzing-mosquito Mitford sisters, but at least they are out in the open where we can watch them." He turned his attention to Caitrin and asked her, "Do you perchance speak German, Miss Colline?"

"I can count to ten."

"So you would not know what *Die Brücke* means?"

"No." She turned her head toward Hector.

"The Bridge," Hector answered.

"Yes, and many of the English aristocracy are sympathetic to the Nazis."

Caitrin noticed Churchill pronounced *Nazis* as *Nazeez* because he had a lisp, of which he was self-conscious, and hid it by making an *S* into a *Z*. She liked it: his pronunciation made him human and the enemy sound sleazy.

"They may well dislike Hitler's boorishness," Churchill continued, "but do approve of the way he put Germany back on its feet. And although they would never admit this in public, they condone his attack on the Jews and would like to do the same thing here. We have a long history of throwing the Jews out of the country."

"And Cromwell let them back in," Caitrin said. "But only so he could borrow money. A most kingly trait."

"Among other things, *Die Brücke* is an organization that links the English sympathizers with Nazi Germany."

"They're English, so surely they wouldn't give him the Crown Jewels?" Caitrin said.

"The friction between monarch and aristocracy is an ancient one. They will give him whatever he wants, as long as he leaves them alone on their estates."

"Will he leave them alone?"

"They think so, but I don't. Holland, Denmark, and Norway thought they could remain neutral, each hoping that if it fed the crocodile, it would eat them last. But don't forget, for centuries there has been a strong Germanic hereditary strain running throughout much of the aristocracy."

"The Battenbergs come to mind," Caitrin said.

"They're the Mountbattens now," Hector said.

"And of course, who could forget the venerable and very German Saxe-Coburg-Gothas?"

"Who became the House of Windsor," Hector said, with the feeling he was being outmaneuvered.

"Timing is everything in life, isn't it?"

"Stop it, you two," Churchill growled. "Unfortunately, apart from a few glaring examples, we do not know who is or is not part of *Die Brücke*. That means you will need to be cautious where you stay and tell them nothing. This might remind you of the country's plight." He picked up a sheet of paper, cleared his throat, and read, "I was sitting bound to a chair in a darkened room, hardly able to see who or what was there with me. Although I could not see, I could plainly hear the groans and whimpers of anguished pain from the friends sprawled at my feet. They had been savagely struck down with blinding speed. And the shifting sound of something horrid slithering closer was a chilling warning that the same appalling violence was about to descend upon me."

He put the paper down and puffed his cigar back into life. "The allusion to what is happening in Europe at this moment is quite clear. What say you to this, Miss Catty?"

"Honestly?" Caitrin sniffed. "It sounds as though it was written by some clergyman from a remote Norfolk benefice cradling the forlorn hope that his genius would find the right intellectual ear and alter the predictable trajectory of his sad, meager life."

Silence made them all monuments. Until Hector broke it by saying, "I wrote it."

"Sorry, vicar." Caitrin's hand flew to her mouth, to hide a smile more than to retract the words.

Churchill thumped the desk, stood, and pointed to the door, partly to prevent himself from laughing. "Go! Away with you both this instant, make up a history of a marriage you can both agree upon, and prepare for the journey. Three days hence."

Caitrin and Hector left, Thompson closed the door, and Churchill collapsed into his chair. "My God, what hath we wrought?"

"Indeed, Sir."

"And it never ceases," he said, glancing at a sheet of paper on his desk. "Listen to this. A Mr. Cyril X. Goslington, I wonder about the *X*, is editor of the campanologists' magazine *Ringing World*. I had no idea such a thing even existed. Regarding my banning of all bell-ringing, so we might use them only as warning of an airborne attack, he writes: 'The ban is a stunning blow to ringing, from which, even when the war is over, it will take a long time to recover.' What say you, Thompson?"

"To be honest, I don't know the gentleman, Sir, but his magazine's name rings a bell."

Churchill paused, cigar halfway to his mouth, but Thompson's expression was detective-blank as he continued, "Excuse me for asking, Sir, but do you really think they're the right couple? They seem so different. Why not choose Lady Prudence or

Lady Anne? Socially they would be a better match for Lord Hector."

Churchill picked up the telephone and barked, "A bottle of Pol Roger, soonest. In my office, not here." He replaced the receiver and said, "You are correct, Thompson, you usually are correct, and if it were a hunt ball or the London season I would agree, but our Welsh spitfire is what Lord Hecky needs to complete this task. They will squabble like a real married couple and so seem authentic. But once Operation Cat is finished, and if they both survive, I fear our Lord Hector, Hecky, will never be quite the same man again."

5

Reginald Bardwell was an educated man and a good husband who dearly loved his wife, even though she came from a lower social stratum than did he. The son of a devout yet impecunious Dorsetshire parson, Reginald met and fell in love with Lilian Gormley, a lass from the slums of Limehouse in London's Docklands. He was frugal and saved enough to buy her a place in Elephant and Castle on the other side of the river. It was not a giant step up, being a modest terraced house identical to its neighbors in endless ranks of terraced houses, and the slums were just a few streets away, but it was a palace for Lilian. It came complete with a large bedroom she didn't have to share, except and delightfully with Reginald, and even had its own indoor flushing lavatory and bathroom. The greatest luxury of all was an Ascot hot water geyser in the kitchen. The whoomph as the gas ring lit when she turned it on was such a comforting sound, it was the sound of security, and Lilian vowed to cherish and never leave her little kingdom. They would grow splendidly old together there, with children, grandchildren, and annual holidays in Skegness.

Not only was Reginald frugal, he was also a proudly patriotic Englishman and gladly went to war when Kitchener called him to service. As a lieutenant in the West Kent Light Infantry, part of Army Corps III, he was the first to leap out of the trenches and go over the top to lead his men to glory. He did so at Amiens in 1918, just a month or so before the war ended, and like thousands of keen young lieutenants before him was cut down by machine-gun fire. Reginald did not reach glory; he hardly got more than fifteen feet away from where he started.

Lilian's life abruptly changed, and she lived in terror of returning to the Limehouse slums. That would mean going back to a communal lavatory and a tin bath hanging on a nail outside that was brought in once a week while water boiled in cooking pots on the fire. And no more whoomph of the Ascot geyser. Reginald had refused to let her work, so she now had no way to support herself. After crying herself to sleep for weeks, Lilian, with regret, decided to rent out her lovely bedroom and move downstairs. She had had several lodgers of varying character over the years and had recently found a nice young lady, who, although she was Welsh, came with good references. As the bombing grew heavier, this young woman, Caitrin Colline, became her vital support. Almost daily, houses were being destroyed all around her, but Lilian Bardwell was determined not to move, and neither would she scurry away to the smelly bomb shelters with the slum dwellers and leave her palace to be looted. Reginald would not have wanted that, and while she lay in her bed downstairs and stared at the ceiling to remember the wonderful times they had enjoyed together in her lovely bedroom, at least she had Caitrin's presence up there as comfort during the blitz.

After enduring an endless, exhausting night of bomb blasts, sirens, and clanging emergency bells, Caitrin slipped into bed, put a pillow over her head to muffle the snoring coming from Lilian downstairs, and finally fell asleep. Only to be rudely shaken awake by a man grasping her shoulders and hissing in her ear, "Caitrin, wake up!"

Half-asleep, she opened her eyes but saw nothing. Blackout curtains sealed off all light and hid any detail in the room.

"I said wake up!"

Training took command of reflexes, and her right fist drove deep into the man's solar plexus as the palm of her left hand clapped hard against his right ear. He released his grip on her and with a whoosh of exhaled breath staggered away to crash against the wardrobe and tumble to the floor. "*Oooossh.*"

She sat up and switched on the light, ready to face her attacker, and saw who it was. "Hecky? What are you doing? How on earth did you get in my room?"

"Mrs. Bardwell let me in," Hector managed to wheeze between tortured breaths.

"Now you're in, why not tell me why you are here?"

"I can't, I'm dying." He groaned and clutched his stomach. "You broke my ribs."

"No, I didn't. You're just winded, and you'll be deaf in one ear for a bit."

"How did you learn to do that?"

"I took lessons from the man who taught bartitsu to the Pankhurst suffragettes. I had to stop, though."

"Why?"

"I broke his arm."

"Why am I not surprised?" Hector got to his feet and inhaled a restorative breath. "We have to go to the Tower."

"It's not Tuesday, is it? My God, did I sleep that long?"

"It's Sunday morning."

"What time is it?"

"Dawn. Our plans have suddenly changed. The Germans bombed the Tower last night, so we are starting Operation Cat three days early." He took another breath, straightened, and noticed a suitcase on top of the wardrobe. He grasped the handle and swung the case onto the bed. "You have exactly five minutes to fill this," he said, raising his right hand, fingers splayed. "Five. Pack your things. I'll be waiting in the car, and five minutes from now I'm pulling away. With or without you."

Wincing and rubbing his right ear, Hector left. Four minutes and thirty seconds later, Caitrin slung her case into the rear of his Humber Super Snipe and joined him in the front seat.

"Made it. This car smells of dogs, Hecky."

"That's because my mother loves cocker spaniels."

"How many does she have?"

"I believe about ten, last count." Hector started the engine and pulled away, the towed horse box rattling behind. The dim streets were deserted. The blue-black air smelled of burning rubber, and smoke coiled above the roofs. A red glow to the east showed the docks were ablaze.

"The Elephant and Castle is an aiming point for the Luft-waffe to bomb the docks," Hector said. "Why on earth did you choose to live here?"

"I didn't choose. It was all I could afford, and the Nazeez weren't bombing us when I moved in."

They passed a burning street to their left, rows of sightless windows flaring orange and the firemen tiny silhouettes battling the flames. A fire engine rattled by, warning bell hammering, as a building wall collapsed in a welter of sparks. The fire-fighting efforts seemed pointless in the face of such an inferno.

"Why were you in your room last night?" Hector said. "That is so dangerous. The underground shelter is only two streets away. You would have been safer down there."

"Because my landlady, Mrs. Lilian Bardwell, had one of her turns. Poor dear gets so frightened sometimes and can't move. I didn't want to leave her alone."

"Next time there's a raid I suggest you do leave her," Hector said.

"I would never do that to Mrs. Bardwell," she said as they crossed Tower Bridge. Mid-river, they could clearly see the docks were a cauldron of flame.

"Those poor chaps in Docklands took a pounding," Hector said.

Caitrin pointed to their left. "So did they over there."

Across the Thames a column of smoke was rising from the Tower of London.

"Looks as though it took a direct hit," she said.

"More than one," Hector said. "Let's hope there's something left."

They crossed the bridge and turned toward the Tower. A policeman waved a torch to warn them away until Hector presented him with a letter. He read with great care and returned it to Hector as though it were some holy relic. "Thank you, Sir. Bombs demolished a big piece of the Mint and the old Hospital Block," he said. "Just missed the White Tower. Killed Yeoman Warder Reeves. He was a good bloke too. Family man. Tragedy I call it."

"Yes, it is," Hector said.

"And the docks got it again last night." The policeman pointed west. "Go through the Middle Tower, turn left down Mint Street and stop at Beauchamp Tower. It's well away from where the bombs exploded. They'll meet you there. Mind how you go, Sir."

"You too, Constable," Hector said and followed his directions.

Inside the Tower walls, Mint Street narrowed at Beauchamp Tower, where a half-dozen men were waiting in the shadows. One of them was Walter Thompson, Churchill's bodyguard. They shook hands, but no one spoke as the cases were loaded into the horse box. A few of the smaller cases were stored in the Humber's boot. Satisfied they were secure, the men covered the cases with hay bales and closed the horse-box door. Caitrin watched, fascinated by their silent toil, and whispered to Hector, "All we need is a horse neighing in there to finish it off."

"No space left."

"You could sit on the hay bales and pretend. Maybe I could get you some coconut shells to clomp." She stopped one of the men from padlocking the horse-box door. "No, don't lock it. Give me the lock."

"But the Jewels," he said.

"If it's unlocked, people will think there's nothing of value inside. Nothing but hay bales. Locked, they'll be curious."

The man glanced at Thompson, who frowned for a moment, unsure, then nodded in agreement. He gave Hector a card. "You are to call this number every morning to report, and only from a telephone box. Do not call from anyone's home; it might not be secure. Do not give away your location. The estates on the list the prime minister gave you are all numbered. When you report in, give only the listed number of the house where you are staying. The telephone is manned day and night, but call at other times only in an emergency."

Hector nodded to show he understood and glanced to the lightening sky. "We've left it rather late. Regardless of the day, we were supposed to depart before daybreak."

"Couldn't be helped. Make sure you time your arrival in Scotland to just before the submarine sails, so the Jewels go directly on board."

Shouts in the distance followed a rumbling as part of the bomb-shattered walls collapsed. Hector stopped and stared in disbelief at the rubble and its rising cloud of dust. As a boy, he had visited here many times and remembered standing close to this spot.

This was the Tower of London; he had drawn it in his art classes and gotten excellent marks. His mother still had the sketch up on a wall in their home. His English teacher wanted an essay about one of their trips, and Hector, while better with a pencil than a pen, had done his best. He wrote that William the Conqueror had built the first Tower in 1078, and Sir Walter Raleigh was imprisoned there, as were the two Little Princes, although he did not know why and forgot their names.

His memory clung to a pristine image of the Tower that clashed with the fallen reality before him and tried to put it back whole. In many ways, he had grown used to the war and its random destruction, but the struggle between the remembered and the real affected him, and he understood why some people eventually went insane. What was happening was insanity, and how would they deal with it, how would they make sense of all the ruin when the war was over? Who would, or could, explain why it had happened?

"Hector?" Caitrin tugged at his sleeve. "Are you all right?"

"I don't know how to answer that question. I cannot believe or accept what I'm seeing."

"Come on." She put her arm through his. "It's getting light. We have to go."

Hector drove out through the Middle Tower and turned west, away from bomb-ravaged London.

A small man standing at a corner watched them leave, went to a telephone box, and called a number.

6

An hour later, ahead of the rising sun, Hector had driven out of London and passed through Windsor with Caitrin asleep, curled up in the seat next to him. She had hardly moved in over an hour, and he appreciated the silence while delighting in taking surreptitious glances at her. Those glorious red curls, begging to have his hands run through them, had fallen across her face, leaving only a closed eye and her lips exposed. Such tempting lips. The eye remained closed, but the lips moved enough to murmur, "Hecky, does your mum really own ten cocker spaniels, or is it just one very active dog that races in and out of the house and gets counted ten times?"

Alarum! Beware, England, the Welsh are awake and across the border. A new day with new challenges has begun.

Caitrin sat upright, stretched, yawned, and smiled at him. Hector felt his heart pulse. Caitrin Colline was a glorious, beautiful, and mercurial force of nature. She smacked her lips and said, "My mouth tastes like the newspaper on the bottom of a budgie cage."

He had no answer to that, so instead said, "Good morning."

"And a fine good morning to you." She squinted at him. "First question of the day. Are you sure you're a real, authentic English lord?"

He arched a curious eyebrow at the question. "Reasonably certain. Why do you ask?"

"Because you're not a chinless chump with only one eyebrow." She improvised a squeaky upper-class English accent. "And because so far you haven't once said spiffing, topping, or what a dreadfully frightful bore, darling."

"That's a different kind of lord."

"What kind?"

"A silly one. Are you sure you're a bona fide member of the working class?"

"Yes. Why do you ask?"

"To start, you have your own teeth." He attempted a working-class accent. "And you haven't once said ee by gum, where there's muck there's brass, lad, or trouble at t'mill."

"That's a different kind of working class, northern England serfs."

"What do Welsh ones say?"

"Nothing. They'd never talk to an English lord. Where are we?"

"On the B4507 and just turning onto Fawler Road, which takes us to the quaint village of Uffington in the county of Berkshire."

"Where, I pray to gods various and sundry, there is a café. I swear I was five years old the last time I ate."

"There is, and a good one too."

The Sixth Bell Tea Shop—set in a chalk block, red brick-detailed, and thatched cottage—was on Broad Street opposite St. Mary's Church, where they could park outside and keep an eye on the car while they ate breakfast. Caitrin refused to say a word until she had drunk her first cup of tea. Then, primed, she said, "Hecky, m'lud, don't you think this is all a bit daft?"

"Uffington?"

Caitrin waved her fork at the tea-shop window. "No, I mean everything. There is yet another war to kill millions, the second in my lifetime, preceded by the Slump with so many people unemployed and going hungry. A week ago, I was leading a predictable life, but not without humble aspirations, and now here I am wandering around England in a ruin of a dog-smelling Humber Super Snipe pulling a horse box full of hay bales, under which we have concealed the . . ." Her voice dropped to a melodramatic whisper. "The Crown Jewels, which we must deliver in eight days to a boat in Scotland to go across the perilous deep to Canada before the perfidious Nazi overruns this sceptered isle and dooms us to forever eat sauerkraut for breakfast. Heaven forfend! That sort of daft."

"Top marks for saying that all in one breath, and while Victoria may be redolent of cocker spaniels, she most certainly is not a ruin."

"Victoria?" She sat back, eyebrows raised. "You actually named your car Victoria?"

"I didn't; my father did," Hector mumbled and forked a generous helping of bacon into his mouth in a bid to end the conversation.

"What's in a name, huh? What *is* in a name? Pray tell all about the double-barreled Neville-Percy name."

"The Neville and Percy families go back centuries."

"Please pretend you're reading me a bedtime story, skip the early centuries and all the begats, and touch the high, scurrilous points before I fall asleep."

"All right, I'll try my best. Since medieval times, the House of Percy has been one of the most powerful families in northern England. They still are and still quite wealthy. The House of Neville was equally powerful, and they were mortal enemies."

"So if you northern chaps were mortal enemies, always bashing lumps off each other, what happened with the Neville-Percy coming together to produce your family bit?"

"No one knows the exact details, or at least no one is telling. I suppose it brought much shame on both houses, but unlike the Nevilles or the Percys, we, the Neville-Percys, are not wealthy. There are actually only two of us left: me and my mother."

"And not forgetting the ten cocker spaniels."

"Tell me about you. Colline. What's in that name?"

"We're not medieval or landowners. When the Welsh colliers sailed to Ireland, they needed ballast after they unloaded their coal. So they filled the holds with Irish immigrants. My grandfather was first ballast and later fodder for the coal mines."

"And Caitrin?"

"Means *pure and clear*."

"Sure it isn't *loud and clear*?"

Caitrin leaned forward, crunching a piece of toast, stared hard at him, and said, "You, m'lud, have dangerous eyes."

"What does that mean?"

"I'm not telling you. But you can tell me where we're going."

"Our first country estate stop is outside Cockleford. My old school friend Roland Ashtonthorpe lives there."

"Old school. Eton?"

"St. Paul's. We couldn't possibly afford Eton. You?"

"Abertillery Grammar School. But only for two years because there was no money after my dad died."

"Where did you get your education?"

"Mr. Hancock was the landlord of our street. There are only twenty houses, small ones: two up, two down, eight-foot-wide rooms, flagstone floors, gas-lighting, outdoor lavatory. I would take the rent to him every week, and when I had to leave school, he and his wife—they had a marvelous library—took over my education. Never asked for a penny. I think I was the daughter they never had. During the day, I worked in Mr. Preece's grocery shop on the corner, and I spent my evenings in their library. I learned so much from them."

"You said you can count to ten in German."

"I can."

"And what if you had to warn me in German that *twelve* Nazis were chasing us?"

"I would shoot *zwei* and tell you there were *zehn*." Her hand darted out and snatched the last piece of bacon from his plate before he could react. "To the victor . . ."

"You have lightning-quick reflexes."

"Because I grew up with lightning-quick brothers. By the way, I also know what *Die Brücke* means."

"Why did you say you didn't?"

"I didn't say anything because I didn't want the meeting to be all about me." Caitrin chewed the last of the bacon and brushed the corner of her mouth clean with a fingertip. "I thought you should have your brief moment to shine in the spotlight."

"How very kind of you."

"There's something else. We were supposed to spend time creating a plausible background story, until the Germans bombed the Tower of London and blew up our plans. We should do it now. Where did we first meet? And please not at the Eton Wall game, old chum."

"Or the Wigan Miners' Gala. Nay, nay, lass."

"I know. The Lyons Corner House on the Strand, where—"

"You were serving me afternoon tea and—"

"No. I was having tea with Princess Elizabeth, and you tripped over her foot and called her a ninny. Whatever that is."

"I did not!"

"Did too! She was not amused and could have had your head chopped off." Caitrin grinned. "This is not going to be easy."

"It will if you let me—"

"Let you have it all your way, you being a man and all?"

"Cat!"

"Hecky, we did it. We're arguing like an authentic married couple. Arguing about nothing."

"All joking aside, we have to work on this. Our marriage must be convincing."

"To be serious, I'm not sure how to make it seem authentic. We're from completely different backgrounds and normally would never have met, unless perhaps if I were a waitress serving little cucumber sandwiches at the village fête, which you were opening as lord of the manor. Then a relationship between us would probably end up not as a love match but more a *droit de seigneur* behind the GUESS MY WEIGHT booth."

"Be serious."

"I am being serious. Our accents place us in a precise location and class the moment we utter more than two words. Listen to more than two words anyone speaks, and I can make a damn good guess what town that person comes from, what their house looks like, and what they do for a living. Morganatic marriages are fine for plays or operas, but in real life they're a different and unlikely matter."

"Perhaps so, but what matters is that for us to be successful, we have to be husband and wife. We have to start somewhere."

"True." Caitrin paused for the briefest of moments. "So let's start with the village fête, which you *were* opening and where I *was* serving cute little cucumber sandwiches. Those dainty crustless pointless triangles that wouldn't feed a mouse."

"All right, good start. And I asked you for one—"

"Not for free, though, even for a lord. Sixpence a piece."

"That's expensive, even for a lord. I bit into it and—"

"Complained because it was bland. Was there ever an un-bland cucumber?"

"I asked if you had any vinegar to add some piquancy."

"And being a lord, and a man, and I only a humble village wench, you were about to pedantically explain what piquancy meant."

"I didn't."

"Yes, you did; I was there. I hurried away before you could display your aristocratic education, found a bottle of vinegar, rushed back, and—"

"*Accidentally* squirted vinegar right into my eye."

"I wouldn't do a thing like that."

"Yes, you would."

"Yes, I would. Continue."

"But, being a gentle soul, even though still only a simple-minded wench, you fetched water and a towel and gently washed away the hurt."

She screwed up her face. "That's a bit soppy, isn't it?"

"Stay with me. You gently washed away the hurt and in doing so floated into my heart."

"I *was* with you, sort of, until the floating into the heart bit. That would never stand up under scrutiny, and if you said it aloud to someone, I'd giggle and give it away."

Hector struggled with his exasperation. "I'm trying my best. You come up with something better."

"I will. Stand back. I bathed your eye, but you still couldn't see properly out of it, so I gallantly set aside my cucumber sandwich sales, volunteered to be a guide, took your hand, and led you around the fête for the rest of the day. I'm generous that way. And as the day progressed, somewhere between the three-legged race and the DUNK THE VICAR booth, we fell forever in love. What do you think?"

"I am blinded, at least in one eye, either by everlasting love or your explanatory brilliance."

"I accept my brilliance but would settle for a yes."

"Yes." He caught a movement outside. A police constable had gotten off his bicycle and was inspecting the horse box. "Before our local copper gets too nosy," he said, "let's get back on the road. We'll talk more about our wonderful marriage on the way."

"At least we now know where we met and fell in everlasting love. That's a start."

7

The road followed an old Roman path through the Cotswolds, passing villages of golden limestone cottages and soft-edged fields beneath a rinsed blue sky. Caitrin was silent as she watched the landscape pass.

"Is this your first time in the Cotswolds?" Hector asked.

"Yes, it's beautiful, and everything here is so clean," she said. "Even the sheep are white."

"Sheep *are* white."

Caitrin put her hands together as though she were praying and opened them to make a steep *V*. "My home town, Abertillery, is in the bottom of a valley, along with a half-dozen coal mines, an ironworks, and a foundry. Oh, and a gasworks. We have gray sheep. Gray everything. Hang the clean white washing on the line, and it turns gray in minutes."

She unfolded a map and traced their progress. The two-lane road was narrow and serpentine, and several times they were slowed by a trundling farm cart or tractor. Twice traffic was stopped while workers removed direction signs.

"Now that is definitely what I call daft," Caitrin said as she watched them unscrew the signs. "How low and slow would the German bombers have to fly to read the road signs?" She held up her road map, turned it upside down, and looked baffled. "*Gott in Himmel, mein Führer!* We iz ordered to bomb zis place called Marston Meysey, but I zink zat is Ampney Crucis. Or could it be being ze Stanton Fitzwarren? Holy sauerkraut, ve just bombeded der Little Coxwell, vot are ve to do? Ve are so lost!"

Hector laughed. "I think it's more to confuse ground troops than Luftwaffe aeroplanes."

"Ground troops?" Caitrin's smile faded. "I don't ever want to imagine or see German soldiers marching over this countryside."

"Me neither, but it's happened before. That's how most of the great English families started. Over the centuries there were waves of invading Angles, Saxons, Vikings, and Normans."

"Who pushed the original British west into Wales and Ireland."

"Yes."

"So I suppose that means the Irish are the Welsh who could swim." Caitrin shivered. "Sometimes I think this island is far too small for so much history."

Hector pulled into a lay-by and turned off the engine. "We're close to Cockleford Manor, and I forgot to give you this earlier." He handed her a small box. She opened it.

"Engagement *and* wedding rings. My goodness." She slipped on the rings and held her hand into the light. The diamond arrangement would not have been her design choice, but she said nothing about that, not wanting to hurt his feelings. "These are so beautiful. Is this Winnie the Churchill's bright idea?"

"No, it was mine."

"Who would have imagined such a thing?" Her face softened. "Behind that proper English exterior of yours lies a big soft puppy."

"With dangerous eyes."

"Yes, but the rest of you isn't. Are these real diamonds?"

"Hardly."

"And the wedding ring, real pretend gold, is engraved with Celtic motifs. That's very loving and thoughtful of you. You must have spent a fortune."

"Three pounds ten, and I get a pound refund if I bring them back undamaged. I got the rings because we have to be careful, Catty. It's the little details that will give us away."

"So this means I am now to be called Lady Neville-Percy?"

"No, you would be addressed as Lady Caitrin."

"That calms my socialist soul, just a little."

"Are you ready to test our marriage out on Charles and Elizabeth Ashtonthorpe, the ancient family of Cockleford Manor?"

"How ancient a family?"

"Charles's great-grandfather was a certain Claude Thorpe, a Liverpool laborer and self-made man in the 1830s who owned lead mines. Couldn't read or write but made a fortune supplying bullets to the British army. He bought Cockleford Manor when it was in ruins and the owners bankrupt; I believe the usual fast women and reckless gambling were involved in the downfall. Claude rebuilt it, and also rebuilt his name into Ashtonthorpe. They're that ancient."

"Gawd, they're mere parvenus compared to us ancient Neville-Percys." She flashed the rings and tapped the dashboard. "Onwards, Victoria, onwards."

Cockleford Manor was imposing. Its honey-colored Italianate exterior stretched across a rise above a lake. Massive yew trees edged it and towered over a walled garden. Charles and Elizabeth Ashtonthorpe were standing at the porte-cochère as they drove up.

"Here we go, heads up, so just you behave," Hector said as he switched off the engine.

"I promise not to pick my nose or drop a single aitch."

"Just don't swipe the silver."

The Ashtonthorpes were effusive in their greeting: Charles, a middle-aged man made of straight lines, except for a prominent, catenary curve of a stomach; and his wife Elizabeth, small, tilted off-center, and with a nervous habit of clasping and unclasping her hands to harmonize with a fluttering smile. She wore an old-fashioned blue dress decorated with a brooch shaped like a swan. The sole servant was named Wendy, an inscrutable girl with a myopic stare, who showed them to their room and left without saying a word. Caitrin collapsed onto the bed, arms outstretched.

"I'm tired. How big is this place?" she asked.

"Thirty bedrooms, maybe more, and the same number of rooms on the ground floor."

"Poor Wendy must spend all day making beds. No wonder she looks so sad."

"They are almost all empty and decaying, though," Hector said. "Roland and I used to play hide and seek in them. So many, we never could find each other. We have to dress for dinner. Elizabeth wants to impress you."

"Roast beef and Yorkshire pud would impress me, and I packed only one dress."

"I'm sure you'll look marvelous in it."

She did, too, wearing a sea-foam green rayon cocktail dress with a simple row of pearls, although she also looked lost, as did the others, in the cavernous oak-paneled dining room. The table was dressed with glittering ranks of cutlery and a centerpiece of flowers that Charles had Wendy remove because they made him sneeze. Hector sat opposite Caitrin in the middle with Charles and Elizabeth marooned at either end of the table. Caitrin noticed Charles had stopped blinking, and his face was flushed. He had apparently been drinking for a while and looked as though he intended to continue.

"What a pity Roland isn't here. He'll be so disappointed to have missed you," Elizabeth said, and Caitrin thought she detected a thickness of tongue. Perhaps both Ashtonthorpes had tanked up well before dinner.

"Where is Roland?" Hector asked.

"He's in Catterick. Knocking new recruits into shape. It's a miserable place, so I'm told. Then, it is in Yorkshire, so what can one expect?" Charles said.

"We were so surprised to hear you were married," Elizabeth said. "There was no official notice. Not even a word about it in *Tatler*."

Hector shrugged. "It's the war, I'm afraid. It's not really the best time for a grand affair. We decided to make it simple."

"Registry office?"

"Yes."

"Which one?"

"Chelsea," Hector said.

"Kensington," Caitrin said at the same time and recovered. "I wanted Kensington, but Chelsea was easier."

Wendy appeared, served, and left looking as though she was about to burst into tears or stab Charles in the neck. Charles drank his wine and poured another glass.

"Your family is in Wales?" Elizabeth asked, and Caitrin knew it was the first question in a series of probes to find out precisely where she would fit in the rigid hierarchy of their world.

"Yes."

"Hector tells me your maiden name is Colline. Are you by any chance related to the Harlech Collyns?"

"No, the County Cork Collines."

"Oh, Irish." There was an uncharted and tragic disappointment in just those two words. Charles intruded.

"You're not enlisting, Hector? I should have imagined a strong chap like you would be out there leading the charge. Follow me, chaps, over the top and all that," Charles said in a louder voice than he intended.

"I tried to enlist in the Guards," Hector said and patted his chest. "But during my physical they discovered a weakness in my heart. It seems there's a faulty valve somewhere. Rather an unpleasant surprise, really, and so disappointing."

Wendy silently appeared again, removed their plates, and served a second course. Caitrin attempted to send her an empathetic smile, but the maid was unreceptive. Caitrin had visions of the girl going downstairs, closing the door, and doing unkind things to the family dog. Charles swallowed another glass of wine.

"I do so love a romantic encounter," Elizabeth said, forging bravely past Caitrin's lack of pedigree and returning to the fray. "Now you really must tell me. Where did you two first meet?"

"Oh, do let me tell it this time, darling." Caitrin inhaled a calming breath as Hector flashed her a warning glance. "I arrested him one Saturday night on Regent Street for being drunk and disorderly in charge of a bicycle," she said. "Then I decided to let him go because he was landed gentry and so frightfully handsome. But I kept the bicycle—for his own safety, you understand—and gave it to my brother to ride to the mine when he came out of prison."

That brought another dismayed *Oh* from Elizabeth.

"Arrested him?" Charles said, astonished at the thought. "You're a policewoman?"

"Yes, I am."

Charles laughed, and it was not at all a pleasant sound. "I remember Sir Nevil Macready being against women police, saying something about he didn't want vinegary spinsters or blighted middle-aged fanatics in the force."

"Perhaps so, but I am neither."

"For a woman I suppose that's quite adventurous really, but of course you will have to give up that sort of silly thing now you are part of the Neville-Percy family," Elizabeth said.

"But of course," Caitrin answered, teeth politely clenched. "Wouldn't want to be silly and sully the good old family name."

"Do you have any fresh news from London about the war?" Charles asked.

"No great changes, I'm afraid. Only that the Germans are still bombing London, and our brave boys are still shooting them down, while across the Channel it appears the Wehrmacht invasion army grows daily."

"Invasion. Lord Halifax was right all along about negotiating with Hitler. He should have been made prime minister, not that drunken fool Churchill."

"You think so?" Hector said.

"The king thought so, and said so too to Halifax. Churchill and his fools don't understand Hitler, and if the French had minded their manners—they're such resentful fools, so, so French—this war would never have happened. As if they ever had manners."

"Do you think it is really that simple?" Caitrin said, but Charles ignored her.

"The countries Hitler went into were rightfully German. The Ruhr was theirs. Sudetenland was German, but it was given to Czechoslovakia, a country that didn't even exist until the end of the last war. No wonder he is angry. He has damn good reasons."

Caitrin said nothing. Charles had become a spinning whirlwind of grievance, turning slowly but increasing in speed. Getting in his way would be dangerous.

"And another thing no one wants to talk about, but we must, he is absolutely right about the Jews." Charles waved an erratic hand at nothing in particular. "Even I got taken by a damn Jew. Clarence Hatry."

"Is Clarence a Jewish name?" Caitrin asked.

"Son of Julius Hatry and Henriette Katzenstein." Charles spat out the names. "That sound Jewish enough for you?"

Caitrin went silent. Charles was getting redder, louder, and angrier.

"He even got Henry Paulet, Marquess of Winchester, involved. I lost a fortune to that filthy Jew. Hitler is absolutely right. We should drive the Jews out. They're not like us, they're nothing but money-grubbing leeches who have latched onto our society. Always have been, always will be. We're of the same stock as the Germans. Anglo-Saxon. True white people."

"Surely you don't want Nazis taking over our government?" Hector said.

"Of course not. That's just a silly hoax perpetuated by Churchill so he can keep control. They would do no such thing. Hitler doesn't want to fight us; we're brothers. We negotiate peace; he leaves us alone and turns to fight the socialists and the Russian Bolsheviks in the east. We should help him with that before they come here in a great ugly tide. And, mark my words, they will swarm all over England if left unchecked and destroy our way of life."

Elizabeth put up a hand to warn Charles, but he brushed it aside. He was not finished. "Instead of shooting each other, we English should be building bridges with the Germans. They are our true brothers, not the French or the Poles. Together we can fight the socialists and the communists. Keep Great Britain great, and our empire too. Bridges, we must build bridges."

"Thank you for dinner," Caitrin said as she got to her feet, emotions barely in control. "Forgive me, but it has been such a long day, and I am so very tired." She left before anyone could reply.

Hector entered their room a few minutes later, slumped into a chair, and they stared blindly at each other for a moment before he said, "That was a veritable Verdun barrage."

"*Sieg heil*, old chap. Kick out the Jews and hug dear old peace-loving, misunderstood Alfie Hitler."

"He was testing me to see if I was a member of *Die Brücke*. He looked right at me when he said, 'we must build bridges.'"

"We also need to get our story straight." She flashed him an inquiring look. "Do you know what is strange, Hecky? They never said a word about us turning up towing a horse box full of hay bales. I know we're in the country, but wouldn't you be a bit curious? They didn't ask where we were going either. It's as if they already knew. We have to leave here."

"Not at night with the blackout, and not until they're asleep."

"Asleep? Passed out is more likely."

"You get some sleep," Hector said. "I'll go to the bathroom while you change."

"And then what?"

"And what then what?"

She spread her hands toward the bed and laughed at his innocence. "That then what then what."

"Oh, yes, of course," he blurted and looked horrified. "I'll sleep in that chair."

"Do you really have a bad heart?"

"No, I do not." He took her hand and pressed it to his chest, the sudden intimacy startling her.

She pulled her hand away. "Then why didn't you enlist?"

"Who says I didn't? Good night, Lady Caitrin. My dear, beloved wife Catty."

8

They slipped out of the house before dawn. It was a cold morning, everything was coated with a heavy dew, and Caitrin shivered as she climbed into the car and quietly eased the door shut. Hector pulled out the choke, pressed the accelerator pedal once, and whispered, "Pray Victoria starts first time."

Caitrin nodded. "Come on, Victoria, or the Ashtonthorpes will not be amused."

The engine fired, hesitated, and roared into life. Hector engaged first gear and let the car roll away.

"That is guaranteed to wake up every Ashtonthorpe right back to old Liverpool Claude." Caitrin giggled and slipped into a "posh" English accent. "This is all rather cloak-and-daggery. A jolly jape, what ho, Jeeves?"

Hector changed gears and switched on the headlamps. With only one on the driver's side working, as required by blackout regulations, and covered, except for a tiny slit, little light escaped, and it barely illuminated the driveway. Windscreen wipers smeared dirt crescents across the glass.

"I can't see a damn thing," Hector said.

"Fortunately, there's nothing to see. Look out, a deer!"

Hector braked, and Victoria skidded to a halt.

"It's not a deer, it's a Wendy," Caitrin said and opened her door. The Ashtonthorpes' maid Wendy, pinned to the darkness by the feeble headlamp light and clutching a pillowcase stuffed with her belongings, looked scared and ready to run. Caitrin got out of the car and went to her. "Wendy, what on earth are you doing out here?"

"I'm going home, Madam," she said, her chin tilting and with an edge of defiance to her voice. "I mean it this time and no stopping me. Not changing my mind."

"Where's your home?"

"Ipswich."

"You're a long way from home."

Wendy nodded, barely, and shivered.

"Aren't we all, I suppose, and your feet are soaking wet," Caitrin said and took the girl's arm. "Hop in the car. We can at least take you away from here."

Wendy climbed into the rear seat, Caitrin sat in front, and Hector pulled away. There was silence until they reached the end of the driveway and turned onto the road. The day was getting lighter. Wendy was motionless. She seemed even to have stopped breathing and clutched the pillowcase to her breast as though it were her only protection against the world. It was.

Caitrin turned to face her and said, "Were you going home or escaping?"

"Madam?" Wendy was startled by the blunt question.

"Don't call me madam; we're all girls here," Caitrin said and poked Hector. "Except for him, and he's just the driver and doesn't count."

Wendy darted a glance at Hector, who looked suitably chauffeur-aloof.

"It's all right, Wendy; we were escaping that dreadful place too," Caitrin said, and that opened the floodgates for Wendy.

"It's not fair. I had to do everything, I did," she said, swiping at her nose with the back of a hand. "There was five servants when I started and they all left and it was just me at the end to do everything."

"There used to be a lot more than five," Hector said.

"Not now there ain't."

"Good for you for deciding to leave. What are you going to do when you get home to Ipswich?" Caitrin asked.

The question seemed to baffle Wendy, and it took her some time to answer. "What would I really like to do?"

"Yes."

"I know it sounds silly, but I always wanted to be a lorry driver and go all over the place. See things I haven't seen before, things I just heard talked about."

"Why didn't you?"

That question too was difficult for her. "Can I whisper?" she said, leaned forward, and whispered in Caitrin's ear before she could reply.

"That's the past, it's ancient history, and there's so much time ahead of you," Caitrin said and patted the girl's hand. "You can still be a lorry driver if you want. With this war going on, the country needs all the lorry drivers it can get, male and female."

"I don't know if I could do something like that. You could."

"And why not you?"

"I'm just a maid."

"I was a maid once too," Caitrin said.

"You were?"

"I was indeed." Caitrin squeezed Wendy's arm. "You can do it if you really want to."

Wendy looked as though she wanted to believe her.

"You can, Wendy."

"You can let me off at that bus stop up there if you like," Wendy said, pointing ahead.

Caitrin wound down her window to say goodbye as Hector

stopped and Wendy got out, but he interrupted by leaning across and handing the girl a banknote.

Wendy stared at it in amazement. "A fiver! Never had one of these before."

"Unfold it. There are two fivers. Use the money to go be a lorry driver, Wendy. Drive all over the place, and see everything that needs to be seen. You deserve it, there's no time like the present, and your country needs your service."

Tears brimmed in Wendy's eyes. "Thank you, Sir. Thank you, Madam. I'll always remember this." She sniffed back her tears, took a step forward, and lowered her voice as she said, "Can I ask a question, if you don't mind?"

"Yes, what?" Caitrin said.

"What's in the horse box?"

"The Crown Jewels."

Wendy's hand flew to her mouth as she laughed. "That's funny, that is. Clever. I would never have thought of that one in a million years."

She waved as they drove away, and Caitrin watched her image getting smaller in the mirror. "She looks so little and alone."

"Aren't we all?" Hector said. "I cannot believe you told her about the Crown Jewels."

"Mum raised me not to lie. And that was a very kind thing you did for Wendy."

"I hope she gets to drive lorries." He gave her a weary smile. "You're not wearing your wedding rings."

"I'm not married."

"But you were a maid."

"Yes."

"Yes? That's it?"

"What would you like to know?"

"Whatever you want to tell me."

"For a start, in service I learned all about the ludicrous display of cutlery Elizabeth Ashtonthorpe laid out last night."

"That was a bit much, and I did wonder how you navigated it so well."

"With the Slump, there was no work, and the family was having a hard time, so I went to be a maid at Quantock Priory in Somerset." Caitrin's face tightened, and she angled away, gazing out of the side window. "I was fifteen and learned to take care of myself in that place."

"You had a difficult time there?"

"The youngest son of the family, he was a big hulk of a creature, had this 'they all belong to me' attitude about the maids. He had already hurt a couple of them before I got there, and he'd gotten away with it."

"But not you?"

"He hurt me too." Her knuckles rapped a hard tattoo on the glass. "But I'm told his limp is permanent."

"What did Wendy whisper to you? Her big secret."

"Wendy said she couldn't be a lorry driver because of having a baby when she was fifteen. They sent her off to a home for unwed mothers, where she had the baby, came back alone, and has no idea what happened to it."

She turned to face him, her expression profoundly sad. "There are thousands of Wendys. They marry early, have babies, and settle into being old before they're twenty-one. They deserve at least a fighting chance at a wider horizon. I don't want to hurt your feelings, Hecky, but the landed gentry have got to go. No more parasites. It's got to be our turn now."

9

Their next stop, Hammersleigh Hall, was an unlovely pile buried deep in a wooded valley. The road through the estate was neglected, as were the flower beds, which had long since gone to seed that spread over the uncut lawns, and Hector had to stop several times to remove fallen branches so they could continue. Wallace, Sir Hereward's butler, stood at the door to greet them. He looked equally decrepit, but his welcome was sincere.

"Lord Hector, it has been so long. Welcome back to Hammersleigh Hall."

"Hello, Wallace. This is my wife, Caitrin."

"M'lady." Wallace bent a little at the waist, his lungs whistling with the effort. "Sir Hereward will be so pleased to see you."

He ushered them inside, and Caitrin shivered. Outside, it was not a cold day, but dampness made it so inside. She guessed that none of the doors or windows had been opened in centuries.

"This way." Wallace led them through the Great Hall, which was guarded by dusty suits of armor commanded by dark portraits of glowering ancient Walters-Hammersleigh aristocracy, and into the library. Caitrin caught her breath. These old buildings never smelled particularly fresh, but this one had the scent of recent decay.

"Lord Hector and his wife to see you, Sir," Wallace announced to a bed set up near the window.

They approached the bed. Sir Hereward was a tiny, low rise in the center of the blankets. He had been reduced to a skeleton over which the skin was stretched taut. His eyes were bright, though, and he spoke in a strong, clear voice.

"Hector, my boy, what an unexpected surprise. Excuse me for not getting up. I can't do that anymore. And who is this lovely apparition?" A skeletal hand slipped out from the bedclothes.

Caitrin stepped forward and took his hand. It was warm, the skin soft, the bones hard ridges. "I am Caitrin, who just married Hector."

Hereward's thin lips creased into a smile. "Hector, your parents will be so delighted to have this wonderful creature in the family."

"Yes, Sir, they will."

To everyone's surprise, Hereward winked. "No doubt you will have strong, healthy babies."

"I should imagine so, but he'll only be making a contribution, while I'll be the one making the commitment," Caitrin said, and Hereward laughed, a rustling sound that sapped his strength. Wallace tilted his head so he could drink water.

"You have a good one here, Hector. Fresh blood flowing in the ancient family's veins."

"I believe so, Sir."

"Sit down, sit down, and tell me more."

Sir Hereward listened intently to their conversations and

laughed at their witticisms, as though he had not heard a human voice in weeks. He stressed how sorry he was to see them go. But the next day they were happy to leave, and Wallace escorted them to the car.

"Thank you both for coming," he said. "We have had no one here for such a long time."

"It was good to see you both."

Wallace seemed to notice his ruined surroundings for the first time, and to him they changed as he spoke. "It's not like it used to be. Twenty-five servants we had back then, if you include the gardeners and stable lads. And such a lively family too. Always people coming and going. And dogs, we had dogs for the children. There is nothing like a child's laughter. Kept me on my toes, I'll tell you, day and night. But it was all worth it."

"The place may be run down, but I noticed the flowerbeds directly outside Sir Hereward's window are well-maintained," Caitrin said.

Wallace looked down at his shoes, his head making little shy bobbing movements. "It's all he's got to look at every day, so I put on Jessup's old smock and hat, he was the head gardener, and take care of the flowers. I wave to Sir Hereward and I'm too far away to be recognized, so he waves back, thinking it's Jessup and everything is like it used to be. It's not much, but I do what I can for him."

Hector put a hand on his shoulder. "You must take care of yourself, Wallace."

"I do my best, Sir, but Sir Hereward's my greatest concern. Life will look after me as it should."

Caitrin bit her lip. This man—this poor, fragile, wonderful little man. She embraced him. "You're a marvel, Wallace, and I'm so glad to have met you."

She stepped back. "Give life a nudge or two to make sure it takes care of you properly. That's important to me."

Wallace blinked back tears. "Thank you, Ma'am."

He stood outside the front door and waved until they disappeared from view.

"Poor Wallace," Caitrin said as Hector drove them away. "Sir Hereward could drop dead there any day. So could Wallace, and not be found for ages."

"They probably will, and they won't be the only ones," Hector replied. "So many estates had one or two sons who died in the Great War, or now in this one, and that is the end of the family."

"How sad."

"The Walters-Hammersleigh family is an ancient one, stretching back to the Elizabethan era. Sir Hereward's son died at Mons, and he was the last of the line."

As the sun rose, they were driving through a different landscape. The countryside was more open, and the Cotswolds' honey-colored, thatched cottages had been replaced by the red-brick, tiled-roof houses of the Midlands.

Caitrin fidgeted in her seat, stretched, and yawned. "Hecky, I am hungry. No, I am ravenous."

"You're always hungry."

"True. My dad used to say with me it was like feeding a donkey strawberries."

"Look at the map. Are there any decent-sized villages ahead?"

She spread the map across her knees and read place names aloud. "Burton Bank, Snudgeley, Westthorn, all tiny places smaller than their names. Oh, here's one a bit bigger: Momble under Neen. That sounds like something a doctor would say about a hernia. Got a bad one here. The lad's got a bad case of Momble under his Neen, nurse. To save his life, we'll have to operate right away and take his head off. Them's Mombles can be deadly if left untreated."

"Sounds more like someone from a Gilbert and Sullivan

opera. Hail, here cometh Pooh Bah, the Grand Momble under Neen."

"It does have a square, a church, and a post office, though, so if we're lucky it might have a tea shop."

"How far away?"

Caitrin measured the distance on the map, raised her hand with the thumb and index fingertips a few inches apart, and said, "That far."

He frowned at her. She grinned back and said, "Where are we going to today, exactly?"

"I do not know, exactly." He pushed the list of stately homes to her. "Why don't you peruse this and take your pick?"

"Peruse, huh?" She held up the list and read aloud, "Castle-morton Manor."

"Too far to the east."

"Ashleworth House."

"Behind us."

"Walvert Frome Hall."

"Home of the Madison-Hardynges. I know their daughter Emily."

"You know Emily in what sense?"

"Stop it. We'll go there for tonight."

"I have been thinking."

"An unsupervised woman working with highly dangerous tools."

"An intelligent, unsupervisable woman." She tapped the dashboard. "If your car is called Victoria, incidentally a charming name, then shouldn't the horse box be called Albert? The man obediently following behind the woman, wherever she may wander."

"I suppose so," he said, sighed, and surrendered. "If you so wish, darling."

"Something else to consider. Have you ever actually seen the Crown Jewels?"

"No. And no, we're not stopping to look at them."

"There's no need to." She slid over the car seat with the ease of an otter, opened her suitcase, and returned with a book. "*The Royal Crown Jewels*. I borrowed it from Mrs. Bardwell. She just adores royalty, and the poor dear didn't know that by renting me a room she had brought a socialist viper into her bosom."

"Some viper."

"Some bosom." Caitrin opened the book. "Some of the Jewels are over eight hundred years old, but most of the recent set are from the reign of Charles II, three hundred years ago."

"Our beloved Oliver Cromwell had the early ones melted down or sold when the monarchy was abolished."

"What a man. If ever I have a son, I'll name him Oliver. Maybe twice." She read, "'In 1282, after Llewelyn ap Gruffyd was defeated by Edward I, the Welsh crown of the legendary King Arthur was surrendered to England. The Scottish Crown followed a few years later.'"

"Sorry about that, but I wasn't there, so don't blame me."

"It says the English kings were forever selling, melting down, or pawning the Jewels. Doesn't seem as if they held them in much esteem. They were keen on swords, though, especially Charles I. Look at this picture." She flashed the book in front of him, and for a moment he lost sight of the road. "Three swords: the Sword of Temporal Justice, the Sword of Spiritual Justice, and the Sword of Mercy, also called Curtana, which has a blunt tip, probably from Henry VIII using it to open a beer bottle. There's more detail about kings and queens and their interminable wars I'll gloss over. Mostly because it's incredibly repetitive and boring." She slapped the book shut. "History lesson over. It's now time for questions."

"Would that be asking or answering, and benign or accusatory questions?"

"Pointed ones. To finish what we started last night. God,

that seems so long ago. Ignoring the wobbly heart fable, are you enlisted?"

"Yes."

"In what service?"

"You are a police constable?"

"Yes, a *woman* police constable. As if the difference isn't already apparent."

"Is it true that women constables are required to walk the beat in pairs, and with a pair of male constables following them ten yards behind to keep them safe?"

"That is ancient history, and I don't walk the beat anymore. What service are you in?"

"Is it true most of your role as a woman police constable is to save growing girls from temptation?"

"Girls like your pal Emily Madison-Hardynge? Again, past history. Are you in the army?"

"And is it a belief that police work will make women hard and superficial?"

"You be the judge. Is it the navy?"

"What department of the police do you actually belong to? Is it even the police? Not going to tell me, are you?"

"And you're not going to tell me, are you?"

"Seems not." Hector put out his hand. "Shall we agree on a draw?"

She gave a rueful smile and shook his hand. "Draw."

Momble under Neen did have a small teashop, the Church House, in the village square. It was nowhere near a church but opposite the post office, which had a red telephone box outside. The tea-shop waitress—a round, cherry-cheeked woman—was surly until Hector made a show of stacking four half-crowns on the table. They did much to change her attitude to match her cheeks.

"Birmingham has been bombed," Caitrin read from a newspaper she had bought from the local tobacconist. "And London again, of course, and they even took a swipe at Liverpool."

They watched a group of men—mostly middle-aged, some older, with flat caps and civilian clothes—amble into the square and create something resembling a military rank. A few of them were self-conscious and made jokes, while others seemed distracted, and one was struggling to light a huge briar pipe. Each of them had a wooden rifle on his shoulder, some of which appeared to be freshly carved, and no two were alike. A tall, gray-haired man, who had grown in all directions since his military service ended and now barely fit into a Great War army captain's uniform, was issuing orders with mixed results.

"And with wooden rifles, just what harm do they intend to inflict on the invading Germans?" Caitrin said. "Shooting nasty splinters?"

"It's a bit sad and desperate if that's all we've got to defend king and country. I read some of the Home Guard directives. They said that any parachutist landing in civilian clothes is to be shot immediately. Another one warned about German parachutists dressed as nuns."

"You're being silly."

"I am not."

"Who would ever want to look up at a nun floating down? What an unholy image."

"Now lodged in my mind."

"Unfortunately forever."

"I read one that said German paratroopers land with their hands above their heads, so you should immediately shoot them because it means they have a grenade in each hand. This ignores the fact that any paratrooper, regardless of nationality, has his hands above his head to control the guide lines."

"The world has gone mad."

"They also killed all the snakes and poisonous creatures in

the London Zoo and have marksmen stationed there to shoot lions and tigers if a bomb drops and frees them."

"*Die Brücke*," Caitrin said. "I was thinking that German is such a harsh, unlovely language, all hard *C*s and *K*s. Not a wonderful wobbly *W* or a slippery *S* anywhere to be found. It sounds as though it was created by a horde of drunken clog dancers in an empty chapel. I don't like the Germans much."

"Yes, we finally agree on something."

"What about agreeing on our background story?"

"The line of least resistance," he said and sighed. "What if you tell the story, and I'll nod my head like a good, henpecked hubby?"

"You talked me into it."

"Just please don't get too creative." He gestured to the post office. "I should call in before we go any farther."

She watched him cross the road and enter the telephone box. In the square the captain had the men marching, or at least moving mostly the same way in two ragged ranks. She was contemplating requisitioning Hector's last undefended slice of bacon when he left the box, dodged between the miniature army ranks, and dropped into his chair.

"Don't you dare," he said, slapping her hand and rescuing his bacon from her predatory fingers.

"Thought never crossed my mind. I was just rearranging it for artistic effect. Any news?"

"No, apart from the bombing is getting worse. Walter Thompson is going out of his mind because, while everyone else runs for the bomb shelter, Churchill insists on going up to the roof to watch the attack. Usually with a glass of brandy and a cigar, and without his helmet and gas mask."

"Death or Glory Churchill. Does he know Mafeking has been relieved?"

"Thompson said he tried being slow to unlock the half-dozen doors to get to the roof until Churchill threatened to shoot him if he didn't hurry up."

"And knowing Winston, he probably would."

"We're still on schedule. Six days to get to Greenock." Hector glanced at his watch. "Shall we go and visit the Madison-Hardynges?"

Caitrin sighed, took the wedding and engagement rings from her pocket, and slipped them onto her finger. "Oh dear, it's back to being married again. Poor Emily will be just so crushed to know you're taken."

10

Emily Madison-Hardynge was not all crushed at Hector being taken. Not even the slightest bit dented, because she was not at Walvert Frome Hall. "Em's gone off to London," her father, Sir Rupert Madison-Hardynge, said as he tore out another rose bush. A broad-shouldered man with prodigious eyebrows, large hands, and a ruddy complexion, Rupert wore Wellington boots, corduroys, and an ancient cardigan as he laid waste to the garden. Helping him was his wife, Penelope, a lady but in no way fragile.

"What is she doing in London?" Hector asked.

"She is down there doing her bit for the boys."

"I'm sure she is." Caitrin whispered an aside to Hector, her face a mask of innocence. Hector shot her an admonishing glance that had little effect.

"Driving an ambulance, she says. All I can say is God protect the pedestrians if she is." Rupert tore out another rose bush and threw it onto a growing pile. "Penelope's been such a rock. The rose garden is hers. It's taken years to cultivate and only a day to destroy."

"I do so hate to see it go, but it is the best soil for a Victory vegetable garden," Penelope said. "So we can do our bit like everyone else."

"With well over a thousand acres of farmland and seven hundred of woodlands and orchards, you'd think we'd be productive enough, but Penelope insists otherwise."

"To do our every little bit helps, and it's a worthy sacrifice," Penelope said as she brushed Rupert's arm. It was a simple yet affectionate gesture, and Caitrin noticed it. "And this garden, no matter how modest it might be, will be my own contribution."

Rupert straightened and dusted his hands clean. "That is enough wanton destruction for now. Let's go inside."

Walvert Frome Hall was not what Caitrin expected. There was no elegant exterior, no grand staircase inside or acres of dark wood paneling. Not even a suit of armor or paintings of ancient ancestors. The white, timber-framed building was constructed of wattle and plaster with a red brick chimney and a moss-studded tile roof. It resembled a large farmhouse rather than a stately home. Even the great hall with its white plaster walls, exposed timbers, and modest minstrel gallery seemed almost intimate. There were few true right angles anywhere, and the sofas and chairs had endured long lives.

"Drink?" Rupert said, pouring whisky without waiting for anyone to reply. He handed around the glasses, and they sat before the fireplace. "So you're married. When did that happen?"

Rupert and Penelope may well have been Caitrin's class enemies, but she found them appealing. Neither had airs and graces, and she especially enjoyed Rupert being so direct. She let Hector answer.

"Just a few weeks ago, actually," Hector said. "At the registry office. Seemed it was the right thing to do in the circumstances."

"Circumstances? Not pregnant, are you?" Rupert asked. "Not you, Hector, you great lummox, her."

"No, I'm not," Caitrin replied. She liked Rupert; he reminded her of her father. "But it's not for lack of trying, though."

Rupert laughed, Penelope smiled, and Hector blushed as he hid behind his glass. Caitrin studied Rupert and noticed something. Unless she was misjudging him, he did not believe a word Hector said, and he knew they were not married. On the drive to the estate she and Hector had discussed ways to discover if the Madison-Hardynges were members of *Die Brücke,* but Rupert was obviously a canny fox and she doubted they could trap him easily.

"Tell me, how are things going in London?" Rupert asked.

"Anxious times, I'm afraid," Hector said. "There is great fear of an imminent German invasion, although no one wants to admit it."

"What about Churchill? Do you think he is the right man to take care of things at this time?"

There, perhaps that was the opening. "I believe he is doing the best he can in the circumstances," Caitrin said.

"Perhaps he is, but will his best be good enough to save the country?"

"I don't know. What do you think?"

Rupert paused and swirled his drink. "Churchill is not a man I would get behind. He is an opportunist, changes parties to suit himself. It can be hard to trust a man like that."

"I understand." Caitrin exhaled a silent calming breath and asked, "Bearing in mind his opportunism, would you say he was the kind of man to deal realistically with the Germans? Do you think he is the sort of man who would build bridges?"

"Bridges?" Rupert swallowed his drink. "I would not normally vote for him, but he knows Hitler is not to be trusted. This is not the time to build bridges; we need walls instead, damn big ones. And if anyone can pull the country together and keep the Germans from invading England, it's Churchill."

Caitrin sat back, relieved, and asked, "May I have another drink? That was good whisky."

Rupert stood and took her glass. "I like this young woman of yours, Hector. She'll keep you in your place."

He went for the bottle and poured everyone a fresh drink, before sitting again to say, "I'm surprised to see you driving, Hector. I thought private vehicles had been banished from the nation's highways. Petrol rationing and all that."

"I'm taking it home, where it can stay for the duration, unless the government needs it."

"Are you on leave?"

"No, I'm afraid I failed my physical," Hector said and tapped his chest. "Wonky ticker. Quite a disappointing surprise, really."

Caitrin could sense Rupert did not believe that either, and she waited for the next question. He was a cat playing with a favorite mouse. "Bad ticker, huh? Better go easy on him at night, Caitrin. You don't want to lose a brand-new husband. Might need to line up a reserve one, just in case. Let me know if you do."

Caitrin laughed. Rupert was truly a fascinating man.

"And you, young lady? Tell me, how do you occupy your time?"

"I'm a police constable."

"Police?" His eyes widened. "Ooh, handcuffs and truncheons."

"Rupert, if you don't behave in front of our guests, I shall cut you off," Penelope said, but with a forgiving smile. "That is going to be your last drink—"

"Before dinner," he interrupted. "All right. Dinner. Nothing elaborate, we all eat out of the same trough here, so don't dress up."

He put down his glass, stood, and said, "Why are you towing a horse box?"

"It's Albert," Caitrin said to deflect him, although she knew he wouldn't be diverted for long.

"Albert?"

"Hector's father called his car Victoria, so I thought the horse box should be named Albert. Always being led by the nose and following one step behind."

Rupert roared with laughter. "That is funny because it's damn true. Well done, Caitrin, well done. Now, what's in it?"

The question came flat and hard and caught her off guard. She said, "The Crown Jewels."

But Rupert Madison-Hardynge was not Wendy the maid. "That's impossible. Too damn small," he said. "You'd need a bigger box. So it's probably just the important parts, right? What the public thinks are the Crown Jewels. The crowns, orbs and scepters and such."

"And such," Caitrin said.

"Why do you have them?"

"To keep them safe. For our country."

Rupert touched her cheek and turned to Hector. "I don't know what you two are up to, but you should marry this girl, Hector. It would be the best thing you ever did for yourself. If she'll have you."

The flagstone-floored bedroom, white-walled and cold, was small, as was the bed. The only furniture was a half-sized wardrobe and a chest of drawers. With a great sigh Caitrin sat on the edge of the bed. "That was unexpected."

"Unexpected? That's a Welsh understatement. It could have been an absolute disaster," Hector said. "Imagine if we found out Rupert was a member of *Die Brücke after* he discovered we had the Crown Jewels."

"That he worked it out so easily is what concerns me. It means the longer we're out here, the more likely someone else will do that too."

"We have just five days left," Hector said as he sat next to her. "What if we stop at only one more home and then go directly to mine? One long day's drive tomorrow, spend two days at home, and we can get to Greenock easily from there in two days."

"You, me, and your mum." Caitrin fell back onto the bed and stared up at the ceiling.

"At least we know my mother's not part of *Die Brücke*."

"Maybe so, but can you vouch for all the cocker spaniels?"

Hector lay on the bed next to her, with their heads almost touching, and looked up at the ceiling. "What are you staring at?"

She pointed to a thin crack edging a rough patch of plaster.

"Looks like the Thames at Windsor to me," he said.

"More like the Webb's Brewery sign in Aberbeeg, or maybe Mussolini's profile," Caitrin said as she stood and moved toward the door.

"Where are you going?"

"I'm going to have myself a nice hot bath."

"Lucky you."

"I'll leave the water for you if you want. And the Madison-Hardynges worked out we're not married, so Penelope graciously made up another bed for me."

"Where?"

"I'll be right next door, so no snoring—or sleepwalking. Good night."

She waved and left before he could reply.

11

The morning was colder, with a frost that promised an early winter as they left Walvert Frome Hall and turned north. At Studmarsh village they stopped for Hector to make his London telephone call before continuing on. The road, narrow and twisting, was empty, as was the color-drained landscape.

"There are no cattle, no sheep, no people," Caitrin said. "Not even any birds. We could be on a different planet."

"We are moving toward the north of England. It's a different country up here."

"What did London have to say for themselves when you called?"

"They agreed that we should go to one more home and then drive straight to Marlton. Soon we'll have to come off the side roads, though, because there are so many small towns and villages to slow us down that we'll never get anywhere."

"Would you like me to drive?"

"I beg your pardon?"

"Don't beg; you're big enough to steal. I'll say it louder: would you like me to drive?"

"You?"

"There's no one else in the car. Me. Why not?"

"I just assumed—"

"Because I was a woman I couldn't drive?"

"Not so much that, but it is rather a big car and towing the loaded horse box makes it handle differently."

"I understand. So, I repeat, at the risk of sounding boring, would you like me to drive?"

"All right, after we stop for petrol. Thank you."

By late afternoon they had crossed the Manchester Ship Canal; filled up the petrol tank at Warrington, where Caitrin got behind the wheel; and taken the A49 north. The daylight was absorbed by a cloud-heavy sky, which made the land dark. The towns, row after parallel row of anonymous houses, were dim, without contrast or detail, and unemployed men clustered at every corner.

"Same country, different country," Caitrin said.

"I beg . . . sorry, what did you say?"

She gestured to the groups of men. "This morning we left the Madison-Hardynges with their thousand acres of farmland and seven hundred acres of woods and orchards, and now we're passing town after town filled with men who haven't worked in years. Poverty and no opportunity. Same country, different country."

She glanced at Hector. He was a handsome man, and kind, but he would never, could never, understand working-class life.

"When we were in the Cotswolds, we were close to Sudeley Castle," Hector said. "The Sudeley name was extinct by the fifteenth century. Other families lived there, made fortunes, wasted them, and the castle fell into ruins, although it was a pub at one point, the Castle Arms. In the eighteen hundreds, John and William Dent bought the ruins and rebuilt the castle. They were not nobility; they were merchants who made their fortune selling gloves. Death duties brought it all to an end about ten years ago."

"I don't understand the connection."

"There's more." Hector continued, "The English revere Richard the Lionheart as a legendary hero, a true-blue Englishman. The country paid a staggering ransom to free him from the clutches of the German king Henry VI, but he spent only six months in total in England, spoke little English, and mulcted the people for money to finance his endless continental wars. Some English hero."

"Now I understand even less."

Hector rubbed his face, blinked, and stared through the windscreen. "What I am saying is that there is no rhyme or reason to wealth or fame or poverty. Your grandfather must have had a miserable life to leave Ireland for work in a Welsh coal mine, but you, his granddaughter, will have a much better one. It's Fortune's Wheel, and we're all on it, Caitrin. It's always turning, and we have no control over it."

"Have you ever had to worry just once in your life about paying the rent, Hector? Or how to afford new shoes, or where the next meal is coming from?"

Hector shook his head.

"I'm going to put a spoke in that damn slow-moving wheel so the people at the bottom can get off and find a better life. And the ones at the top need to climb down and help them. Or get torn from their privileged perch."

Hector inhaled a deep breath and blew out his cheeks. "I confess you are a very good driver."

She laughed, and it relieved the moment. "I'm sorry. My apologies for the diatribe."

"I suppose we must each look after our own diatribes," Hector said and unfolded the map. "Hadnall Hall is just a few miles ahead."

Hadnall Hall was at the end of a wide, mile-long drive flanked by ancient beech trees. What was left of it. It had been one of the grander homes in the Midlands but was now a blackened, smoking ruin, an alien presence in the center of immaculately groomed lawns and flowerbeds.

"It was incendiaries that did it," a groundsman said. "They say the bombs was meant for Birmingham or Manchester, but the Germans got lost. I think it was done deliberate."

"Why do you say that?" Caitrin asked.

"Because Sir Basschurch hated them Nazis more than anything and wasn't at all shy about saying so. If you ask me, I believe some spy told the Nazis where he lived, and I think it was them getting back at him. They dropped high explosives first to rip the roof off and then followed up with incendiaries to burn the place down."

"Where did the family go?"

"They've all gone to live at their Mayfair house in London. But that's not much safer, from what I hear."

"Thank you," Hector said and turned the car around. "We'll head straight for Marlton."

Heavy rain clouds grew and brought on the night faster than they expected. There was no traffic and fewer and smaller villages. Soon they were driving alone over an empty moor, still some distance from Marlton, and the map showed no villages close. Caitrin pulled over and parked under some trees at the edge of the road.

"It's too dark to drive, and I think we should call it a day," she said and peered up at the sky. "Because this day is over."

"All right. I'll take the front seat, you can take the back bedroom," Hector said.

Caitrin cleared the back seat, pulled several sweaters and a coat from her suitcase, and curled up to sleep. "Are you all right there?"

"I am just marvelous, thank you for asking," Hector said, paused for a long moment, and said, "Caitrin, you do appreciate it isn't my fault, or Rupert's. We didn't ask to be born into our families."

"I know that, and I don't want to send you both down a coal mine. I just want a better balance in life for everyone, so people at the bottom don't slide off the edge. That's all. Good night."

"Good night."

"I have never slept with a lord before."

"Nor I with a commoner."

"Touché."

A sound outside woke Caitrin first: a scrape of metal, followed by a man muttering. Hector woke up an instant later, but she was already gone, slipping silently out and leaving the car's rear door ajar. He followed and found her standing at the open horse-box door, with hay scattered on the ground and two men kneeling with their hands in the air. Neither man looked as though he ate or bathed regularly.

"What we have before us is a pair of right villains," Caitrin said in the calmest of voices. "Thieving villains."

Hector was struck by the expressions of terror on both the men's faces—and by the Webley-Fosbery revolver in Caitrin's hand. He recognized it by the distinctive zigzag grooves on the cylinder. It was aimed at the men and unmoving: she and it could have been carved from a single block of granite.

"What to do? Do you think I should shoot one of these villains as an example to the other?" she said to Hector. "Or perhaps shoot both because they could be German spies. Or even worse, evil saboteurs."

"No, we're not German spies; we're English villains," the younger one squeaked.

"Speak for yourself. I'm not English, I'm Scottish," the other one said.

"We're British villains, then."

"What were you doing out here?" Hector asked them. "Stealing?"

"No, no," the older one said. "We was just looking for a warm, dry place to kip."

"That's it, that's right. It's perishing out here," the other one said and waved a raised hand at the horse box. "I thought it would be nice and dry in there with all them hay bales."

"Honest, missus. We wasn't going to steal nothing."

Caitrin continued as though she had not heard them. "And if I off just one, which one would you like me to execute?"

Hector knew his mouth was open, but he seemed to have no words. Caitrin turned away from the men and winked at him. She lowered the revolver and turned her back fully on them. "What if I do shoot them both, to be on the safe side, just in case they really are German saboteurs?"

She laughed as the men scrambled to their feet and sprinted away into the tree shadows.

"I didn't know you were armed."

"Now you do, and I'm sure you are too, right, Hecky?"

"Right. That's a Webley-Fosbery automatic revolver .455 caliber, six-shot," he said, gesturing to her gun. "A rara avis. Heavy thing that hasn't been manufactured in what, fifteen years? And complicated."

"Complicated, just like a woman?" Caitrin engaged the safety. "Accurate, and deadly too."

She was not smiling. He had just seen another facet of Caitrin Colline. This journey north had become an odyssey. And if he remembered his classics correctly, the first odyssey was a long and strange one too.

12

The road threaded its way through bare fields as the land ahead rose and changed. This was border country, and much of it lay hidden by a morning mist. Gradually, hedgerows were replaced by endless ribbons of gray drystone walls, and the few stunted trees were curved into submission by the prevailing wind. Although it was not raining, everything looked damp. The scattered villages, small and compact, were huddled in hollows, while isolated farmhouses sat shouldered into a protective hill. Thinly laid over granite, the soil was too poor for anything but grazing.

"I can tell we are way in the back of beyond because the road signs are still up. That means they're not expecting the Hun any time soon," Caitrin said as she gazed out of the side window, Hector having been allowed to drive again. She read the passing signposts aloud, "Bupton, Hoon, Snittlegarth, Whelpo. Impressive."

"I'm glad we can impress you."

"You have, and what's impressive in your pocket?" she

asked and laughed at his reaction. "Don't look so embarrassed-English. I meant what firearm are you carrying?"

"Browning Hi-Power .40."

"Which means you're probably Parachute Regiment, commando, or SOE."

Hector shot her a startled glance.

"It's SOE. If you didn't know Special Operations Executive existed, you wouldn't have been surprised I knew. Top secret stuff, right?"

"I am saying nothing."

"Which merely proves I am right. Don't worry, I won't tell the nazty Nazeez."

"All right. What is your organization?"

"The Women's Institute, the elite Welsh Virtue Division. Committed Baptist chapel-goers and expert long-range tut-tutters, every one of us."

"You are without a doubt the most infuriating woman I have ever met."

"Thank you. It took me countless years of hard work and sacrifice to reach that dizzy height," Caitrin said and turned her attention to the map. "Your place is not on the map."

"Look for Houndale. It's the nearest village."

Caitrin searched the map. "Got it. Right next to Callow. Fifteen minutes or so?"

"I'd say closer to twenty-five. It's uphill, and Victoria's not getting any younger."

"When she's towing Albert, what do you expect?"

"Stop it, or you're walking the rest of the way."

They stopped at a sub-post office in Houndale, and Hector went to a telephone box. He returned minutes later, looking worried. "I got no answer."

"Perhaps that's why," Caitrin said and pointed to a newspaper placard outside the village shop that read: LONDON BOMBED AGAIN. MANY CASUALTIES.

"I'll try again later."

The road into Marlton ran alongside a brook for some considerable distance before turning a right angle toward the house. Built of gray stone in the lee of a hill and surrounded by trees, the house was smaller than Caitrin expected. Three people came to meet them as they stopped. A tall, elderly, slender man with an equally tall woman; and a smiling shorter, middle-aged woman wearing a tweed skirt and an Aran sweater. At her side was a dog. A beagle.

"That's a beagle. One beagle. The beagle," Caitrin said. "So where are the ten cocker spaniels?"

"What cocker spaniels?" Hector said.

"The cocker spaniels that made this car smell like a wet kennel."

"Oh, you're mistaken. I once loaned the car to my friend Jeremy who used it to transport his foxhounds to the hunt. Smelly creatures. I know nothing about cocker spaniels."

Caitrin shook her head. "You are the most infuriating man I ever met."

"Thank you. Took me countless years of hard work and sacrifice to reach that dizzy height," Hector said behind a wide grin. "And his name's Alfred. The beagle."

"Wedding rings on or off?"

"As you wish," Hector said.

"Off. It'll be simpler, especially at bedtime."

"Let's go meet the family." He opened the car door and got out.

"Bobby, how wonderful to have you home," Hector's mother said as she embraced him.

"Bobby?" Caitrin said.

"Mother, this is Caitrin Colline. We are working on a hush-hush project together."

"Pleased to meet you, Caitrin. I'm Elinor."

"Pleased to meet you, Elinor," Caitrin said. "You called him Bobby? He's got yet another name?"

Elinor laughed. "Not really, but he's always been Bobby to me."

"And this is Edmund and Maude Broadcastle." Hector introduced her to the older couple. "They've been with the family since before I was born."

"Madam, pleased to meet you." Edmund bowed from his considerable height, while Maude settled a quarter of an inch in a curtsey.

"Shall I take your luggage, Sir?" Edmund said.

"No, no, I can manage," Hector said, worried Edmund might do himself irreparable damage if he picked up anything heavier than a newspaper.

"I'll go and put the kettle on," Maude said as they entered the house.

The thick-walled living room was neat, nothing was new, and it smelled of mold and wood smoke. They sat at the fireplace, where burning logs gave some warmth to one side while the other remained cold. A portrait of a man in an army captain's uniform hung over the fireplace, and it took no great imagination on Caitrin's part to see that it was Hector's father. He had the same erect posture, blond hair, and clean, open features.

"I am going to chop more wood—we need it—while you two get to know each other better," Hector said, as through the window he saw Edmund, ax in hand, tilting toward a wood pile. He hurried out to avoid catastrophe. Moments later, Maude brought in a tray, and Elinor poured them both tea.

"Bobby—"

"I'm sorry, Elinor, but I cannot get used to him being called Bobby," Caitrin said.

"I really shouldn't say this, but I never liked the name Hector and have always thought of him as Bobby."

"Then why didn't you call him Bobby from the beginning?"

Elinor gave her a wise smile. "If only it were that simple.

Hector is an old family name." She gestured toward the painting. "His father's name was Argus. In the misty past someone decided ancient Greek names were dignified, I suppose, and we're stuck with the tradition now."

"Poor Bobby Hector."

"It could have been worse. The other names under consideration were Herakles and Horace."

"Horace? That's habsolutely horridly hawful."

Elinor laughed. "You have a sense of humor."

"It was a present from my mum, and it's the only thing that keeps me alive sometimes." Caitrin put down her cup, stood, and went to inspect the painting. It also put her closer to the fire's warmth. "He was a handsome man, and Hector looks just like his dad."

"He and Bobby were so close. They went hunting and fishing together. They loved riding. Do you ride?"

"Bikes and buses."

"We don't have a stable anymore anyway."

Caitrin glanced at a row of photographs beneath the painting. They showed a group of boys at a ski resort. Hector stood in the middle between two boys with huge grins, but he was not smiling.

"In their final year at St. Paul's, Bobby went with his friend James Gordon and the class to Kolbensattel for skiing. It's a quaint little place near Oberammergau, you know, where they hold that Passion Play every ten years, when the year ends in zero."

"Probably not this year."

"No, probably not for a while. All the other boys took their fathers, but my husband was not well enough to travel. Bobby didn't say anything, but you can tell he was disappointed."

"I understand. It must have been difficult for him."

"It was for both of them. Now, enough about us, tell me about your family. You're Welsh."

"Yes. Dad was a coal miner. Died of black lung. Mum is the rock in the family. Older brother Evan was killed at Passchendaele—"

"That's where my husband was badly wounded."

Caitrin saw pain flicker through Elinor's eyes. The pain blurred a little over time, losing an edge but not its weight, and would never go away. "I'm sorry."

"And I'm sorry for your brother."

"I was a little girl when Mum and Dad got a letter from King George V apologizing for losing Evan. At the time I didn't understand how anyone could lose Evan because he was my big brother who I loved very much and was easy to spot. I wasn't at all impressed with King George V. Didn't he have hundreds of dukes and lords to help him keep track of his subjects? Later I learned Evan was not lost. He was killed in the war. I remember thinking that although King George V said he was sorry, I didn't think he was, and one day I would go to London and tell him exactly how I felt. But George died before I could set him straight."

"George was a fortunate monarch to have passed away before you got to him."

"Yes, he was. My middle brother, Dafydd, is an RAF flight instructor at Kinmory, some godforsaken place high up on the west coast of Scotland; and Gareth, the baby, is away on the high seas with the Royal Navy."

"My husband died five years ago. The pain of his injuries was always with him, and he never fully recovered. When he came back from the war, he tried so hard for so long but was not the same man."

And at that moment Caitrin *saw* the woman. She saw the hurt and the loneliness. Elinor was landed gentry, and so of a different class, but far more than that she was a woman who had lost her husband, the man she loved. She remembered Hector saying that only he and his mother remained of the family.

Who then could Elinor turn to in this isolated place? Surely not the superannuated servants. Elinor didn't have what she had, a loving compassionate family. *Elinor would like my mum, and she would like Elinor.*

"I shan't ask about your task because it's probably all very hush-hush," Elinor said, "and I suppose you both swore a dreadfully serious secret oath not to reveal anything."

"It started that way, but now it's beginning to feel silly, wandering around England discovering the daftest place names."

"We have a few of our own here."

"Yes, you do. Thackwaite."

"Flusco."

"Sockbridge."

"Mockerkin."

"Conksbury."

"And for the classically trained mind, although I have no idea what it means, I give you Aspatria."

"That's the winner."

"Hector likes you. Do you like him?"

"Oh, that was direct. I didn't expect that."

"Sometimes you have to put aside being English to get the answer you want. Do you like him?"

"Yes, I do, but—"

Hector returned, arms filled with firewood. "I see you two are getting on well."

"We are indeed, Horace," Caitrin said.

"Horace?"

"That's just habsolutely horridly hawful," Elinor said, and laughter rendered her incapable of saying another word.

13

The sun had lowered behind the hill, leaving the house in shadow, and the air was a deepening crystalline blue as the day faded away. Caitrin, wearing a woolen scarf and one of Elinor's overcoats against the rising chill, walked with Hector toward the brook. A few yards away, a fox broke cover, froze when it saw them, and spun on its length to disappear into the trees.

"What a beautiful creature."

Hector watched him go. "Edmund's chickens will have a different opinion."

"At least they're safe for now," Caitrin said as she stretched her arms wide and inhaled a deep breath of cool evening air. "It is so good to have time away from sitting in a car. And to be out of the city."

"We still have one more day off tomorrow. After that, two days to get from here to Greenock will be easy. Job done, Jewels on a sub, across the ocean, and then safe in a Canadian bank vault."

They stopped at the water's edge. Caitrin picked up a stone

and skipped it across the surface. "Why do we do that, do you think, throw stones into water?"

Hector shrugged. "An offer to the ancient water gods, perhaps, or to keep wicked monsters at bay?"

"Or perhaps just because it's fun. This is a pretty stream."

"Up here it's called a beck. What is it in Wales?"

"*Ffrwd* or *nant*."

"That which we call a brook by any other name—"

"Would still be wet."

They walked upstream in silence for a while, and the first bat of the evening flickered past. The land had a bleak beauty. It was self-sufficient in its simplicity.

"My father and I used to walk here often," Hector said and pointed to a far hill, its curved edge just visible against the cobalt sky. "When I was little, he would carry me on his shoulders, and we would continue on right to the top of Marlton Fell. He loved this place. Then it was a summer home only, though. We had property in Durham, Belgravia, and the City of London. Did my mother tell you anything about him?"

"Just a little. She said you two were very close."

"Yes, we were, and after the war he tried so hard to be a good father, even though the pain interfered so much at the end. Did she tell you how he died?"

"Not exactly."

"He shot himself."

She looked at him, surprised at his blunt, un-Hector-like statement.

He seemed surprised too. "I don't know why I told you that. I've never mentioned it to anyone before."

She took his hand.

A door, long closed, opened. "The pain was growing more intense, and he was gradually going blind. I think he could have stood the pain a little longer, but his pride could not accept the blindness too. The thought of being in agony and helpless for the rest of his life was too much for him."

"I am so sorry, Hector."

"I found him. My mother thinks it was an accident. I told her it was, managed to convince the coroner too, and I wouldn't want her to ever believe otherwise."

"You know I would never tell her."

He stared at something invisible in the far distance. "We lost everything to death duties, except for Marlton. It survives, barely, on farm rents," he said and turned to face her. "So you see, I am a member of the ancient aristocracy you want to eliminate, but I assure you I am a harmless and rather, no, very impecunious one."

"I'm not Robespierre, Hector, I don't want a French Revolution."

"Would you accept dinner instead of my head? My mother is so excited about having company she has pulled out the fine linen, china, and silver. Edmund is sacrificing the chicken the fox won't get."

"I still have only the green dress to wear."

"You'll look wonderful in it, and my mother will be so happy. And, apart from you, we have two surprise guests."

They were two surprised and somewhat bewildered guests, who were on familiar ground yet in foreign territory. Edmund and Maude, with Elinor's help and guidance, had prepared the dining room for dinner. The room was lit solely with candles and a wood fire, which coppered every surface, and the table was covered with an antique Irish linen cloth. On that tablecloth was displayed Elinor's finest china, crystal, and silverware. Once they had finished, Elinor told them they were her guests for the evening. It stunned both Broadcastles because in their forty years of service they had never eaten at the same table as the family. Elinor brushed aside their concerns and insisted they join her in this homecoming dinner for her son. They hurried off to their rooms and returned at the appropriate time, shining, polished, and unsure of what to do next. Edmund wore his funeral suit and best boots, while Maude wore a bright floral dress with a lace collar and a huge yellow rose on the front that smelled of mothballs.

Elinor, wearing a midnight blue dress with pearls, sat at the head of the table with Edmund on her right and Maude to her left. Both protested as Hector and Caitrin served dinner, but she demanded they sit quietly and for once in their lives let themselves be looked after. Once everyone was seated, she raised her wineglass. "I would like to propose a toast to my son and his hush-hush companion Caitrin, and also my faithful friends—they are so much more than servants, they are part of the family—Edmund and Maude Broadcastle."

Glasses were raised, Edmund gulped back an emotion, and Maude wiped away a tear.

Hector raised his glass and turned to face his father's portrait. "To friends and family past and present. And to my wonderful mother."

Elinor blinked back her own tears and said to the Broadcastles, "We are friends and family but also strangers. In these troubled times I think being unknown to each other should come to an end. I would like to know how you met and how you became a family. And, if you like, to break the ice I'll start."

Caitrin watched Elinor. Hector looked like his father, but his character, his strength and resolve, came from her. She glanced across the table at him. His eyes were fixed on his mother as she began her story.

"I was a young thing at the Braes of Derwent Hunt. I had fractured my arm so couldn't ride, but I went to watch and inspect the field, and look at the horses too. Earlier I had noticed a handsome young man—blond, clear hazel eyes, impressive shoulders—who was riding. I learned his name was Argus, but you can't have everything. I leaned on a gate as the hunt raced by, and Argus was in the rear but going full tilt to catch up. He bellowed a tremendous *tally ho!*, put his mount to a drystone wall, and the horse stopped dead."

Maude was transfixed by the story, while Edmund helped himself to another glass of wine.

"But Argus didn't let that stop him. He rocketed out of the saddle, flew over the wall in a grand arc, and, like a circus acrobat, turned a perfect somersault in mid-air before landing with an awful thud on his back. I was sure he was dead—and we hadn't even been introduced."

Maude was not alone in her rapt attention. Caitrin and Hector were transfixed by her story too, while Edmund gazed at her through the bottom of his wineglass.

"I rushed over to him, knelt at his side, and said, 'Are you all right?'"

"He looked up at me, put his index finger to his lips, and said, 'It hurts badly right here, but might you kiss it better?'"

"And?" Caitrin asked, because Elinor had stopped and picked up her wineglass.

"I kissed him."

"And?"

"He put his hand on a—a different part of his anatomy, said it hurt, and asked me to kiss that too."

"Did you?"

"I slapped his face, and then I married him," Elinor answered. "And he got a taller horse. Maude, you're next."

Maude's eyebrows shot up to her hairline. She rescued them, cleared her throat, and began. "I was living in Mungrisdale at the time. It's a very small village, and there isn't much to do, so I went to a lecture about George Armstrong Custer at the Church of St. Kentigern."

"Goodness, I wasn't expecting that," Elinor said.

"Yes, I wasn't either," Maude said. "Usually it was the vicar talking about his brass rubbings from famous cathedrals or George the postman and his stamp collection. And in walks this tall, handsome man who knew everything, and I do mean everything, about Custer. It was certainly an information-packed evening."

"I was fifteen when Custer was killed," Edmund said. "I couldn't believe a white man with such a glorious military record could be outwitted by half-naked savages. Custer was a Union Army general when he was only twenty-three. He—"

"He was," Maude said loudly, to regain command of the story and deflect Edmund from recounting Custer's whole life in minute detail. "We had refreshments after the lecture, and I boldly introduced myself. I said: 'Your lecture was lovely. My name's Maude and—'"

"Amazed at her loveliness, I stepped back, like this," Edmund said, standing up and stepping back to show everyone exactly how he did it. "And then I sang to her."

"Sang what?" Hector asked.

"I sang this." Edmund straightened, inhaled, spread his arms wide and sang,

> *Come into the garden, Maud,*
> *For the black bat, night, has flown,*
> *Come into the garden, Maud,*
> *I am here at the gate alone.*

They all heard his resonant bass voice, but he was looking at and singing to only one person: his Maude.

> *And the woodbine spices are wafted abroad,*
> *And the musk of the rose is blown.*
> *For a breeze of morning moves,*
> *And the planet of Love is on high,*
> *Beginning to faint in the light she loves,*
> *On a bed of daffodil sky,*
> *To faint in the light of the sun she loves,*
> *To faint in his light—and die.*

His outstretched arms dropped to his side, and he bowed the smallest of bows as everyone applauded.

"We courted for a little bit, got married, came to work here, and have never left," Maude said, her eyes glistening. "And that's how we became the Broadcastle family."

"And an essential part of the Neville-Percy family too," Elinor said.

Edmund took his seat, feeling pleased with himself.

"Hector and Caitrin?" Elinor said. "I know it's all terribly secret, but do tell us what you can about the first meeting."

"We were introduced by a short, bald, round man smelling of whisky, puffing a stinking cigar, and wearing a sky-blue velvet romper suit," Caitrin said. "And I suggested that Hecky here might want to think about playing nicely with the other children by sharing some of his names."

It was quiet.

Elinor turned her gaze from Caitrin to Hector. "Would the defense like to respond?"

Hector sat back in his chair and spread his hands. "Guilty, m'lady. Strip me of my names and banish me to the dungeons."

"Instead I think we should have brandy," Elinor said.

Edmund got to his feet. "I know where it is."

Later, once the Broadcastles had gone to bed, Edmund singing, "Come into the Garden, Maud," all the way down the hall as they went, Elinor, Hector, and Caitrin huddled around the fireplace.

"What a wonderful and unexpected evening," Elinor said. "I so enjoyed hearing voices and laughter again and—"

"Edmund singing," Caitrin said.

Elinor laughed. "And imagine him being an expert on George Armstrong Custer. I would never have thought it."

"Neither would I. You have broken the separation between them and you."

Elinor shook her head. "It would be nice to think so, but no, I very much doubt that. We're English, so I'm sure tomorrow it will be back to yes, Ma'am; no, Ma'am; very well, Ma'am. Nothing will change."

"But things are changing," Caitrin said.

"This awful war?"

"No, much worse than that," Hector said. "Caitrin is an ardent socialist."

"What exactly does that mean?"

"It means I want a better life for working men and women and their children."

"But what exactly does that mean?"

"Would you mind if we didn't talk about it?" Caitrin said. "This has been such a pleasant evening, and I would hate to spoil it by talking about political differences."

"Agreed."

"I will tell you this, though," Caitrin said. "I know my mum would like you."

"And I'm sure I would like her." Elinor shot a pointed glance at Hector. "One never knows, perhaps a day will come when we will find the perfect occasion to meet."

14

Caitrin sat upright in her bed and glared at Hector, or at least at what little she recognized of him in the darkness. "Again, Hecky? You've come barging into my room at, let me guess, the crack o' dawn, to wake me up. Again?" She noticed he had taken several precautionary steps away from her. "Don't worry, I won't flatten you this time."

"I came because we have to leave, now."

"Why?"

"I couldn't sleep, so I went down to Houndale and called London. You were right about a bomb dropping on the telephone exchange. Direct hit caused havoc. But now the damage has been repaired, not all of it because it was—"

"Hecky, is there any chance we, you, could get to the heart of the matter? I'm sorry, but I'm a grumpy bear in the morning until I've had my first cup of tea."

"The *Talisman*."

"The *Talisman*?"

"The submarine *Talisman* we were supposed to meet at Greenock. I was told there's a bit of a problem."

"Some tea, some tea, my kingdom for some tea."

"It seems the Royal Navy is chasing a German battleship around the Atlantic, and the *Talisman* will be involved covering the shipping routes. It will tie up in Greenock tomorrow evening and leave on the following tide."

"With or without the Jewels?"

"Yes. So we have to go now."

"We lose a day off, but that still gives us two days, though. You said that's enough time to get to Greenock."

"Yes, plenty."

"If we're too late, what do we do, stick a stamp on the Jewels and shove them in the nearest pillar box?"

"We'll be on time easily enough, but only if we leave this instant."

"I'll meet you downstairs. I suppose there's no chance of breakfast?"

To Caitrin's surprise there *was* breakfast, made and served by Elinor.

"I heard Hector rushing around and assumed there was a sudden call to arms," Elinor said as she poured Caitrin a cup of tea.

"You're such an angel."

"No, I'm just a mother," Elinor said as she put a plate of bacon and eggs on the kitchen table in front of Caitrin and sat opposite her. "And I thought we should not wake Maude, and certainly not Edmund, just in case he starts singing again."

"And it's not the time to learn about the white man's tragedy at the Little Bighorn either," Caitrin said and put her hands to her face in mock horror. "George, mah dear, look at all those pesky Injuns!"

Caitrin sensed she was being studied. Elinor poured milk into her tea, concentrated on the roiling surface, and said, "I always wanted a daughter."

"You would have enjoyed each other. But not named with a female version of Horace."

Elinor looked up, and their eyes met. "I did actually have a Greek name for a girl. Atalanta."

"I like that. It's strong."

"In Greek myth Atalanta was exceedingly beautiful, and she had a forceful personality."

Caitrin said nothing but listened.

"She agreed to marry any man who could outrun her and speared anyone she passed. But wily Hippomenes had three golden apples and in the race he dropped one. Atalanta stopped to pick it up and lost when he shot past her, so she married him."

"Beware of butterfingered Greeks bearing apples."

"She was what we might today call a lusty lass with a passion for life. More than a bit like you, I should think."

"Thank you."

Elinor leaned forward and took her hand. "I do have a favor to ask of you."

"Of course."

"My son is strong and honest. Like his father, he believes in what he considers to be right and will defend it to the death," she said and took both of Caitrin's hands. "That does not necessarily mean he is worldly-wise. But I can tell that you are. My favor is, will you look after him for me?"

"I'll try my best."

"When my husband killed himself, Hector covered it up and said it was an accident. He did it for me, I know, but that is a heavy weight for him to bear alone. And an unfair weight."

The English stiff upper lip will be the death of them all. Caitrin thought for a moment and said, "You could have told him you knew the truth."

"I wasn't brave enough."

For Caitrin it was odd to listen to Elinor's precise English diction while she opened her soul. It was so different from the emotional trilling of a Welsh voice. "You're both bearing the weight, but separately, alone, because you don't want to hurt him and he did it because he loves you."

Elinor straightened, surprised. "We were a close family and cared about each other, but I don't remember any of us talking much about love. It just wasn't the done thing and would probably have embarrassed him and his father. Did your family tell each other?"

"Yes."

"How fortunate. I feel the loss now. I really should have been braver," Elinor said, and to Caitrin she was the loneliest woman in the world. Once she and Hector left, there would only be the Broadcastles for company, and they would revert to the safety of their cocoons of being servants. On her street in Abertillery—that smelly, dirty little coal town—Mrs. Parker lived next door to the Collines, and the happily boisterous Griffith family were on the right. Opposite was the Hughes family with their many children, who spent most of their time streaming in and out of Caitrin's house, and next to them lived Jimmy Lummis, who looked after his mum, worked on the buses, always went on holiday by himself, and came home happy and filled with secrets. And he never forgot a birthday. They were all her family. It was always noisy on her street, at times annoying, but she was never lonely.

"Are you ready to leave?" Hector said as he appeared in the doorway. They followed him out to Victoria and Albert, who were, like Elinor's old Wolseley, coated in frost.

Elinor embraced her son and walked around the other side of the car toward Caitrin. She pushed a package into her hands. "Some sandwiches. I know you will be in a hurry."

"Thank you."

Elinor hesitated for a moment, stepped closer, flung her

arms around Caitrin, and whispered, "Another favor. When this is all over, will you come back and see me? I would so much like that."

"I promise. Who's going to stop me?" Caitrin kissed her cheek and whispered, "Not some wily Greek with gold-plated balls."

"Caitrin!" Elinor said, suitably scandalized.

"Elinor!" Caitrin replied, suitably contrite. "Sorry. Apples. I meant gold-plated apples."

They grinned at the joy of being wicked together, embraced again, and Caitrin felt Elinor's tears wet on her face. Hector gave an impatient cough as he started the car. Caitrin took her seat and waved as they drove away. In the mirror Elinor was small, overshadowed by the house. They turned a corner, and she was gone.

The first miles were driven slowly because the sun had yet to rise and the headlamp was too feeble to illuminate the road properly.

"You love your mum, don't you?" Caitrin said and startled Hector. He mumbled a few words and fell silent. "It was a simple question. I wasn't asking you to reveal your most personal secrets or chat about wearing women's underwear, Hector."

"Yes, I do, then," he said, and in a bolder tone added, "Of course I do."

"She knows the truth about your father's death," Caitrin said. "And I suggest that if you were to talk openly to each other, it might make the pain easier to bear. Might bring you closer together. You don't have forever, and there are only two Neville-Percys left in the world. You need to be honest with each other."

Hector grew quiet.

"I didn't mean to upset you, Hecky. Now I'll mind my own business."

"No, it's all right, thank you," he said and sighed. "When I called London, they told me something I wasn't going to mention."

"Let me see. The war is over, or the zipper jammed, Winston's stuck in his romper suit, and we have to race back to London to save him?"

"No. They think we're being followed."

15

A caped police constable with sad eyes above a red nose and a splendid walrus mustache waved them to a halt at the border town of Carlisle. Hector got out of the car and went to meet him, smiling, arms spread and calling out, "*Bonjour, monsieur policier. Comment ça va?*"

"*Je vais bien, et vous?*" The constable replied in heavily northern English-accented French.

"My apologies," Hector said, stunned by the policeman replying in French. He recovered. "How silly of me. Wrong language. I was daydreaming of France and the terrible things happening over there. *C'est la vie.*"

"More *c'est la guerre, non?*"

"*Oui.* Yes, you're absolutely right. What may I do for you, Constable?"

"You can start by assuaging my curiosity, Sir. First by telling me where you're going to at this hour of the morning."

"Scotland. Greenock."

"I see. And where have you come from?"

"Marlton."

"Uh huh," the billowing walrus mustache said because Hector could see no sign of lips moving. The constable took a step back, tilted his head, and squinted an inquiring eye along the horse box. "And what might you have in there?"

"Hay bales. We're taking hay bales to Greenock."

"Towing hay bales all the way to Greenock from Marlton. Are you aware, Sir, that civilian motorcar traffic is no longer allowed? The exigencies of war, you understand. *La guerre* and all that."

"Yes, of course I am aware."

"Would you mind opening the horse box for me?"

"Ah, that might be a problem," Hector said and raised a finger. "Give me one second if you don't mind." He opened the car door, found the letter he had shown the policeman at the Tower of London, and offered it to the constable. "Perhaps this might clear things up."

The constable read the letter with great concentration, folded it, and handed it back. He raised his hand and touched the rim of his helmet to salute Hector and gave a little bow. "I beg your pardon, m'lord. Carry on."

"*Merci bien*," Hector said with a wink and climbed into the car.

"*Bon voyage*," the constable's mustache said as Hector pulled away.

"What the dickens was that all about?" Caitrin asked. "*Bonjour, monsieur policier?*"

"It was an unexpected lesson in humility, for me. Once upon a time, and not too long ago, a chap rattling off a few words of French, or even Latin, along with some odd, vaguely foreign gestures"—he fluttered his hands, shrugged, and wiggled his eyebrows to look foreign—"would utterly bewilder the local, rather uneducated gendarmerie. Flustered, they would let you go rather than deal with a pesky foreigner. Now it seems they're getting more educated. He even used the words *assuag-*

ing and *exigencies* and looked as though he knew exactly what they meant."

Caitrin looked smug. "That's what will happen under socialism. No more of the effete elite hoodwinking the unwashed, uneducated masses. They will be more educated, smarter, and it's only going to get better."

"Or worse." He made a face at her.

"What's in that letter?" she asked.

He handed over the letter. "Why don't you find out for yourself?"

She read it. "My goodness, you've been given the keys to the kingdom. 'Failure to render all and any services requested by Lord Marlton will be considered a direct contravention of the Defense of the Realm Act and be most severely punished. Signed, Winston Churchill.'" She folded the letter and handed it back. "With this in hand, you could even get an extra helping of chips at Bertie's Fish Shop in Clapham."

She sat back and watched the outskirts of Carlisle disappear. With most of the large cities behind them and the Scottish border a few miles ahead, Hector had stopped using the side roads and entered town by the main London Road. It was an eerie experience. The sun had just risen above the horizon to light the spires and rooftops, but the streets were still in shadow. And deserted.

"Empty streets, no lights. This is what the end of the world must look like," Caitrin said. "No life."

"Until the walrus mustache attached to a police constable makes its appearance. We'll cross the border soon and head toward Dumfries."

Caitrin pulled out the map. "Dumfries. Got it."

"Then it's the A76 to Kilmarnock, Ardrossan, and up the River Clyde to Greenock. We're almost home."

Caitrin scanned the list of stately homes. "North of the border we seem to be lacking a choice of accommodation."

"There is one. We'll stop at Mauchline House. My friend

James Gordon lives there. We were in the same class at St. Paul's. We went skiing and played rackets together."

"You wicked little Al Capone you."

"Not *the* rackets. Rackets. It's an indoor game played with rackets. Began at the Fleet Debtors' Prison, and the public schools picked it up. It's where lawn tennis came from. Did you play sports?"

"Where I come from, little girls only get to play house, and then mother."

"But not you."

"Not me."

"I have a question. If, as you surmised earlier, I might be a member of SOE, what might you belong to?"

"Five twelve."

"That's it? Not Section 512, Department 512, or Regiment 512?"

"Five twelve."

"I have never heard of it."

"You're not supposed to," Caitrin said and spread out the map. "This country has some strange places. Listen: Cargen, Duncow, Auldgirth, and let's not forget Enterkinfoot."

"Good job at changing the subject. At least, unlike Welsh, they have vowels. What's that outrageously long place?"

"It's Llanfairpwllgwyngyllgogerychwyrndrobwllllantysilio-gogogoch."

"Amazing."

"You wouldn't know if I just made it up."

"Or care that much, actually." Hector swung the car off the road and up a country lane.

"Where are we going?"

Hector jabbed at the map. "There. A disused quarry."

The lane dropped into a shallow valley and Hector turned onto an even narrower track that led to the quarry. He stopped the car, got out, went to the boot, and retrieved two tins. He held them up as he passed her window. "Come on, and bring that antique howitzer of yours."

"Why?"

"If the chaps who are following us catch up, I want to know how good a shot you are."

Caitrin got out with her revolver and followed him. "Baked beans? That's good food, and I could get a shilling apiece for those tins."

He lodged the tins horizontally into a stone wall with the tops facing them. "What distance? Five, ten yards?"

"Twenty."

"You jest. We can't even see the tins at that range. Be lucky to hit the wall."

"Then use an effigy of Oliver Cromwell instead. Twenty yards."

"All right." Hector paced off twenty yards, raised his Browning Hi-Power, aimed, and fired.

"Six inches left and low," Caitrin said.

He fired three more shots and hit with the last one. "Your turn."

Caitrin aimed and fired. And fired and fired, eight times until the revolver was empty. "I just ruined supper."

Hector stared at her in disbelief. "You hit your target four times and then mine four times. Eight shots."

Caitrin held up her revolver. "This is a Webley-Fosbery .38, not, as you thought, a .455, and holds eight rounds, not six. May I?"

She gave him her revolver and put out her hand for his automatic, and he watched himself give it to her. She seemed to raise, aim, and fire in one sweeping movement. The first two shots missed—they were sighting shots—but the rest struck home. She handed it back and reloaded her revolver. "Verily you have a fine and manly weapon, Sire, but I prefer mine."

16

Caitrin leaned forward, peered up through the windscreen, wrinkled her nose, and said, "I don't care who he is, I am not going in there. We go in, we'll never come out."

Hector peered up through the windscreen too. "I understand, but when I called Sir William, he did assure me we were quite welcome."

Mauchline House was a massive building set high on a hill overlooking a wide valley. The house, built of red sandstone blocks, was a perfect cube with little decoration to soften its harsh lines: a desultory arch over the front door and a small pointed turret at each corner. A steep slate roof held it in place, rain streaks stained the walls, and it was not in the least bit welcoming.

"This is our last stately home, and the last night of our honeymoon, dear," Hector said, raising his left hand and tapping his finger. "Rings."

Caitrin slipped on the wedding rings and asked, "Have you been here before?"

"No. Only met James's parents at school."

"Egads, then there's still time yet to flee back across the border," Caitrin said.

The heavy front door swung open, Sir William Gordon strode out, and fleeing was impossible. Sir William resembled his home. He was a square, solid man who stood anchored to the earth on sturdy legs. He squinted at them and bellowed, "Hector, away in here, man, and bring that lass of yours."

"Too late to flee now," Hector said and opened his door.

"A warning. I'll starve to death before I eat haggis," Caitrin said as she got out of the car and they went to meet Sir William. He embraced both with bone-crushing hugs and shepherded them into the house with the zeal of a Border Collie. Inside it was dark, and Caitrin recognized the familiar smell: wood smoke and damp. All stately homes smelled the same, some with a tint of wet dog or last night's brandy. The great hall was hammer-beamed, oak-paneled, and decorated with circular displays of claymores and muskets; the Gordon coat of arms hung over the ubiquitous fireplace.

They had heavy crystal glasses of whisky in their hands before they could react. Sir William added a dash of water to them. "It's Laphroaig, thirty years old. Nectar of Islay in the Hebrides. Sip and taste; don't gulp. Let the taste come to you. Now sit and tell me what brings you to Scotland."

They sat, and Caitrin and Hector glanced at each other, each waiting for the other to speak. Finally Hector said, "We're on our honeymoon."

"No, you're not."

"What?"

"You're not married."

Hector coughed into his drink. "Why do you say that?"

Sir William pointed at him and then swung his finger across to settle on Caitrin. "Any man who had just married this beauty would be sitting next to her. You're not."

"What do you think of Churchill?" Caitrin asked, because

she did not want Sir William to take command of the conversation.

"That was an unexpected and deflecting question," Sir William said. "What do I think of Churchill? He made a complete arse of Gallipoli, but that wasn't all his fault. The return to the gold standard fiasco was, though. But to give him credit, when he was dismissed for the Dardanelles disaster, he upped and joined the army and went into the frontline trenches in Flanders. I can't imagine another Westminster minister doing that, even if he did turn up like an English Napoleon on a bloody great black charger, and with ten times the allowed personal belongings, including a tin bath and a boiler. Still, he's too much of a shifty political weather vane for my own taste."

"In London there are calls to negotiate with the Germans. Do you think Churchill is the man to build bridges with Hitler?"

Sir William leaned back and sipped his whisky. "You have yourself a lassie and a half here, Hector."

"I think so," Hector said and smiled at her reaction.

"You should have married her. What's in the horse box?" Sir William asked.

"Tell me your thoughts about Churchill first," Caitrin said, focusing her attention on Sir William and ignoring the rows of deer-head trophies staring myopically at her from the wall behind him.

"A lassie and three-quarters, right enough. Churchill's not the man to build a bridge to a lunatic like Hitler, who intends to rule the world and needs to be eliminated. And the sooner the better. What's in the horse box?"

"Hay. Bales of hay."

Sir William slapped his knee. "Hector, they say that some of the strongest-spirited women come from Wales and the West Highlands. QED. Can I see these bales of hay?"

"No," Caitrin said and met Sir William's gaze.

"No? And what if I were to tiptoe down when you were sleeping and poke about?"

"I am a light sleeper and would be forced to shoot you the instant the horse-box doors were opened," Caitrin said.

Sir William gazed at Caitrin with open admiration. "I believe you would. So let's assess the situation. We have a healthy young man who is not in uniform. To me that suggests a more clandestine service. And next, we have a beautiful young Welsh-woman who can easily out-think any man I know —"

"And outshoot," Hector said.

"And added to all that, a horse box full of hay bales that no one is allowed to see. Tip-top secret, no?"

"Yes," Caitrin said. "The hushest of all hushedy-hushes. Nice whisky."

"Where is Lady Alice?" Hector asked, to redirect the conversation.

Sir William's smile faded. "In a sanitarium in Peebles. Has been there for a while."

"Because of her son James," Caitrin said.

"My goodness. How did you know that?"

"Because Hector and James are close friends, and you would have mentioned him sooner, except for . . . ?"

"Dunkirk. Jamie always loved the army and joined the Territorials as soon as he was old enough," Sir William said and sipped at his whisky. "He was a captain in the 153rd Brigade, part of the 51st Highland Division."

"Who stayed behind to fight the Germans and let the others be rescued," Caitrin said.

"Yes."

"What happened?"

"We don't know. They were rushed over there badly trained and with poor equipment. They still fought hard, though."

"No news?" Hector said.

"Not yet."

"So he might well be a prisoner of war," Caitrin said.

"I hope so, but I have my doubts after all this time. We should have been informed by now," Sir William said, staring at his whisky. He changed the subject. "You know the Home Guard came calling last week and asked for weapons. I gave them some shotguns and a couple of deer rifles. They even took a dozen claymores. The thought of those old men galloping across the heather blasting away and waving claymores at the Nazis would be funny if it were not also so tragic."

"Perhaps so, but it does mean we will all do everything to defeat the Germans," Caitrin said. "If they come, they will learn that invading Britain was a terrible mistake."

"You're right, lass," Sir William said, and added with a wicked grin, "I hope you are also hungry. My cook, Angela, brought us a fine, freshly butchered haggis."

The next morning, Sir William stood at his front door, feet firmly planted and hands on hips, to watch them drive away. Caitrin waved until he was out of sight. "A lovely man and another poor soul rattling around all alone in his ancestral home. I hope his son is safe."

"I hope so too. James is a good man," Hector said as Caitrin slipped off the wedding rings and gave them back to him. "You don't want to keep them on?"

Caitrin's expression softened as she shook her head. "No, Hecky, not yet."

Caitrin stopped at the post office in Mauchline so Hector could call London, then drove north as he surveyed their route on the map.

"They want us to call again when we reach Greenock," he said.

"Nothing serious?"

"I don't think so, just being extra-cautious." He folded the map, put his hands behind his head, and stretched out. "Almost over. Now for the easy leg of the journey."

"My mum used to say that nine-tenths of the journey was only halfway there."

"Very profound, and I have no answer to that."

"I never did either. I do know being the sole civilian motor-car on the road means we're no longer inconspicuous. Then again, neither is the man following us. Or men."

"If they still are. I haven't seen anyone." He glanced at her. "After spending a week with the landed gentry, have you changed your mind at all about them?"

She shrugged.

"That's your answer?"

"I liked your mum a lot."

"She liked you."

"Now tell me where we're going."

Hector opened the map. "We'll take the A76 to Kilmarnock and the A71 to the coast. Then it's a leisurely drive up the east bank of the River Clyde to Greenock. We should be there in plenty of time."

The car engine hesitated, then raced. Caitrin pulled to the side of the road, switched off the motor, leaped out, and opened the bonnet. She stepped back as steam billowed out. "The belt snapped," she said.

"I don't carry a spare."

They were in the middle of open farming country, and the road in both directions was empty.

"I do, sort of," she said, went to the rear seat of the car, opened her suitcase, and took out a nylon stocking. She wound the stocking around the pulley wheels to get the right length, tied a knot, and chafed her hands clean. "That should take us to the nearest garage. But you and Victoria owe me a new pair."

It did get them there. Belt replaced, they drove through Kilmarnock and by midday turned west for the coast. Now there was traffic, lines of army lorries, with military police who waved them off the road until the convoys had passed. The day was slipping away.

"We should get off this road and take a B-road inland," Caitrin said.

Hector scanned the map and said, "It will be slow going."

Caitrin pointed to another approaching lorry convoy. "It can't possibly be any slower than this."

"Take the next turn right, through Braehead, Carruthmuir, and Auchenfoyle. It's a gradual climb uphill, and Greenock will be on the bay beneath us."

Caitrin drove as fast as she dared along a narrow, winding road, and the light had faded by the time they reached the hill above Greenock. The town was in blackout, and only dim shapes and edges showed the buildings and docks. "You can hardly see the town. How do we possibly find the *Talisman*?" she asked.

"I'll call London and ask them," Hector said as he glanced at his watch. "We still have three hours."

They found a telephone box. Hector made the call and returned to the car with a frown. "It seems no civilian vehicles are allowed on the dock, not even us. They're sending a Captain Murray with an army lorry to meet us."

"Where?"

"At the Highland Mary monument in the Greenock Cemetery." He shook his head. "I have no idea who she is, was."

"She was Robert Burns's great love. '*O' my Sweet Highland Mary.*' Burns was a maudlin man at best, and she wasn't his only one. Where's the cemetery?"

"They gave me directions. We follow this road for two miles and turn right on Murdieston Road." Hector pulled a small reporter's notebook from his pocket, flipped it open, and read. "'Go through green gate entrance and travel uphill. It gets steep, and about three hundred yards in and on the left is Highland Mary's grave. It is a tall monument surrounded by a low black fence.'"

"Let's go see Sweet Highland Mary," Caitrin said and put the car into gear.

*   *   *

Greenock Cemetery was completely black, and their sole headlamp caught only edges of the road as it got steeper. Hector held a torch inside the car to hide the beam and scanned the passing gravestones. "There it is," he said.

Caitrin stopped on a rise just above the monument and switched off the engine. "We're running out of time."

"We have no choice. It would be impossible to find the *Talisman* in this blackout."

They waited. The night was silent, apart from the ticking of the engine as it cooled.

"So you think the great Scottish poet Rabbie Burns is maudlin?" Hector said.

"I do. He's soppy and a bit daft and, like most Scotsmen, was born a half-bottle under par."

"Who do you like?"

"Dylan Thomas."

"Welsh?"

"Naturally."

"Never heard of him."

"You will. But he's a bit of a daft drunk too. Listen."

They heard an engine complaining as it climbed the steep hill and saw the horizontal slit of a headlamp appear. A canvas-topped army lorry stopped next to them, and four uniformed men got out.

"Here they are."

"My woman's intuition tells me there is something not quite right about this," Caitrin said and reached for her revolver as Hector wound down the window.

"Lord Marlton?" one of the men, no more than a silhouette in the darkness, said in a strong Scottish accent.

"Yes," Hector answered.

"I'm Captain Murray. We have to move fast. Time and tide, Sir."

Hector patted Caitrin's arm. "I think we're all right, Cat. Let's help them load up."

The horse box and car boot were quickly emptied, and Captain Murray opened the lorry door for Hector and Caitrin. "Your part of the operation is over, but I thought you might like to see the Jewels being loaded onto the submarine."

"It's not over until I see them aboard," Caitrin said. "But I'll sit in the back with the Jewels, if you don't mind."

"Me too," Hector said.

"I believe I'll join you," Murray said with a grin. "Not often you get to travel with such riches."

"What about my car and horse box?" Hector said.

"It'll be safe enough here, and we'll bring you right back as soon as we're offloaded."

As they climbed into the lorry bed, Caitrin glanced at Captain Murray. He looked familiar, but from where? She struggled to focus her memory, but he would not come to the surface. But she had seen him before, of that she was certain. The journey downhill was slow, and when they reached Port Glasgow, the lorry turned right.

"You're going the wrong way," Caitrin said. "Greenock's to the left."

"You're right, but we're not going to Greenock," Murray said, and his automatic rose from the darkness until it was aimed squarely at Caitrin's face. "Now I would like you to hand me your revolver, slowly. Yes, I know you have one. And then you, Lord Marlton, do the same. Any heroics, and Miss Colline will die first."

They surrendered their weapons, and Caitrin leaned back against the canvas top and groaned at her failure. Full attention should always be paid to a woman's intuition.

17

To bodyguard Thompson's eternal despair, almost every night Churchill—wearing his blue siren suit under an RAF overcoat and sometimes, reluctantly, a tin helmet but rarely his gas mask—insisted on climbing up to the Downing Street Annexe roof to watch what he insisted on calling "The Grand Show." Five floors down were the underground Cabinet War Rooms, safely reinforced against bomb blasts with steel girders and five feet of concrete, but Churchill thought them claustrophobic and wanted to be up on an exposed rooftop in the middle of the Blitz.

He sat in a favorite chair with a glass of brandy nearby, a cigar clenched in his jaws and binoculars in hand. Thompson had managed to get a low sandbag wall built around him, but it would be no defense against a near-miss or shell splinters, let alone a direct hit. He submitted to his own fate and stood in the protective lee of a brick chimney, silently praying the Luftwaffe would take the night off. They were prayers unanswered.

"Here it comes," Churchill growled as he shifted in his chair and raised the binoculars. "The Grand Show."

In the streets below, wardens shouted and shook their warning rattles, air-raid sirens moaned, the first anti-aircraft guns barked, and searchlights lanced up into the night sky. The drone of approaching aircraft engines grew louder, followed by the first whistling of bombs.

"Yes, I know, I know," Churchill answered Thompson's unspoken thoughts. "People are about to die, here in the city and up there in the sky. That is the way of war, always has been, and that will never change. But this is a rare moment, Thompson, in which we are privileged to be witnesses to the savage creation of history. Look at that!"

An aircraft was struck squarely by an anti-aircraft shell. Its high-explosive and incendiary bomb load ignited instantly, and the blast flared across the sky as the aircraft vanished into burning remnants floating to the ground. Now the engine drone was louder, insistent, rattling windows, and the guns fired with increased fury. Fire engines added the sounds of their emergency bells, and the building shuddered as a bomb exploded somewhere close. The smells of cordite and burning buildings rose, smoke thickened the air, and shell splinters rattled down on the rooftops. London was burning.

"Sir, we really should go down," Thompson said. "It's getting far too dangerous up here."

"No, not yet, and please do not worry so much, Thompson," Churchill grunted and pointed heavenward. "He who put me here will take care of things. He will not let harm befall me until my work is done."

"While you were in discussion with Him about your immortality, did you perchance put in a word for me?"

"I'm afraid I did not," Churchill said and laughed. "But your proximity to me gives you immunity from disasters great and small. Another one! Hope it's one of theirs, not ours."

A burning aircraft tumbled out of formation, and Churchill

followed it through his binoculars. "A Heinkel, I think." He turned in his seat to face Thompson. "The Germans are a precise people who can be relied on not to make small mistakes but always the big ones. By concentrating their bombers on London, they have given our brave fighter pilots a rest. Soon Mr. Hitler and Mr. Der Dicke Göring will come to regret that decision."

The rooftop door opened a few inches, and a woman's hand shot out, clutching a file as she squeaked, "Mr. Thompson." The hand vanished, and the door slammed shut the instant he took the file.

"Read it for me," Churchill said, his binoculars fixed on the aircraft armada passing overhead.

Thompson opened the file. "It says our newlyweds are on their way to Greenock. It all goes well."

"Thank God something is, because Norway was a horror. I wonder if our Welsh tigress has driven Lord Hecky insane yet?"

They had been rattled around, blind, for what seemed like hours when the lorry lurched hard left and stopped. The canvas cover was untied, and the tailgate unlatched. Captain Murray nudged them out to where his men, now all armed, were waiting for them as they dropped to the ground.

It was silent, dark, with black hills on one side and a vast lake, a dull hammered gray, on the other. A star-speckled sky stretched above them. There were no signs, no lights, no buildings.

"Where are we?" Caitrin asked.

Captain Murray sniffed the air, coughed, and said, "On the bonnie banks of Loch Lomond. It's a pretty enough place in daylight; they even wrote a song about it. We won't be here to see the beauty, though." He gestured to a stand of trees a few yards away. "My apologies, but that's the best I can offer for your . . . your conveniences. The lady first, and just so you know, if you run away, I will shoot Lord Marlton. Off you go."

Caitrin slipped into darkness under the trees. There was something strange, some odd dissonance she could not comprehend, about what was happening. Captain Murray was familiar to her, although she still could not retrieve him from memory. Why were they not told sooner about civilian vehicles being barred from entering the dock? Was that actually true, and surely Hector's "magic" letter would have gained them access anyway? Murray knowing exactly where to meet them with the lorry meant there was a spy—more than a spy, someone deep in the government who was making decisions. Someone who probably knew everything about the operation. The lorry had a civilian number plate, and apart from blackout white visibility stripes, there were no military markings. She noticed the men were no longer wearing uniforms. And last, they were heading north, away from any major towns, ports, or airfields. Why?

Caitrin was shivering on her return to the lorry because the night was cold, with damp air drifting in from the loch, and she was wearing just slacks and a light blouse. Hector slipped his jacket around her shoulders as he passed and went into the trees.

"Captain Murray," she said. "You were kind enough to tell us where we are, now would you mind explaining where we are going?"

"I cannot possibly do that, I'm afraid." Murray grinned, but his automatic pointed at her was unwavering. "I want you to think of it as a free grand tour of Bonnie Scotland. Unfortunately it will remain a mystery, though, because it's night."

Caitrin put a hand to her stomach.

"Would you at least ask your man to drive a little more smoothly? I travel badly."

"I will try my best, but the road follows the contours, and we are heading into the Highlands."

Hector returned, they were pushed back into the bed, the tailgate was shut, and the lorry moved north, away from Loch Lomond.

18

In London that week German bombs killed over two thousand people, wounded two thousand eight hundred, and destroyed countless homes and warehouses. The numbers were heartbreaking, as were the totals of the previous weeks, and the future promised to be worse. The Blitz had become a malign presence that was a constant and jagged thorn in his side, but Churchill had other problems to face, and he intended to share them with the two people who had just been dragged from their beds.

On the other side of his desk, Brigadier Sir Alasdair Gryffe-Reynolds, a slender, ascetic man who rumor had it was once destined for the church but instead chose the army, sat upright, eyes blinking away what remained of his sleep. Churchill knew Gryffe-Reynolds quite well and had in fact suggested him to the Special Operations Executive. A secret organization, the SOE had recently been established to run espionage and sabotage in occupied Europe. It had been nicknamed the Ministry of Ungentlemanly Warfare, although Churchill much preferred the other title: Churchill's Secret Army.

Winston's command to them was *Set Europe Ablaze*.

The other person was Bethany Goodman, a neat, middle-aged woman dressed in a tweed suit. He knew little about her or 512, the organization she commanded.

"So it seems Caitrin Colline is not a policewoman but instead a member of your organization?"

"She is both. I encourage my women to maintain their civilian occupations while not on service. It makes a good cover."

"Why is your organization a complete mystery to me?" he asked.

"That's because it was, and is, supposed to be a secret, Sir," she said.

"Not to me, your prime minister."

"We were created during the last government, Sir. My apologies—actually it was initiated at the tail end of Stanley Baldwin's office. I naturally assumed they would have told you."

"That is an incorrect assumption. Now tell me, what does 512 actually do?"

Goodman's mouth tightened as she glanced at Gryffe-Reynolds, who diplomatically pretended to be fascinated by a picture on the wall.

"Sir, my remit is to keep the organization confidential. Perhaps you—"

"Perhaps you, Miss Goodman, should appreciate we are at war."

"I am well aware of that, Sir, and it is *Mrs.* Goodman. My husband served on the *Exeter* fighting against the *Graf Spee*. He was killed on the bridge."

"My sympathy. Brave fellow, and we are forever in his debt. However, as prime minister I need to know about 512, and Gryffe-Reynolds here is in the SOE and so knows all about keeping secrets. You said: I encourage my women."

Goodman hesitated before saying, "Five twelve is an all-female organization."

"My goodness. Why?"

"Because we are excluded from male-dominated organizations. Women are unseen and underestimated. Nothing is expected of us, so we try harder."

Churchill wanted to say something, perhaps make a small protest, but could find no adequate response and stayed silent.

"Our work involves uncovering spies and saboteurs within the country."

"All right." Churchill sat back, picked up the telephone, and ordered tea. He put down the receiver and said, "We have a member from each of your organizations working in Operation Cat. What do you know about it?"

"Very little," Goodman said. "Just that you wanted our best operative."

Gryffe-Reynolds nodded in agreement. "Ours too."

"And it will remain that way. Operation Cat involved the transfer of the Crown Jewels from the Tower of London to Scotland and then by a Royal Navy submarine to Canada, where they would be safe. Masquerading as a married couple, Lord Marlton and Caitrin Colline were to drive the Jewels, hidden inside a horse box, to Greenock."

He searched their faces, but both were professionally blank. "Sounds far-fetched, I know, but to be successful it was essential the operation be inconspicuous."

"You said *were to drive*," Goodman said.

"They left the Tower with the Jewels, but several days later the horse box, empty, was discovered in a cemetery in Greenock. The Jewels, Lord Marlton, and Miss Colline have vanished into thin air."

"Was it a robbery?" Gryffe-Reynolds said.

"There were no signs of a struggle, both motorcar and horse box were seemingly abandoned. And the mystery is, why were they in a cemetery at night, just a few miles from their final destination at the docks?"

"You believe one or both of them might be involved?" Goodman said.

Churchill rolled a cigar across his mouth. Bethany Goodman was, like Caitrin, already steps ahead in the conversation. If all the women in 512 were of the same caliber, it needed to be put to greater work. He faced the brigadier. "Gryffe-Reynolds, what are your thoughts?"

"It's possible, of course, but highly unlikely. Lord Marlton is, well, he comes from a well-respected family that goes back centuries, and—"

"Caitrin Colline does too," Goodman interrupted. "She just doesn't have an estate filled with moldering portraits of her fine and ancient ancestors."

"She is an avowed socialist, though," Churchill said. "Who stated to me she would like to see the Royal Family working for a living."

"Let's be honest, would it hurt them? We all have to be a benefit, not a drain, to our society, don't we?" Goodman said. "The pertinent question is, what are we going to do?"

"What is Lord Marlton's role in SOE?" Churchill asked Gryffe-Reynolds.

"He's a scallywag."

"Explain that for Miss Goodman."

"*Mrs.* Goodman."

"Scallywags are small groups of men who will form a resistance if the Germans invade. There are hidden bases and arms caches all over the southern counties."

"Brave patriotic men who practice the arts of subterfuge and concealment," Churchill said.

"Which might also be ideal training for a smash and grab," Bethany Goodman said.

Gryffe-Reynolds looked mortally wounded. "Madam, you forget he is a British lord—"

"So is the Right Honorable Lord Arthur Nall-Cain, Second Baron Brockett, who did nothing but be lucky enough to be born into a wealthy English family and is a well-known Nazi sympathizer," she replied. "I believe he attended Hitler's fiftieth birthday celebration in Berlin last year. Took time off from evicting his Scottish crofters from his sixty-two-thousand-acre estate to do so, because he preferred shooting game to caring about their livelihood. That kind of lord, you mean?"

Gryffe-Reynolds struggled to find the right words, but Bethany Goodman had no such problem. "I will vouch for the loyalty of all my staff, because I interviewed each woman, researched her background, and then trained her. Can you say you did the same for yours?"

"Yes, I suppose, not individually, but . . ." Gryffe-Reynolds spluttered to an end.

"Operation Cat," Goodman said with an amused little head turn. "Who would ever imagine the Crown Jewels being spirited away in a humble horse box?"

"Precisely," Churchill said, feeling a little smug about his ingenuity and grateful he was not dealing with both Bethany Goodman and Caitrin Colline at the same time.

She sighed, like some weary schoolmistress dealing with an especially dense pupil. "Before this operation got underway, I suppose no one bothered to point out that it would be odd to have a horse box at the Tower of London?"

"Why so?"

"Because although the Tower of London once had a menagerie, it has no stables or horses."

Churchill could not remember the last time he felt intellectually bested. Perhaps it was the first time he met Caitrin Colline. The thinking behind creating 512 was becoming clearer, and it promised to be a formidable force.

"Prime Minister, I am sure you are concerned that losing the Crown Jewels would have a demoralizing effect on the nation," Goodman said. "I am equally concerned about the health and safety of my agent, Caitrin Colline."

Caitrin was not well. For hours the lorry ground uphill, and the serpentine road made it constantly sway. The night had grown much colder, and through gaps in the canvas she glimpsed the outlines of steep, snow-covered hills in the darkness. From what little she could see it was desolate, treeless country. Finally the lorry began a long downhill haul, the driver keeping his foot on the brake, which made the ride even more jarring. She retched, waved Captain Murray's help away, and croaked to Hector, "Help me."

The lorry slowed on a corner as Hector took her to the tailgate. She pushed open the canvas, pretended to be vomiting, unhitched the tie-down line, and said, "Follow me. Now." In one rapid movement she was through the canvas cover and over the tailgate. She rolled away from the road the instant her feet touched ground and had a half-image of Hector's startled face staring down at her from the lorry. The world dropped away, and she was falling. Her hands grasped desperately for a grip, but the hill was almost vertical. She ricocheted off a rock and groaned in pain, for a brief moment stood nearly upright, but slipped and was shocked to be underwater. The river spun and rolled her. She fought to reach the surface, she fought to breathe, and she fought hard against the current, until it slammed her against a rock, and the fight was over.

19

Bodyguard Thompson—his job title had long since become his name—did as was requested, entered Winston's bathroom, and sat on the toilet.

"Loofah please, Thompson," Churchill said from the bath. He was sitting up with a board across the bath on which lay his papers and an ashtray. On the right was a tall stool for his brandy. "It's that long thing at your feet."

Thompson gave him the loofah, and Churchill pushed his spectacles up his nose to inspect it. "It's a fruit, did you know? Popular in India and China, but they insist it must be eaten before it ripens. Do you think she did it, or perhaps him, or was it perhaps a larcenous partnership?"

"*Hmm*," Thompson said, to delay answering, because he had not expected the abrupt question and had no answer ready.

"Do not *hmm* me, Thompson. You know better than that," Churchill said and emitted a great cloud of cigar smoke. "Take off your bodyguard hat, and put on a detective one. In your opinion as a professional sleuth, was it our mercurial Welsh socialist, determined to ransom the Jewels for her own perfidious political ends—a Cromwellian Britain or perhaps even a Welsh one—or is Lord Hecky a member of *Die Brücke* and about to bring the country to its knees? The question is, whodunit?"

"I do not know, Sir."

"There are no clues? All mysteries have clues."

"When we loaded the Jewels at the Tower, Miss Colline did ask me not to padlock the horse box. She said if it was unlocked, people would assume there was nothing of value inside."

"A clever lass, that one. Go on. Tell me more."

"I was wondering about the actual theft. The horse box was found in Greenock, but that might be to send us off on a wild goose chase, so to speak. They stopped several times on the way, and each stop was an opportunity for theft."

"I hadn't thought of that. Well done. The Jewels could have been taken anywhere along their route. Where did they stop?"

Thompson pointed to the board. "There is a list there, Sir."

Churchill shuffled through the papers, dropped several into the water, ignored them, and found the list. "The Ashtonthorpes of Cockleford; the Madison-Hardynges of Walvert Frome; Marlton, Hector's home; and Mauchline House, the Gordons." He made a sour face. "All good British families of impeccable pedigree. Do we have any information on them?"

"The Gordons' son, James, is missing at Dunkirk, believed killed, and there is a rumor that the Ashtonthorpes might be inclined toward *Die Brücke.*"

"I hope not; they are such an old family. Should we have them watched?" Churchill said.

"A careful eye wouldn't hurt."

"A brisk search of the estate would have better results. An immediate one, and investigate all the others too. We will tell them there were reports of German parachutists landing in the area, so we are concerned about their safety. Take this." Churchill handed him the board and stepped out of the bath. Thompson was a modest man by nature and had never gotten used to Churchill being oblivious of his own nakedness. "Towel."

Thompson handed him a towel. Winston sat on the edge of the bathtub and wrapped it around his belly, where it remained for only a few seconds before sliding to the floor. He seemed not to notice. "Lord Hector comes from an old, if sadly diminishing family, the bedrock of England, and I cannot see what he could possibly gain from such a theft. Caitrin Colline is a shining, brilliant creature, who I thought was inherently honest. Is it possible she dazzled me with her intelligence—the Welsh are mercurial and quick-witted by nature—and in doing so fooled me about her true intentions?"

Bethany Goodman's immediate answer to his question about the existence of the all-female 512 organization surfaced: "Women are invisible, so we try harder." *We do underestimate women at our own peril.* "We have to find them, Thompson, and time is not on our side."

Something soft, wet, and cold snuffled in Caitrin's ear. She opened her eyes and looked up at a bright-eyed, black and white Border Collie staring down at her.

"That is Fiona," a woman's voice said. "She was the one who found you, and finders keepers; you now belong to her. Don't move or she'll lick you to death."

Fiona licked Caitrin's face to show she would do just that as the woman took a seat on the bed. She was a vision, a tiny angel. White hair cascaded down her back, and she wore a long robe of some homespun material cinched at the waist by a cord belt. But it was her eyes that held the focus. Hector had dangerous eyes, even though he himself wasn't, but this woman's eyes could make you cry. She saw you, saw who and what you were.

"Fiona found you, Wee Wendy brought you home, and I put you to bed."

"Wee Wendy?" Caitrin said. She was wrapped in flannel sheets, lying in a bed, in a cottage. The room was small with book-lined walls, and her clothes were hanging to dry in front of a peat fire.

"Wee Wendy's my pony. I'm Maggie Mhòr. Mhòr's Gaelic for big. Big Maggie."

"You don't look big."

Maggie laughed. "My old name was Margaret Little. The locals have their own sense of humor, so I am now Big Maggie."

Caitrin sat up, wincing at her bruised ribs. "Where am I?"

"In Iolaire Cottage in Glen Coe."

"How long have I been here?"

"An hour or so at most, I would imagine. I have no clock."

"Are my clothes dry?"

"Almost."

Caitrin stood and wrapped a blanket around herself. "Where's the road?"

Maggie pointed to the outside.

Fiona followed Caitrin to the door. It was low, making her stoop as she went through it. Outside there was no road; there were only white peaks looming over her and a primitive empty valley stretching ahead. The river was barely visible in the distance, and a feathering mist was erasing detail. The cottage, whitewashed and sod-roofed, was tiny in the landscape. She shivered and went back inside. "You said locals. What locals?"

"The village of Ballachulish, on the loch some way farther down the glen," Maggie said and waved a vague hand at the distance. "You should eat for your strength."

Caitrin sat with a thump, all tensile strength gone. "I'm sorry, I was being thoughtless. Thank you for saving me."

"Thank Fiona, not me."

Caitrin put out her hand, and the dog wriggled under it for attention. An emotion shot through her. She had had a dog once, a Border Collie like this one. *Roced*, Rocket, named because he was fast and agile, and she loved him. She scratched

Fiona's ear. "I was escaping from some bad men when I fell into the water."

Maggie said nothing as she prepared food, pushed the plate in front of her, and sat opposite. "Capercaillie and potatoes," she said and explained, "it's a Scottish grouse. We eat mostly the males because they're twice the size of the females."

"Teach them to show off." Caitrin ate while Fiona's nose nudged at her hand for attention. "You don't ask questions, Maggie."

"Asking questions has never been my favorite form of conversation, and besides, it encourages people to lie."

"I was in a lorry and escaped. My friend is still with them, so I have to catch up, but with the morning gone—"

"Were they going north or south?"

"North. What is in the north, what cities?"

"Fort William, and, although it's a long way around, Inverness. They're heading into the Highlands, which is rather unpopulated country. And they will not have traveled far. The Ballachulish ferry takes pedestrians but only two vehicles at a time, or one lorry, with the army getting priority. If there is a convoy, which is likely, they will have to wait for hours, if they can get on at all. The only other choice is to drive a very long way around Loch Leven. And the bridge is being repaired at Kinlochmore. That will take even longer, but at least they will be moving."

"Which means, if they took the road, I could catch up by taking the ferry?"

"Aye, and if they took the road, which is most surely what happened, you would probably be well ahead of them."

"If I went now?"

"Yes."

Caitrin rose and sat again. "I have no idea how to get there."

"That's simple. Take Wee Wendy. She knows the way, and of course Fiona will have a proprietary interest in coming with you too."

"Thank you. How do I get them back to you?"

"You don't need to because they know the way in both directions. I send them into the village once a week for my groceries."

"It just dawned on me. Your accent. You're English."

"I am."

"Living in a remote Scottish cottage alone."

"I'm not alone. I'm with me," Maggie said and smiled at the thought. "My husband was so proud of being a station manager for the London Necropolis Railway. Two separate stations at the cemetery: North for Catholics and Nonconformists, South for Anglicans. He loved his job, but all I could see was one day being just like another until my corpse was transported on one of his trains. One pound for first class, five shillings in second, and two shillings and sixpence in third."

"Even in death, the different classes are maintained, and all one way, of course."

"One day, a bit like that Émile Zola short story about a housewife, I could take no more of whatever my life was going to be. I put on my coat, walked out, left everything and him behind, and came to Glen Coe. When I die, it will be here, in a beautiful place, first class. But not alone."

Fiona ran in happy circles as Caitrin mounted Wee Wendy bareback and Maggie put saddlebags across the pony's neck. "Wee Wendy will go on to the shops after you're gone."

"There are no reins?" Caitrin said.

"We have no reins," Maggie said. "Wee Wendy has never known them. But she does know the way there and back. The road wriggles all over the hills and takes forever, but Wendy goes in a straight line, right down the center of the glen. One moment."

Maggie hurried inside the cottage and returned with a small homemade knapsack. She opened it and produced a book. "This is a guide book of Scotland and has some very good maps that fold out." She took out a knife from its sheath and held it up. "It's called a *sgian dubh*. It's not much, but you don't want to meet the bad men completely unarmed."

"Thank you, Maggie. Good—"

"I never say good-bye," Maggie said. "That's for just once, at the very end. The one pound for first class one-way ticket good-bye."

"I will see you again long before then," Caitrin said.

"Let us hope so." Maggie tapped Wee Wendy's rump, and the pony ambled away, to Fiona's demented joy.

Caitrin looked back, but the mist had settled, and Big Maggie and her cottage had disappeared.

20

Fiona sat quivering at the water's edge, shifting the weight on her front paws, bright eyes fixed with devotion on Caitrin standing at the ferry rail as it moved away across the loch. Caitrin almost waved to the dog but did not, scared she might leap into the water and swim after her. "Fiona," she murmured, and made herself a promise. Once this was all over, she would find a better place to live, a green and quiet place, and have her own Fiona.

Behind Fiona on Rannoch Street in Ballachulish, Wee Wendy was wandering home with her saddlebags full. True to Big Maggie's word, the pony had made a straight line from the Glen Coe cottage to Ballachulish, aiming in particular at MacDuff's Greengrocers. MacDuff hurried out with Maggie's groceries, loaded up Wee Wendy, and sent her on her way with a carrot before she could show interest in the cabbages displayed in crates outside the shop.

Caitrin looked inland, down the water. The west coast of Scotland was grooved with narrow sea lochs, and Loch Leven was a long, jagged-edged stiletto thrust deep into the hills. This was not an easy country to traverse. She turned back to the south shore, and Fiona was gone, her adoration of Caitrin discarded and left in the grass as she ran to catch up with Wee Wendy and go home.

There were a few minutes for Caitrin to reflect before the ferry reached the north shore. She had made some elementary mistakes. The first and biggest one was deferring to Hector about communications and decisions. On their journey north, he was the one who called London every morning, and he alone knew about their rendezvous at Greenock Cemetery. It was a sobering thought to realize she had relinquished all control simply because Hector was a man. Bethany Goodman was right, gaining their equal place in the world would not be easy for women, and the biggest changes would need to be within themselves. She also wondered what had happened to Hector and guessed Captain Murray had stopped him from leaping out of the lorry after her. Murray still bothered her because his face was familiar, but still she could not remember where she had seen him before. There were other things—little prickles in the mind, her mother used to call them—elusive, half-formed clues that needed to be developed further.

It was cold out on the water. She shivered and was grateful for the protection of Hector's jacket.

The ferry slowed, butting against the tidal race as it inched toward the shore. A row of army lorries was waiting at the ramp to board as Caitrin went ashore. Ferrying one lorry at a time across the loch would be a slow process. She found a spot at the end of a row of cottages where she could watch the Kinlochmore road without being seen and hoped it was not too late. The ferry came and went, back and forth. Across the road from her a Riley 16 Kestrel pulled up, and a young man bounded out. He wore plus fours, a Cairngorm tweed jacket, carried a Gladstone bag, and had a stethoscope draped around his neck. He was sharp-nosed and eager-eyed, with a long, darting stride. She leaned against the wall, feeling its rough texture against her back, and watched him disappear through a gate.

There was no other motor traffic. An old man grumbling grudges to himself passed on a bicycle. A little boy with a stick appeared, searching for magic or mischief. Either would do; neither would surprise him. The day was quiet, endless, and Caitrin knew she was too late; the lorry had probably gone. A robin dropped to the ground at her feet and jabbed at something in the grass. She watched it pursuing an invisible prey and looked up to see the doctor returning to his car—just as the lorry passed between them.

The number plate was different, and signs on the door and along the side read MACDUGALD & SONS, FISHMONGERS. But it was the same lorry. It was past her before she could react.

She leaped to her feet as the lorry disappeared and caught a movement to her right. The doctor was opening his car door. She reached him just as he closed it and rapped on the window. He wound it down.

"This sounds so lunatic, I know," she blurted out. "But would you follow that lorry?"

"Yes!" The doctor's eyes widened with glee. He jammed the car into gear, floored the accelerator, and screeched away—leaving Caitrin standing on the pavement. Open-mouthed, she watched him leave.

Fifty yards away, the doctor braked hard, reversed to her, and said, "Got a wee bit ahead of myself there. For this to work properly, I suppose you should come along too?"

"That would be very nice," Caitrin said, ran around to the passenger's side, and was hardly in her seat before the doctor took off again.

"Those dirty, yellow-bellied rats," the doctor said from the corner of his mouth in a passable James Cagney impersonation.

"What?"

"You a shamus?"

"What, again?"

"A copper."

"I am."

The doctor turned his lapel. "Show us ya buzzer, then."

"Buzzer?"

"Cop badge, for undercover detective work. George Raft."

Caitrin rubbed her eyes. "Forgive me, I thought I was in the Scottish Highlands."

"You are," he replied, and went back to being Scottish again. "Sorry, I'm a huge gangster film fan. Go to the pictures in Glasgow as often as I can. Doctor Munro Finlay at your service."

"Caitrin Colline, and you might want to slow down, or they'll be following us."

"Right, right," Finlay said and eased off the accelerator. "OK, sister. Give with the lowdown. Why are we chasing them dirty bums?"

"They stole some . . . family heirlooms."

"They gonna be throwing lead at us?" Finlay/Cagney said.

Lead—bullets—guns. "Yeah, they got roscoes," she said in her best moll accent, to Finlay's wide-eyed delight.

"I've got a twelve-gauge in the back."

Caitrin glanced into the back seat, which was filled with horse blankets, Wellington boots, waders, and strange medical instruments. "What kind of doctor are you?"

"A vet. Large animals, small animals, everything except penguins and porpoises. Even them, I suppose, should the need arise. Are you carrying a gat?"

"No, and we're not getting that close. There will be no shooting."

That disappointed Finlay. "So why are we following them?"

"To see where they're going."

"And then what? You'll bring in more cops to help the local constabulary, actually constable? There's only one, that's Wully, and he's not exactly fleet of mind or foot."

"I tried to call London, but the line was dead."

"That'll probably be Archie MacPherson's doing. He's a farmer up in Drumgan convinced the telephone wires make his sheep go bald. So he cuts down the telephone lines and steals the copper wire to make bracelets for his arthritis. It will be repaired by tomorrow, perhaps."

"Maybe someone should shoot Archie," Caitrin said and pulled out her Scotland book. "Where are they going?"

"Only one place. The road leads straight to Fort William. Oh, oh."

She looked up to see what had alarmed Finlay. A hundred yards ahead of them, the lorry was parked in the center of the road.

"What do I do? I can't turn around, and they're blocking the road," Finlay said.

Caitrin slipped over the seat, curled up in the footwell, and pulled the horse blankets over her. "Drive down slowly, and see if you can inch past them. And please, no gangster stuff."

Finlay drove forward as a man came from the front of the lorry and waved him to stop. He wound down his window and called out, "Good afternoon to you. Are you having a spot of bother with your lorry?"

"No, just making sure we don't. Would you mind turning off your engine?"

As the engine died, Caitrin recognized Captain Murray's voice and unsheathed her *sgian dubh*. A knife would be no match for armed men, but the battle was never over until one side surrendered. And she was not about to do that.

"Fair enough," Finlay said. "Do you think I could squeeze by there on the left?"

"It would be a wee bit tight," Murray said as he peered into the back seat of the car. "We stopped because I thought you were following us."

"And there you'd be right. I *was* following you," Finlay said, and Caitrin's heart pulsed as she heard Murray's sharp intake of breath. She was on the wrong side of the car and too far back to surprise him. He would kill her before she rounded the car's nose.

"Why would you do that?"

Finlay laughed. "If you know another way for me to get from Ballachulish to Corrychurrachan to attend to Brenda MacConnell's bowed tendons I'd be glad to hear of it."

"*Hmm.*"

"Terrible afflictions, bowed tendons."

"I'm sure," Murray said.

It went quiet, until Finlay whispered over his shoulder to Caitrin, "It's all right, I fooled the mug."

"What's happening?" Caitrin whispered back.

"He's going back to the lorry," Finlay said, then poked his head out of the window and shouted to Murray, "One more thing before you go, Sir."

Murray stopped and spun on his heel. "Yes?"

"What are you doing?" Caitrin whispered, her blood going cold as she heard Murray's footsteps returning to the car.

"Stay quiet, I'm in control," Finlay said.

Murray stopped at the window. "What is it?"

"When we were talking just now, I didn't want you to go away thinking I was hiding anything."

"Like what?" Murray said.

"The bowed tendons," Finlay said. "I said Brenda MacConnell's bowed tendons, but what I really meant was Brenda MacConnell's horse's bowed tendons. Brenda herself has a fine set of gams. Best and straightest tendons in the west o' Scotland."

There was a silence that seemed eternal to Caitrin.

"I'm a vet, you see, not a doctor," Finlay broke the silence. "An animal sawbones, as they say in America."

"Isn't that good to know?" Murray said, and she heard him walking away and the lorry engine start.

"You can come out now; they're leaving," Finlay said, and Caitrin raised her head above the seat.

"Why did you call him back?"

"I wanted to convince him that we, I mean I, was harmless."

"If he thought you were lying, that man would kill you without a moment's thought and then put a bullet in me."

"I'm sorry. I suppose I was a bit zealous there," Finlay said. "Should I follow them?"

"Yes. But slowly, and at a safe distance."

Finlay started the engine and put the car into gear. "I always thought it would be grand to be Bugsy Siegel. Out on the town every night. The Mocambo, Cocoanut Grove, Ciro's, driving a Cord or a Duesenberg with the hood down along Sunset Boulevard, and all the Hollywood dames you want, and everyone scared of you."

"You don't want people scared of you." Caitrin said nothing more; instead she watched the lorry as it slowed. "They're turning left. Where are they going?" She opened her book and scanned the map.

"Not to Fort William. They're taking the *North Argyll*; that's the Corran ferry across Loch Linnhe," Finlay said.

"I don't understand," Caitrin said. "I don't see any towns west of here. Just a sea loch."

"There is nothing but a few scattered crofts and a wee harbor in Kilcanan at the dead end of the road. Nobody ever uses it anymore."

"How far?"

"About forty miles on a winding and badly kept road. Shall we wait a while before we go across ourselves?"

"No, Doctor Finlay. This is as far as you go," Caitrin said.

"If we cross, they'll know we're following them, and they are very bad men."

"Are you sure?"

"Sure, I'm sure. I'll take it from here," she said, reached over, kissed his cheek, and slipped out of the car before he could answer.

He called after her. "So sorry about being silly. I got excited and lost my head."

The sudden change in his demeanor startled her. The exuberance was gone. He looked so sad, deflated, and she thought he might cry. And if he did, she might too.

"You did really well."

"It's just that being a vet can be so disappointing sometimes. Not at all what I expected. You were fun, different."

Caitrin was lost for an answer.

He held out a thermos and a paper bag. "A peace offering? You'll be getting hungry. Here's a thermos of tea, an apple, and some slices of very tasty haggis my housekeeper Janet made for me."

"Thanks."

"Thank you," he said, waved, turned the car and drove away.

She watched the lorry drive off the ferry and turn south down the only road. She waited for the ferry to return and boarded. It would be dark soon.

21

Bodyguard Thompson was rightly proud of his handiwork and hoped Churchill would be too. He waited until nightfall to present it, because that was when his gift would be most effective.

"This is for you, Sir," Thompson said. "A custom-crafted gift from me. I made it myself."

Churchill peered at the gift and growled, "You do know that's my own walking stick you're holding, Thompson."

"Yes, Sir, it is, but this is the gift part. See?" Thompson pointed to a leather holder fitted to the handle. "It holds a torch pointed toward the ground so you can see where you're walking at night."

Churchill took the stick and switched on the torch. "That's damn clever of you."

"Thank you, Sir. I checked, and its brightness is well within blackout regulations, and if you like"—Thompson clipped a filter over the torch lens—"you can have blue light, or red."

"This will save lives, or at least your face," Churchill said with an impish grin. They both remembered a recent blackout walk through St. James's Park when it was so dark Thompson walked right into a tree and moments later saved Churchill from a similar fate. He wagged the stick at Thompson. "But you must never ever call it a gift. It's a present."

"Why not?"

"Because in German *gift* means poison."

"Beware of Nazis bearing poisons?"

"Clever of you, Thompson, clever and unexpected. Shall we go out and test your present?"

"Now?" Thompson said, knowing it was a pointless question to ask because Churchill was already marching to the front door.

He would never get used to stepping out of the Annexe building into a darkened London. It felt as though the wounded city was holding its breath, hibernating to heal. This strange period would linger in his mind until he died. He would remember two things most of all: the barrage balloons swaying above their heads like so many creaking gray elephants, as if they were listening to you; and the sound of footsteps. In the absence of the usual city sounds of cars, buses, and lorries, footsteps could be heard clearly. And after a raid they would become a constant brittle crunching over shattered glass.

"We'll cross Horse Guards, go up to Duck Island Cottage, and make a loop around the lake and back over the bridge," Churchill said. "That will give your present a good tryout."

They crossed Horse Guards Road, and Thompson was relieved that, so far, it seemed the Germans were taking the night off.

"Convoy SC7 lost twenty out of thirty-five ships to U-boats on the Western Approaches," Churchill said. "They got all the way across the Atlantic and died in sight of home."

"That is terrible."

"It is a grievous loss of men and matériel. And that flying fool Lindbergh is making speeches everywhere attacking Roosevelt about wanting to drag the Americans into a European war. The Americans lack a tradition, a history essential for a nation's foundation," Churchill said and pointed his torch at Duck Island Cottage. "Even that little cottage is part of English history. There's been a version of it there since the 1600s. Once had pelicans, a gift from the Russian ambassador, and a crane with a wooden leg. And now there is a Victory garden planted—good work, if the ducks don't get in there first."

"We can always eat the ducks if they do."

"We damn well might need to. Our men scared the families with warnings of Nazi paratroopers but found nothing untoward at any of the estates. Not a single crown or jewel. Not a Hector or a Caitrin. Where, then, are they?"

Air-raid sirens began their primeval moan, in the far distance at first, but the chorus grew louder and nearer. Thompson had been mistaken; the Germans were not taking the night off. The first anti-aircraft guns opened fire as searchlights stabbed into the night sky.

"I heard that a little girl in one of the bomb shelters referred to the air-raid sirens as the Wibble Wobbles," Churchill said. "She was right. Out of the mouths of babes."

"Don't you think we should go in, Sir?"

"Go in—why?"

Thompson glanced up at the night sky. "This could be a bad one."

"They're all bad ones, and if the Londoners have to face them, so will I. There is one thing I do not understand, Thompson. The car and horse box arrived in Greenock a day early. The *Talisman* hadn't even docked. Why do you think that happened?"

"I don't know, Sir."

"Lord Marlton and Miss Colline are both very capable people, and neither seem to me the sort that would get their arrival off by a whole day. Why don't you give it some of your excellent detective thought?"

"Yes, Sir, I will. Perhaps a police bulletin sent out country-wide might help?"

"Good idea, but without divulging the Jewels. Pictures, though. Caitrin Colline will be easily identifiable with that mass of curly red hair. Mention her Welsh accent too."

Aircraft engines throbbed over the sirens, and the first bombs exploded to the east, in the docks. Churchill seemed not to notice them as he pulled a piece of paper from his pocket. "I have been working on the radio speech I am to give the French people. Shall I read it to you in French or English?"

"English, Sir, if you don't mind. I don't know the other language," Thompson said, which was true, but he was also well aware that Churchill spoke the most atrocious schoolboy French, made even more unintelligible by his speech impediment. Unfortunately he considered himself fluent, which meant that any discouragement to him giving the speech in French would surely be appreciated by the French people and spare him embarrassment.

"Very well, English it is. Listen to what I am considering saying." He coughed, shook the paper, and read aloud, although Thompson was not fooled for a moment. Churchill knew his speech by heart; he just didn't want to seem like a second-rate actor expounding to the world. "We fully intend to hammer the life and doctrine from Hitler and his creed. So, my French comrades, sleep well and prepare for the morrow, when the brave and the true will fight for their deliverance. The bright rays of freedom will shine on them and their path to glory. *Vive la France!* The common people will stride confidently toward their just and deserved inheritance. A new and promising age awaits those who dare to face their oppressors. On the horizon, yet close, is your France, brave, victorious, and forever the home proper of its heroes." He slapped the paper. "There, that's it. What say you to that, Thompson?"

"I would say it is incredibly moving, Sir," Thompson said, being honest. It *was* moving—thrilling, in fact—and he knew he had just witnessed an unforgettable, historic moment in his own life. For all of Churchill's flaws, drama, and Victorian sense of heroism, Thompson believed he was the only man who could lead the country to beat the Nazis. But he did not have the words to tell Churchill how he felt.

Bombs struck closer, and the ground trembled. A fire engine rushed past, bells clamoring, and an air-raid warden shook his warning rattle and shouted at them to get to a shelter.

"I was thinking about that one sentence of yours, Sir. The bit about the common people striding confidently toward their just and deserved inheritance. That would appeal to Caitrin Colline."

"Yes, it would, wouldn't it?"

As they reached the Annexe door, a bomb struck the western edge of St. James's Park with a thunderous roar. "Methinks we just made it," Thompson said.

"We did."

"I don't know much about this stuff, but it seems to me to be the kind of socialist sentence she would write, you know, about the common people getting their inheritance. Is that what you intended, Sir?"

"Not really, but if she wrote that sentence, it would say, the common people, *women* and men, in all the lands," Churchill said. "I wonder where she put the Crown Jewels, and what she did with poor Lord Hecky. Where is our proud Welsh socialist?"

Caitrin was sitting on a long, slanted rock overlooking the wide expanse of Loch Linnhe and eating the tastiest breakfast she could remember. The tea had stewed in Bugsy Finlay's thermos, but at least it was warm. The apple was cold, crisp, and astringent, while tasting the haggis slices dispelled all myths and Sassenach slanders about its doubtful ingredients. Whatever haggis was made of, and she had no wish to ever find out, it was nutritious.

The morning was cool and clear, the loch mirror-calm until a gull skimmed low across the water and its wingtips dimpled the surface. Last night, she had slept in the crub bed of an abandoned croft, after finding enough sacks, straw, and bits of canvas to prevent herself from freezing. It was a silent night, apart from the occasional rustling and squeaks of the croft's more permanent inhabitants.

Breakfast over, she shook straw from her curls, washed in a burn, and set out afoot on the road to Kilcanan. She knew the average adult walking speed was three to four miles an hour. But that was on well-surfaced flat ground, and this road was neither. It rose and dipped, turned and twisted as it clung to the edge of the loch, and the surface varied from potholed tarmacadam to potholed dirt. The forty miles to Kilcanan would take her at least fifteen hours, likely more; she had seen no one on the road since leaving the ferry, and the chances of finding another Doctor Bugsy Finlay along the way were slim.

It was not harsh country but, in a way, elemental and uncaring: bald green hills deeply cleaved by tree-fringed sea lochs. The day warmed a little as Caitrin walked, and the cadence of her footsteps led to thoughts of her actions. Perhaps what she was doing was a mistake. It was certainly against her 512 training, but Bethany Goodman had consistently encouraged them to have confidence and act on their instincts. In Caitrin's final class, only two of them remained from an intake of twenty. Goodman said quite plainly: *We have been taught since childhood to defer, based solely on our sex. And that is because, supposedly, being born male automatically bestows on them a superior intellect. They might think so, but it is not and never was or ever will be so.*

Caitrin clearly remembered Goodman ending with her inscrutable smile and saying, *Begin by gathering the facts, assess them, and then make a decision. But never dismiss your intuition. Do not be afraid to act alone, and always, always finish the job.*

She had done that and was now, unarmed and alone, walking down a winding road in the Scottish Highlands toward a dead end where four men with weapons would be waiting. The thought crossed her mind that she might need a little more than intuition to survive. And alone meant outnumbered.

The light was failing. Caitrin stopped to rest, estimating she had walked for about four hours, which, optimistically, translated into twelve miles. In her heart she knew it was probably less. Color was draining from the day as a westerly Icelandic wind swept in over the Hebrides, darkening the horizon and driving rain squalls across the loch. The temperature dropped; Caitrin pulled her coat tighter and found shelter under a stone bridge. She decided to stay there until the squalls cleared before resuming her journey.

It rained all night.

22

As though it were an act of contrition for the dreadful night, the morning broke bright and clear. Caitrin crept out from beneath the stone bridge and groaned as she straightened. She was stiff, aching, and had hardly slept. She was also hungry, and the last slice of haggis was so welcome it cured her of ever making jokes about it again. After washing her face in a burn where the water was bone-chilling cold, finger-combing her curls into some kind of shape, and brushing twigs and dry leaves from her clothes, Caitrin stepped out onto the road. Today she was determined to walk faster.

The guidebook map was not at all helpful. It was devoid of any detail, showed not a single road, and offered only the vaguest outline of the coastline. So it came as a surprise when she rounded a corner and found a plain stretched in front of her. It was a modest plain, certainly no great prairie or pampas, but there were open fields on either side of the road. After so much time spent walking along a road cut hard against rock faces and canopied with trees, it was odd to be out in the open, and she felt exposed.

Caitrin had reached the middle of the fields when she heard a distant engine. She darted glances left and right, but the fields had been harvested and were separated by wire fences. There was nowhere to hide. It grew louder. She ran toward the shadows in a corner of the field, ready to drop and curl into a ball so her body shape might not be noticed, but then recognized the sound, a throaty sewing-machine growl, as a yellow RAF Tiger Moth biplane trainer flew low over the plain. It banked, turned into the wind, and gradually became a tiny dot until it vanished, the engine note dying away last. The ensuing silence made Caitrin feel even more alone.

She walked away from the loneliness, determined that there would be no more uncomfortable nights spent in a crofter's cottage or crouched under a stone bridge. There would be no stopping until she reached the end of the road and the harbor. The passing fields diminished in size before becoming narrow, pie-shaped wedges and then disappearing altogether, to be replaced by a now-familiar seaweed-strewn rocky shoreline. The other side of the road was hemmed in by stone outcroppings and trees arched over it to make a dark tunnel. There were fewer turns but more undulations; seemingly every dip was deeper, every rise steeper.

As she walked along, words surfaced, her "mental prickles," and she let them run. First to mind came Kolbensattel, where Hector had gone skiing. Oberammergau—Passion Play—Kolbensattel is in Oberammergau, Oberammergau is in Germany. Germany! And one domino fell after another. In Marlton, while having tea with Hector's mother, she had gone to the fireplace to look at his father's painting. Under the painting was a photograph of Hector and his friends skiing at Kolbensattel—and here was a mystery of her memory solved. There was Hector's friend, James Gordon, grinning in the photograph and now missing, presumed dead at Dunkirk, but very much alive in Scotland as Captain Murray. That was where she had first seen him.

Another mind prickle. At Marlton, Hector had woken her to say they should get underway. He mentioned driving down to the village to call London, but it was a cold morning, and when they drove away, both Victoria and his mother's Wolseley had frost-covered windscreens. Neither car had been driven that morning.

She stopped walking, hot from her exertion, took off Hector's jacket, put a finger through the hook-loop, and threw it over her shoulder. Something hard dug into her shoulder blade, so she opened and searched the jacket. Hector's reporter's notebook was tucked away in an inside pocket. It was buckled and stained from her fall in the river—and every page was blank. She turned the notebook over in her hand, checking both sides of every page. In Greenock he telephoned London and supposedly was told no civilian vehicles were allowed on the dock and they were sending a Captain Murray with an army lorry to meet them. Then Hector read precise directions from this notebook to her. She clearly remembered them: *Go through green gate entrance and travel uphill. It gets steep, and about three hundred yards in and on the left is Highland Mary's grave. It is a tall monument surrounded by a low black fence.*

The telephone call was obviously false, and the directions did not exist on paper. She walked on, faster, not noticing the first strands of a sea *haar*, a fog, settling in the road hollows.

Supposedly close friends Hector and James did not recognize each other at the cemetery, which meant Hector was included in the plot. That was why he rushed in that morning at the Gordons' home and said they had to leave immediately because the submarine's schedule had changed. The sudden change knocked her off guard, and arriving a day earlier meant no one would be expecting them. It gave James and Hector an extra day to escape with the Jewels.

Now for the first time she noticed the sea *haar* because at the bottom of the next dip it was thicker and waist-high.

Along their journey north, Hector had said that they were being followed. If that were so, it was probably by one of James's accomplices, which meant they were being shepherded, not followed. And now she knew why Hector had not escaped from the lorry with her in Glen Coe. He had no need to escape because both he and James were members of *Die Brücke*.

At the next dip, she was swallowed by the sea *haar* and slowed to find her way through the whiteness until she climbed higher up the rise.

Caitrin bit back a flooding anger. They had tricked her, and she had allowed herself to be fooled. The failure to be smarter was hers and hers alone. Now the question was: what would and could she do about it?

She crested a rise and stopped. At the tops of the previous rises she had seen the other hills ahead, like a string of islands in a white sea. But now she saw nothing. Everything—the land, sky, and water—were completely erased, replaced by a featureless white void.

23

Caitrin submerged into a white sea. It was cold and damp, had no dimension or detail, and she could see nothing, not even her feet. After wandering off the road several times, she inched forward by keeping her right foot on the edge, so she could be guided by the surface difference between dirt road and grass.

She could hear only her own breathing until the lapping of water off to her left broke through the silence. A few minutes later, the lapping was replaced by waves breaking on rocks. At long last, she was near the harbor and close to the end. A sound, metal striking metal, froze her in place. It was followed by a man's voice with a Scottish accent shouting instructions. He was some distance ahead. She calmed her breathing and eased forward. A second voice, this one speaking in German, called out a question—from directly behind her and close. He was answered by a man just a few feet to her left—it was Hector. Anger caught at her throat. She was in the middle of them, she could reach out and touch Hector, preferably with her automatic, if she had it, but only if she could see him. But if the fog cleared, they would just as easily see her. She swallowed hard to control her emotions.

An engine grumbled into life and settled into a steady burbling. It was a fishing boat. Caitrin was motionless as she heard chains rattling and the men grunting as they carried heavy loads. Hector issued orders to be careful loading, and she sank to the ground. From there, she could hear approaching footsteps better, and looking up could see the denser shapes of men against the lighter sky, while she remained invisible. She ran an exploratory hand across the dirt road surface and her fingertips touched a furrow made by the tread of a tire. She was close to the lorry.

She crept forward, fingers tracing the path of the tread pattern until she reached the tire. She slid under the lorry and heard the men above her unloading cases. Feet scraped close by, and one man ground out a cigarette with his boot inches from her face. Her hand closed over the *sgian dubh*. It was a feeble weapon against so many men, but all she had.

The lorry bed was emptied, and gradually the fog thinned.

First, Caitrin saw the outline of the boat ramp, followed by the breakwater. Next came the top of a mast as the fishing boat edged away from the mooring. The engine note increased; white water foamed at the stern; and the boat, now visible as blue-hulled with a white wheelhouse, left the harbor.

The sun burned the day clear as Caitrin darted glances around but saw and heard no one. They were all gone. She waited a few moments, crawled out from beneath the lorry, and crept to the harbor's edge. The fishing boat was moving faster, ploughing into the waves as it neared the headland.

Caitrin saw two men leave the wheelhouse to step out on deck and was just able to recognize one of them as Hector. Her anger swelled, and she watched the boat plunge and rear as it met the stronger open waters past the headland. The bow slewed left, and the boat slowed to regain its direction. Against a freshening wind it promised to be a hard journey, wherever it was going. But no matter how slowly the boat went, she was being left farther behind by the minute. *And what do I do next?*

She needed to take action, any action, and that meant not being marooned on this desolate spit of land. She remembered the lorry parked at the top of the boat ramp. They had taken the ignition key, but wiring an engine without one was one of the first things taught in 512's elementary skills lessons. It took only a few seconds to start the engine. She put the lorry into gear and drove east, away from the fishing boat steaming west. And as she drove, she assessed her options. Churchill needed to be contacted and told what had happened while she continued her own pursuit. To do that, she needed help and, driving past the fields, remembered the Tiger Moth and knew exactly where to find it.

The sky above RAF Kinmory was filled with buzzing yellow Tiger Moth trainers as Caitrin pulled the lorry up to the main gate. She noticed rows of stones encircling the grass around the guardhouse. They were precisely spaced and painted a dazzling white, mute testimony to both the RAF's devotion to order and the Sisyphean toil of poor airmen who had committed grievous sins and were handed a paintbrush as punishment. The corporal who stepped out to meet her was not impressed with her or the lorry. Understandably, because both were worn and grubby. Caitrin gifted him her warmest smile as compensation.

"I know this is a little unusual, Sergeant, but I wondered if I might speak to my brother? Just for a minute."

He was not at all swayed by her elevating his rank. "It's Corporal, Miss. This is an active RAF station, and you might not be aware of this, but we are at war with the Germans."

Who probably couldn't find Kinmory if you laid a trail of Apfelstrudel *from Berlin to the village center.* "I understand,

and I'm not German, promise. Could you please give him a message from me? It's very, very important." Caitrin almost put a teary tremor in her voice, but that was a little too simple and a bit demeaning.

The corporal's demeanor softened. "Half a tick, Miss. Stay there." He left for the guardhouse and returned with a notepad and pencil. He gave them to her. "Write it down. What's his name?"

"Dafydd Colline."

The corporal nodded his head with approval. "He's a good 'un, that man. Write what you want, and I'll make sure it gets to him."

Caitrin scribbled a note, returned the notepad, and noticed he tore off the paper and folded it without reading. "You're a good 'un yourself, Wing Commander."

He grinned. "The blokes go down to the Claymore pub in the village when they're off-duty. Turn right at the junction, and it's a couple of hundred yards on your right. They'll be landing soon, and I'll tell him to meet you there."

"You must have sisters."

"I do. Oh, I certainly do." He winked and saluted her as she turned the lorry around and drove into Kinmory.

She had been in her room, a small one over the bar, just long enough to wash her face when someone rapped on the door. She opened it to see her brother Dafydd grinning his Dafydd grin. Her heart pulsed as she embraced him. She resembled their mother, in the sense that she looked like her, but Dafydd *was* their father. He looked and acted like him; had the same voice, the same mannerisms, and the same generous soul. They embraced again and for the first time in weeks, she felt safe, she *was* safe.

"What a wonderful surprise, but with my beloved and adventurous sister, not really. Corporal Kevin Waterfield at the main gate wants to know when he should organize the wedding, and would you like to honeymoon at Lyme Regis or Blackpool?"

"Tell him I will have to give it some serious thought."

He took both of her hands in his, stepped back to study her, and frowned. "I am worried about you."

Caitrin shrugged and looked down at her ruined clothes. "I do look a bit as though I've been dragged sideways through a dead haggis. Damn! I just reneged on my solemn vow to never again impugn Scotland's favorite dish."

"What are you doing up here?"

"I'm chasing some very bad people."

"Alone?"

"It didn't start that way, but yes, alone."

"Who?"

"Can't tell you."

"Can't or won't?"

"Both." If there were one person in the world she could rely on, it was her brother Dafydd. But she could not tell even him about this operation.

"Do you need help from me?" he asked and waited for the long pause that would come. Caitrin was fiercely independent, and usually her answer was no.

"Yes, I do need your help," she said, and that answer surprised him. "The men I'm after are in a fishing boat."

"What kind of fishing boat?"

"Fifty feet long, traditional wooden-hulled coastal fishing boat, carvel-planked with straight grain larch, high raked oak stem, and a blue hull with white painted wheelhouse."

"My hawk-eyed sister hasn't lost her touch. You probably saw it for all of two seconds," he said with an admiring laugh.

"Close the door," she said, took out the guide book, spread the map on the bed, and pointed to the Kilcanan harbor. "They left from here and went northwest. Question is: what's out there?"

Dafydd peered over her shoulder at the map. "Two things are out there, the Atlantic Ocean and the tip of the Outer Hebrides Islands. Being a coastal vessel, they would not go into the Atlantic, and anyway that would make them a sitting duck for a U-boat or surface raider. The land directly on that heading would be the island of Barra. Castlebay is on the southern end of the island, and it is the only harbor."

"That's exactly what I thought too. But what's in Castlebay?"

"Kisimul Castle, which is a ruin, a scattering of cottages and fishing boats, and that's about it."

"Then why would they go there?"

"Without you telling me more about them, I can't help."

"I can't do that." She shook her head. "How long would it take them to get to Barra?"

"It's over a hundred miles, and their top speed is around five knots, probably less with this weather shift."

"At least twenty hours, then."

"I'd guess nearer twenty-four," he said. "Which gives us time to get you fed, cleaned up, and ready for battle again."

"Do battle again? How do I get to Barra in time?"

"I'll take you."

She glanced at the map. "It's an island, and I see no airfield."

"That's because there isn't one."

"Then—"

"Believe in your little brother. I'll get you to Castlebay long before they arrive. You'll be sitting there waiting for them."

Fed, bathed, and wearing clean clothes, thanks to Dafydd, Caitrin had decided to enlist support, which is why she was in the tiny Kinmory police station, standing across the counter from PC Hardy, a horizontal man who filled most of the available space on his side.

"You want to use my telephone to call Winston Churchill?" he said, repeating her request as though she had just asked him how to build an exact model of Edinburgh Castle from porridge.

"Yes."

"May I ask why, Miss?"

"Yes, you may."

"You do understand there's a war on, consequently telephone use is highly restricted to urgent matters of state security, and Winston Churchill's a very busy man?"

"He'll accept my call."

"It's also expensive to call London."

"Reverse the charges. Tell them Caitrin Colline is calling about Operation Cat."

PC Hardy produced a pencil, and Caitrin, barely containing her irritation, prayed he wouldn't lick the point.

He licked the point and said, "Would you kindly spell your name for me, miss?"

"C-a-i-t-r-i-n C-o-l-l-i-n-e."

"C-a-i-t-r-i-n C-o-l-l-i-n-e," he repeated. "And it's Operation ... ?"

"C-a-t. Cat."

"C-a-t. Cat."

He wrote down each letter with the greatest of care, picked up the telephone receiver, and turned his back to Caitrin so she could not hear him. He spoke quietly, listened, replaced the receiver, and said, "They'll call back as soon as the connection is made. You can wait in here, if you like. It'll be more comfortable."

PC Hardy came from behind the counter and opened a door. Caitrin hesitated, but a hard push sent her stumbling into the room. He closed and locked the door behind her before she could react.

"Let me out!" she shouted.

PC Hardy went behind the counter, picked up the bulletin he had recently received, and read it again. "It says here you're wanted and should be held for inquiries, Miss Colline. They'll be sending a man up from Glasgow once they know I have you detained."

Caitrin pounded on the door. "It'll be too late by then. Let me out, let me talk to them."

"Sorry, can't do that. Explicit orders. Keep her isolated, the bulletin says," Hardy called back. "She is well trained in unarmed combat. Extreme caution is advised."

Caitrin groaned. "Will you at least call my brother, Flight Lieutenant Colline, at the station? If I don't come back, he'll be worried to death. Please, if nothing else, do that for me."

PC Hardy rolled the pencil in his fingers and considered her request. He cherished order in his life. For PC Hardy, everything there had its precise time and place, especially since the station was also his home. Should he, or should he not? Plenty of time to consider the question while he had a wee dram or three.

24

Caitrin was angry. PC Hardy hadn't fooled her; she had underestimated him and in doing so fooled herself. The room was windowless; the lock was old and could not be picked; the door hinge pins were countersunk, covered in decades of paint, and would resist removal. Although her escape options were few, she needed only one.

She could take a leg off the bed that was pushed in one corner, call out she needed to go to the lavatory, and disable Hardy the instant he opened the door. First, though, she would remove the light bulb so the room would be dark when he entered. But PC Hardy was a big man, forewarned about her fighting skills, and in such a small room there was no guarantee of winning. Another 512 rule: *Never fight a big man in a small space*. Also, he was just a man doing his duty, and she did not want to hurt him.

Perhaps she could start a fire and blow smoke under the door. That assumed Hardy was in the office to notice it. Or she could short-circuit the electrical system to blow all the fuses and then . . .

She heard the station's front door open and several men enter—only men would make so much noise—followed by much foot stamping and complaints about the cold. She put her ear to the door.

"I'm Flight Lieutenant Dafydd Colline," a man said in a puzzling accent that came from somewhere deep in the Yorkshire dales. "Caitrin Colline's brother."

"And I'm Archibald, her other brother," another man said, and that baffled her too because she had no brother Archibald. Most certainly not one who spoke with such an upper class, syllable-perfect voice.

"I'm Osgood Protheroe, Caitrin's fiancé," a third voice announced to make matters even more confusing. She had no fiancé.

"I'm just the driver and don't know her at all," said a fourth voice in a broad Cockney accent. "But I'm not waiting in the car to perish. It's cold enough out there to freeze the balls off a snooker table."

She heard arguments between PC Hardy and the men, in which she was declared to have severe claustrophobia that would no doubt be triggered by the tiny room, followed by impassioned pleas *for her very life* from her "fiancé" guaranteed to thaw the coldest heart. Hardy finally agreed to a visit of a few minutes; the door was unlocked; the men flooded in and filled the room. They all wore heavy RAF overcoats with raised collars, hats, gloves, and tightly wound scarves.

"Dear sister," the man who purported to be Dafydd said. He looked nothing like her brother. He sported a tremendous handlebar mustache, had an eye patch and a healthy tan. Also very unlike Dafydd, this man had a proud Father Christmas stomach. He wrapped his arms around her and said in an overly loud Yorkshire-accented voice, "There, there now, lass, don't go fretting. Right as rain soon enough."

The other men surrounded her, all with grand mustaches and one carrying an extra overcoat, "because the lass must be freezing," and there were murmurings of sympathy as Hardy watched from outside the room. Not that he could see much with the men crowded in such a small space.

Their concern finally satisfied, they filed out of the room, leaving Caitrin curled up on the bed and wrapped in the spare overcoat.

"Thank you, PC Hardy. The lass is right cold and weary," "Dafydd" said. "Best leave her alone to sleep 'til morning."

Hardy nodded in agreement, closed and locked the door, turned out the light, and ushered the men out. Not until the next morning would he discover Caitrin had magically metamorphosed overnight into an RAF student pilot who said he had lost his memory, had no idea where he was, and remembered only his name: Nigel Pendlebury.

The night bombing raid lasted hours, and while the spire, the tower, and the outer wall remained, the rest of Coventry Cathedral lay in ruins. Churchill and Thompson navigated their way through the still-smoking rubble.

"First built in the fourteenth century, Thompson," Churchill growled. "The town center is gone too, all medieval buildings."

"It's a crying shame, Sir."

"It is that," Churchill said and gave a wry, twisted smile. "Of course they'll blame it all on the Germans, but the city council tore much of it down before the war because they wanted a *modern* city. Now, for their collective sins, they'll get one and later, presumably wiser, will lament the loss."

He stopped, straightened, and turned slowly on his heel to survey the devastated cathedral. "We've lost Wren churches in London, almost lost St. Paul's to incendiaries, and now this. How like the Germans to negotiate by beating you over the head."

"Negotiate?"

"They still promise to stop if we call an armistice. The Hun is always either at your throat or at your feet," he said and stopped, surprised at his own words. "I like that and may use it in the near future. Mr. Hitler, the failed Austrian painter and Charlie Chaplin impersonator, does not understand he is not just attacking us, he is fighting tradition and hundreds of years of stalwart Englishmen. From this day to the ending of the world, but we in it shall be remembered. What news of Operation Cat?"

Thompson took a sheet of paper from his pocket and offered it to the prime minister.

"Read it to me," Churchill said as he poked at a piece of charred wood with his cane.

"We have had numerous sightings of the Welsh woman."

"She has a name, Thompson."

"Miss Colline."

"How many sightings?"

"Eighty-three."

"The Welsh always were fleet of foot, but that's exceptionally agile, even for her. What places? Examples."

Thompson stretched out his arm to bring the paper into focus. "Includes Ramsgate, Holyhead, Tooting, Birmingham, the Isle of Wight, and Auchtermuchty."

"Do you know what Auchtermuchty means?"

"No, Sir, I had enough trouble saying it."

"It means Field of Boars. First time I heard that I thought they were referring to Parliament." Churchill puffed on his cigar and allowed himself a chuckle at his wit. "Field of Bores."

"Oh, and there was another one from a police station in a place called Kinmory in Scotland. But the constable called back and said he was mistaken."

"An elusive lass."

They left the cathedral and walked into what was left of the city center. Churchill stopped outside a shop, Suttons Bakery, to watch firemen and air-raid wardens digging out survivors. One of them, a dazed old man, dust-covered gray from head to foot, sat on a low wall. Churchill sat next to him. It took a moment for the old man to recognize him, and he said in a trembling voice, "We're going to be all right, Sir, aren't we?"

Thompson saw tears forming in Churchill's eyes as he patted the man's knee and answered, "With Englishmen like you, how could we fail? What may I do for you?"

The old man managed a smile. "I think a cuppa tea and one of those big cigars of yours would do the trick."

Churchill laughed and offered him a cigar. "Here's one, and I'll arrange for the cuppa."

"Thanks ever so much, Sir, and keep smiling."

"You too. Keep buggering on."

"Keep buggering on," the old man repeated. "I'll do that."

Thompson helped Churchill to his feet. "We cannot lose, Thompson. That old man would never forgive me."

25

An early morning autumn sun gave light but no heat, and the Tiger Moth's propeller blast made it no warmer as a lacerating cold drove Caitrin deeper into her seat. She glanced to her right, where an identical Moth was also preparing for takeoff. In the front seat William Watkins waved to her. A redheaded man with a front row forward's body and a lunatic chimpanzee smile, William was the Osgood Protheroe who had declared himself Caitrin's devoted fiancé in the police station. Behind him sat Giles Hyde-Harrington, who was supposedly Archibald, her nonexistent upper-class, other brother. Caitrin thought he could be Oscar Wilde's doppelgänger, although she would never dare tell him. Scion of an ancient English family, Giles, she imagined, had probably never said Mum or Dad in his life; mater and pater perhaps, but although he was a member of the oppressing upper class, Caitrin could not help but like him. And they had saved her.

Enveloped in a huge RAF overcoat and a hat that bent her ears double, she had been spirited away from the police station, shoved into Giles's Bentley, and raced through Kinmory to the Rowan Tree pub a mile outside of town—avoiding the Claymore pub, it being PC Hardy's local. Poor Nigel Pendlebury was left behind for PC Hardy as a consolation prize. Before entering the pub, they divested themselves of their disguises, Caitrin gleefully ripping off their handlebar mustaches, only to find Giles's splendid foliage had taken years to cultivate and was firmly anchored to his face. Profuse apologies from her, tears of pain from him. Dafydd removed his eye patch and Father Christmas belly pillow. While Giles ordered drinks, Dafydd hurried away to clean off his makeup. They were sitting around a table waiting as he returned and dropped into a chair next to Caitrin. "Aye, looks like rain, right enough," he said in his Yorkshire accent. He picked up a pint, sipped, and added, "Tastes like bloody rain too."

They all groaned.

"Drinks are on you the rest of the night for that antediluvian chestnut," Giles said.

"Gladly. Caitrin, let me introduce these reprobates who are my dear friends. Giles Hyde-Harrington and William Watkins."

"Pleased to meet you. Whose idea was the Gilbert and Sullivan wardrobe?" Caitrin asked.

"Guilty as charged, m'lady." William raised his hand.

"Well done, William Watkins."

"Why do you use my full name?"

"Because I like the double-U wubble-U sound. William Watkins."

"Fair enough. We dressed up because we couldn't have PC Hardy recognizing us and thus ending our illustrious RAF careers."

"The big belly was my idea," Dafydd said.

"His eye patch and the tan were my brilliant contribution," Giles said. "Dafydd always looks so coal-miner pale."

"And what about those atrocious accents?"

"The Yorkshire one was all mine," Dafydd said. "But Nigel doing his Cockney accent came as a complete surprise."

"What about poor Nigel? What will happen to him?" she asked.

Giles waved an aristocratic hand. "We will bail him out later. I must say, though, he is rather good at acting dense."

"Acting?" William said.

"I want to thank you all for getting me out," Caitrin said, paused, and added, "and for not asking why I was in there."

William looked serious. "I assumed it was hush-hush."

"Mum's the word," Giles said.

He just said Mum, Caitrin thought, but it didn't really count. "I need to ask one more favor."

"Caitrin has to get to Barra first thing in the morning," Dafydd said for her.

"That's easy," William chimp-grinned. "She can join us and be a scarecrow."

Dafydd and Giles opened the throttles of their aeroplanes at the same time, the Tiger Moths rocked as they accelerated, tails lifted, and they were airborne. Caitrin pulled her coat tighter as they crossed the coast and headed west. The Minch, the channel between the mainland and the Outer Hebrides, was a dappled blue across which fishing boats nudged white-laced Vs, a Royal Navy submarine—low, gray, and sinister—pushed north past the Isle of Skye, and Caitrin could see the arc of the Hebridean Islands ahead.

As William had suggested, she was temporarily a scarecrow. Britain had a shortage of aircraft, and Tiger Moths were being operated in pairs over shore waters, under the control of Coastal Command. They were called scarecrow patrols, and the theory, although it had yet to be put into practice, was for one Moth to circle a surfaced U-boat, forcing it to dive, while the other one raced off in search of a Royal Navy vessel that could come and give it a good walloping for trespassing. The Moths were un-armed, save for a Verey flare pistol, and had no radio. Dafydd considered it a monumental foolishness, while Giles thought it reckless enthusiasm triumphing over sanity. William asked what happened if the U-boat didn't dive but instead fired its deck gun at them. A Tiger Moth flying low and turning lazy circles at fifty miles an hour was a bright yellow target for any Nazi with a marble and a catapult, let alone a gun. And what was the flare gun supposed to do—set their beards alight or dazzle them so they would sail into something solid, like a convenient island? And what if . . . ?

The whole idea surely belonged to some alcoholic boffin who had never been nearer the ocean than the Buckingham Palace fountain. Fortunately for the scarecrows, so far U-boat commanders appeared to show no interest in surfacing anywhere near the Hebrides.

Dafydd tapped her shoulder, pointed ahead, and shouted, "There's Barra."

Caitrin could make out the island of Barra but, try as she might, saw no airfield, only a white shell beach. The Tiger Moths throttled back, bucking on the ocean air current as they descended, and Caitrin was sure they were going to crash into the water. She braced for impact, the waves were so close, and then behind her, and the aeroplane was glowing from sunlight reflected up by the broad white beach. The Moths landed together, taxied away from the water's edge, and stopped. The silence was immense as the engines cut, until a light wind filtered in, bringing the calls of gulls and the complaint of a distant sheep.

They climbed out of the aircraft, grunting and stretching, slapping their arms for warmth.

"I know coming in low over the water must have been a bit of a fright, but how do you like the airfield?" Dafydd asked.

"Trying to scare your big sister?" Caitrin said, pushing the toe of her shoe into the white shells.

Dafydd made a *who-me?* face. "It's called Traigh Mhòr, Big Beach."

"Didn't work, not scared," she said and poked him in the belly. "Never did, never will. It's a lovely beach."

While they secured their aircraft, Caitrin took off her flying helmet and goggles, walked a little distance away and up a short rise to the road. She turned in a circle and in all directions saw nothing but water. There was the island, of course, but it was flanked by water. They had landed on the outer edge of the country, where the world was reduced to its elements: land, sea, and sky, which were not separate but each a continuation of the other. It was the strangest experience. Everything was preternaturally clear, and Caitrin, for the first time in her life, sensed herself standing on the Earth. She was aware of her own presence. Of her own being and mortality.

Dafydd appeared next to her. "Magical, isn't it?"

She nodded.

"There is something wonderful about this island. It makes you see things differently. Or perhaps see them as they are for the first time." He pointed to the horizon. "Out there, nothing but Atlantic Ocean between Barra and Newfoundland. Full of U-boats."

She gazed out at the ocean for long moments. "This is such a stupid, pointless war."

"Aren't they all?" He slipped his arm through hers. "Cat, why don't you wait and call in the cavalry?"

"Because it would take too long and scare them off."

"Where are they going to go in a fishing boat?"

He saw her chin tilt and mouth tighten. He knew his sister. Once she began, she would not be dissuaded or deflected. It was both her strength and her weakness. "You're taking this personally. That's unwise—"

"No. It's more than a personal matter, Daf. Yes, I was betrayed, but more than that, my—*our*—country was betrayed."
I don't care about the Crown Jewels. Get them back, and I'll

gladly melt them down to buy people decent housing. She inhaled a deep, cleansing breath of sea air. "But Lord Marlton, Hector Neville-Percy, son of a venerable English family, *le chevalier sans peur et sans reproche*, betrayed his country and I want him to see me when he meets his fate."

She squeezed his arm and smiled at him. "William Forbes-Sempill, Nineteenth Lord Sempill, gave military secrets to the Japanese in the Twenties, but because he was aristocracy and his father was aide-de-camp to George V, William was set free—lest there be embarrassment. Even then, he did not stop, and British men died while he went on his exclusive, treacherous way. I will not let Lord Hector slip away and do the same thing."

She ruffled his hair. *My wonderful, marvelous brother.* "Do you know what I have discovered these past weeks?"

"Tell me."

"I learned one thing. I have been in stately homes and met the descendants of ancient families. I learned you and I are from good stock, Dafydd."

"We are," Dafydd said. *My sister, my sister, you surely are.*

"Have you heard of the Certainty Principle?"

"No."

"In 512 Bethany Goodman taught us that in a situation where you are not expected, perhaps even a dangerous one, if you are well trained and believe utterly that you should be there, it will be accepted without suspicion. But you must believe without even an iota of doubt."

"I couldn't carry it off, but you could."

"I'm supposed to be here to finish this. Of that I am absolutely certain."

"Hey, Collines!" William Watkins shouted, and they turned to see Giles wheeling a bicycle from behind his aeroplane. They ran down to join them.

"A bicycle?" Caitrin said. "You strapped a bicycle to your aeroplane?"

"It *is* almost ten miles to Castlebay," Giles said and shrugged. "I was going to bring the Bentley, but it was rather grubby for a Grand Tour. Would have been a poor show."

Caitrin flung her arms around him and kissed his cheek. "Ta ever so much, my dear brother Archibald." He looked bemused, as she knew he would.

"If ever you're interested in a fiancé," William said and spread his arms wide. "We've already had a successful trial run."

She embraced him and kissed his cheek too. "I shall add you to the list, William Watkins."

"Fair enough, but not alphabetically."

"When you get to Castlebay, look for a large granite house right above the harbor, at the end of Pier Road," Dafydd said. "It belongs to Mrs. Barbara MacNeil. Tell her you're my sister, and she will look after you."

"Flown the odd WAAF or two onto the shiny white beach for a naughty weekend, have we?" Caitrin said and saw his color rise.

William saved him. "There's no telephone service yet, the closest exchange is in Lochboisdale, and the radio station is down. It's always going down, but the MacNeils have carrier pigeons. I know, I know, but it works better than smoke signals."

"You know, you know." Caitrin laughed. "So you're a gay Lothario too, William Watkins. And I suppose Giles also brings the odd dolly or two over here?"

Giles straightened, looked down his nose at her, and said in his most upper-class voice, "Young lady, that is a State Secret."

William raised four fingers as he nodded at Giles. "Only dolly officers, though. Oh, by the way, when you're introduced to the locals, immediately tell them you're Welsh."

"Why?"

"Gaelic is the first language here, but they will speak English, as long as *you're* not English."

Dafydd went to his Moth and returned with a knapsack. "We put some serious thought into what you might need. There are sandwiches, a flask of whisky—"

"It gets rather cold at night," Giles said.

"Twenty feet of parachute cord, wrapped up with four strong elastic bands," Dafydd said and saw the question on her face. "You'll be surprised how handy elastic bands and parachute cord can be. I always carry a couple."

"Thank you." *My brother, always a boy in his own world with secrets to share, but not with everyone.* When he was little, she was forever discovering his finds in her pockets: a feather, a marble, a tiny piece of coal that was almost a perfect cube. *My lovely brother Dafydd, with his excited grin when he watched me discover one.*

"I barely stopped him shoving in a whole parachute," William said.

"I suggest jamming a regiment of the Coldstream Guards in there, horses and all," Giles said. "Or a tank. Small one."

Dafydd was deaf to them. "A pair of binoculars, some cash, and Sandra put in some, um, female things."

"*Hmm*, Sandra? Does this Sandra know about MacNeil's too?" she teased.

Dafydd ignored the question, brought out a small object wrapped in a handkerchief, and unfolded it to reveal a compact automatic pistol. "Walther PPK. Seven rounds, .32 caliber, if things get serious." He stuffed the pistol into the knapsack, offered it to her, and glanced at his watch. "You should be in Castlebay before they arrive."

"If you haven't heard anything from me by the end of the week, call Churchill. Mentioning Operation Cat will get you right through." She slipped the knapsack over her shoulders, took the bicycle, looked at each man in turn, and said, "Thank you. Fly wisely and be safe. And don't go shooting flares at U-boats."

Without looking back, she pushed the bicycle up onto the road, gave a wave, and pedaled away.

They watched her until she disappeared around a corner. Dafydd thought his sister the bravest person he had ever met, but riding alone into the island she looked so small.

"Damn, the Empire will be so proud of her," Giles said.

"Whatever it is she's up to," William said.

"That's my sister."

26

Caitrin had never been on such a small island before. To her right, the Atlantic Ocean drove waves forward with so much insolence it seemed as though she was looking up at them. One after another, they transformed from ranks of collapsing green walls into hissing plains of brilliant foam. The sky was immense, the air felt cool and clean, and Caitrin inhaled deep breaths. She was newly alive. The road meandered across the *machair*—the undulating, thin-surfaced land peculiar to the Outer Hebrides—but there was something missing, although she could not at first discern what. There were rocky outcrops, tufts of wild grass bending against the wind, and sheep dotted everywhere, along with a few tiny houses scattered at random. But the landscape was not complete. What was missing? She finally saw the absence. Trees. There were no trees on the island.

Caitrin's legs were tired, her hair wild, and her face flushed from the wind by the time she got to Castlebay. The village was aptly named. It was a scattering of stone cottages built around a semicircular bay with a half-dozen fishing boats, and the ruined

Kisimul Castle, a square block of granite sitting on a small island in the middle. Pier Road, composed of a half-dozen slate-
roofed, granite-block houses with the post office in the middle,
ran along the western side. Caitrin had no trouble finding Barbara MacNeil's house. She knocked on the front door. A middle-
aged woman wearing a floral-pattern pinafore answered, and
Caitrin knew instantly it was Barbara MacNeil. She had a
mother's face and seemed unperturbed at a total stranger
knocking on her door so late in the year.

"Hello, I'm Caitrin Colline."

"Would you be Dafydd's sister?"

"So he *is* known abroad."

There was a glimpse of a secret smile as Barbara answered,
"He is, and William and Giles too. They bring their *wives* here.
I'm Barbara MacNeil."

"Hello, Barbara. I'd like a room for a few days, and Dafydd
said this was the best place on the island."

The smile grew a little stronger. "The best place for what?"

Caitrin had no answer.

"I'm teasing you the way your brother and his friends tease
me. Come in out of the wind. We're having Arbroath smokies
for lunch. Duncan brought them from Auchmithie."

The interior was small but gleaming, florally decorated in
both carpet and wallpaper, and smelled of furniture polish. It
was a comfortable house.

"Your room is upstairs at the front," Barbara said, as
though she had known all along Caitrin was coming. "It has a
grand view of the bay. When you're ready, come down and eat
with us."

"Us?"

"We'll have no visitors this time of the year, so it's just you,
me, and my son Duncan."

"Thank you," Caitrin said and hurried upstairs. The double
bed filled most of the room and the bedspread, like the walls

and carpeting, was floral-patterned, this one made up of gigantic red roses with large bees. There was a small wardrobe with a mirrored door, a bedside table, and a light. She went to the window. Barbara was right. It *did* have a grand view of the bay, and through her binoculars she could easily read the fishing boats' names. She washed, dragged a brush through her curls, and went downstairs.

And instantly fell in love with Duncan. He was close to her height, slender, with the reddest of hair to match hers, and an open, charming face. She guessed he was about sixteen. He vibrated with eagerness—a big-pawed, flopping-tongued puppy of a lad. He heard her coming downstairs, introduced himself, and led her into the kitchen. She felt at home. Barbara sat at the head of the table, while Duncan sat opposite Caitrin with a constantly mobile smile on his face.

"You are Welsh?" he said.

"You have a good ear."

"It was easy." His smile became a grin. "It's a soft-edged accent, a lot like ours."

"Help yourself and do not be shy, or Duncan will devour everything." Barbara pointed to the dishes in the center of the table.

The Arbroath smokies were smoked haddock and with potatoes and neeps made a nourishing meal.

"I have come to like haggis, capercaillie," Caitrin said as she sampled the fish. "And now I like Arbroath smokies too."

"Are you staying long with us?" Duncan asked.

"Just a few days."

"I'll show you the island."

"Thank you, Duncan, that's very kind of you, but I need to stay in Castlebay."

"Why?"

"Duncan, manners," Barbara said, but it was the gentlest of admonitions. It was obvious Barbara dearly loved her son.

"Sorry," Duncan said. "Before you go, you have to climb Heaval, though; it's the highest point on Barra."

"I might."

Duncan was not to be so easily deterred. "You can see your future from the top."

"Oh, is that a good thing?"

Duncan shrugged and tried again. "You'll have a fine view in all directions."

That got Caitrin's attention. "Can you see from the mainland to the harbor?"

"Yes."

"Will you show me the way?"

"Yes, of course. When?" a delighted Duncan said.

"As soon as this smokie is gone."

A short while later, Caitrin and Duncan—she half-expected him to scamper, barking in mad circles around her, and chase after a stick—climbed Heaval and sat on its peak. To their left, the Minch glittered under a vaulting sky; below, the tiny island of Vatersay politely pointed the way south; and to her right the Atlantic Ocean rippled its muscular indifference to the world. She scanned the waters through her binoculars. "What are the islands?"

"That's Vatersay. Sandary, Pabbay, and Mingulay are beyond it," Duncan said, pointing to the islands. "Lady Gordon Cathcart owns all this, and she's never even been here."

Caitrin was surprised at the anger in his voice and patted his hand. Duncan plucked a stem of grass and scissored it between his teeth. "There was a big storm, and my father's boat was wrecked on Mingulay. But there was no one there to help him because they had all been cleared off the island. Lady Gordon Cathcart has a magnificent country estate in England."

"Things will change, Duncan. After this war, we're going to make it different for people like us."

Through the binoculars, she scanned from the islands across to the Minch. And stopped. "After —"

"After what?"

A shock flashed through her. There was the fishing boat. It was just a few miles offshore, cutting through the reflected glare and heading for Castlebay. They were coming to her. She saw something else. Off to her right a bank of dark clouds was growing. A late autumn storm would hit Castlebay about the same time the fishing boat anchored.

"After what?" Duncan repeated.

"Let's go, Duncan. Now." She was on her feet and running, half-tumbling down the hill, too fast for Duncan to keep up.

27

The storm formed high in the Arctic and swept over Iceland to slow and scatter a homeward-bound convoy in the Western Approaches. As a saving grace, it also made the predatory U-boats ineffective by driving them deeper underwater. It howled down onto the Outer Hebrides, pivoted left at the southern islands, and swung toward Castlebay. The rain sluiced in horizontally, obliterating all shape and color, hissed across the quayside, and hammered against the MacNeils' windows.

In the sitting room, Caitrin lowered her binoculars because it was impossible to see anything through the rain-smeared glass. But she knew they were out there, moored off the castle; there was just enough time before the storm struck to read the fishing boat's name: *Island Star*. Only a few hundred yards across the bay separated her from them, but it might as well have been a million miles.

"Tea?" Barbara entered with a tea tray and set it down on a table in front of the sofa. "I have homemade shortbread, marmalade, and Dundee cake too."

"Oh, yes, please," Caitrin said as she sat with Barbara.

"Being so isolated out here, and with this war rationing, it's getting harder to enjoy life's little luxuries. Soon almonds and sultanas are going to be impossible to find," Barbara said, and added with a conspiratorial smile, "but we islanders do manage to look after each other. There are always unexpected little miracles."

Caitrin bit into a piece of cake. "This is delicious."

"Dundee cake was supposedly first made by Keiller, the marmalade company, for Mary, Queen of Scots, because she did not like glacé cherries in her cake."

"A fussy eater was our Mary."

"They do say she was a girl known to lose her head over the silliest of things," Barbara said and grinned.

Caitrin laughed.

"It's good to see you laugh," Barbara said. "I have been a little concerned about you."

Caitrin's smile faded. "I wondered when you'd ask why I'm here this late in the year."

"As I was going to St. Ives."

"What?" Caitrin was puzzled, then understood. "As I was going to St. Ives, I met a man with seven wives. Our three lusty musketeers."

"Yes. Well done. I do not inquire about their matrimonial status, although they are not the Casanovas they imagine themselves to be, especially your brother Dafydd. He is very much smitten by his young lady, Sandra. And she with him. I'm sure you'll get to meet her soon."

"I hope so, and before the wedding."

"However"—Barbara sipped her tea and looked over the rim of her cup at Caitrin—"if I *were* the inquiring kind, I would say your presence in Castlebay probably has something to do with the strange fishing boat moored in the harbor. The *Island Star*."

"And you would be right."

"*Hmm.*" Barbara raised an eyebrow. "Try the shortbread."

"The men on the boat took something very valuable, and I intend to get it back."

"Something of yours?"

"No, something of ours, the whole country."

"Oh, that is serious. You're doing it all alone?"

"Yes, so far."

"The island's radio is broken, and we sent the pigeons with messages for a boat to bring new valves. It will take a while before we're in touch with the mainland."

"At least no one is going anywhere while this storm persists."

"How may we help you, Caitrin?"

"I don't know, Barbara. These are dangerous men."

"Dangerous? Duncan will be delighted at the thought, but he's all I've got. While you are concocting a plan of attack, there is one thing you might do for me that's not dangerous."

"Gladly."

"I have a list of groceries I need for dinner, once the weather clears a little. Fergus MacLeod's shop is just down the hill on the right. It's the only shop on the island."

"Of course."

"And taking Duncan with you would be a blessing, for him and me. Being cooped up is hard for him, difficult for me, and I think he's madly in love with you. I believe it was F. Scott Fitzgerald who called it puppy love."

Caitrin laughed. "I'll scratch his ear, buy him a bone, and tell him he's a good boy."

The weather did not clear, but it did lessen enough for Duncan and Caitrin, she dressed in oilskins with her hair tucked up under a sou'wester, to scurry through a now vertical rain to the grocers. The shop was small and smelled of sawdust, which was scattered on the floor, and vinegar, from a broken bottle at their feet. Fergus MacLeod held the neck of the broken bottle between finger and thumb and surveyed the pool of vinegar.

"An accident. Only two bottles left now," he said with the sorrow of someone who has just tragically lost his most dearly beloved. A short, round man, completely bald and with the fingers of a concert pianist, Fergus knew every item in his shop and its placement on the shelves. They were his family.

"Hello," Caitrin said and handed him Barbara's grocery list, which he scrutinized with great care.

"I don't have all of this in stock," he said in Gaelic.

"We'll take what you have," Duncan answered, and added, "It's all right. Caitrin is Welsh, not English."

"Ah, then I welcome you to Barra," Fergus said in English.

"Thank you."

Fergus studied the shelves behind him and placed each item on the counter. He ticked them off the list and patted their tops with affection before looking for the next one. Fergus was nothing if not methodical.

Duncan grabbed Caitrin's arm hard enough to make her flinch and hissed, "They're coming!"

"Ouch, Duncan, that hurt! Who's coming?"

"A man from the boat."

"You were listening to my conversation with your mother."

"Doesn't matter now," he said and repeated, "One of them is coming in here."

Caitrin glanced over her shoulder and through the window to see Captain Murray/James Gordon cross the quay and head directly for the shop. He was too close for them to escape.

"I don't have nutmeg," Fergus said with a sigh. "Probably won't have nutmeg for a while. Oh dear, this war."

Caitrin pulled the sou'wester lower, leaned over the counter, and said, "Fergus, I need help. The man who is about to enter is after me, and to avoid being recognized I am going to speak

Welsh. He won't know the difference between Welsh and Gaelic."

Fergus listened, winked, and said, "That's a good enough reason to speak Gaelic."

The doorbell rang as James Gordon entered, and Caitrin cursed herself for not carrying the Walther pistol.

"*Byddwn yn cymryd yr hyn sydd gennych,*" she said.

Fergus took items off the counter and placed them in a cardboard box, settling each one in place with a great deliberation that made Caitrin want to scream. She heard James's feet scuffing the sawdust close behind her as he hummed some tuneless melody. Fergus studied the list again. "I'll put it on your mother's account, shall I, Catherine?"

"*Diolch yn fawr iawn,*" Caitrin said, picking up the box and turning away from James Gordon so he would not see her face as she left.

After they were gone, James Gordon pointed to the cigarettes on a shelf behind Fergus and said, "Forty Senior Service and a box of Swan, please."

Fergus spread his arms wide, bestowed his best smile on him, and answered, "*Chan eil Beurla agam. Tha i na chànan grànda. Mar d'aghaidh. Ach bheir mi d'airgead.*" *I do not speak English. It is an ugly language. As is your face. But I'll take your money.*

He also charged him a shilling more and gave him the oldest stock.

28

The *Island Star* was gone. Lord Hector, James Gordon, and the Crown Jewels had vanished. A dull and overcast morning brought a moment of panic as Caitrin scanned the harbor through her binoculars and saw that the mooring was empty. Until she looked farther left and noticed the fishing boat's stern behind Kisimul Castle. For some reason, during the night they had shifted away from the village and closer to the mouth of the bay. *Does that mean they are getting ready to leave?*

The move helped her because they had moored closer to shore, which made them easier to observe. She pedaled around the east side of the bay, found a derelict cottage on a rise that shielded her from view, and sat deep in what had once been the kitchen to watch the boat through a broken window.

Caitrin noticed there were never more than two men on deck at any one time. James Gordon, smoking a cigarette, appeared from the wheelhouse, and a moment later Hector joined him, although he stood half-hidden in the doorway. They were laughing about something Hector said, which proved what Caitrin already knew—Lord Marlton, Hector Neville-Percy, was a traitor. For a moment he looked directly at the cottage, and instinctively she leaned farther into the shadows, although it would have been impossible at that distance for him to see her. Anger rose and tightened her throat, partly in response to his betrayal and partly because he had so effortlessly fooled her.

She felt the weight of the Walther PPK on her thigh, pulled the pistol out of her pocket, and aimed it at Hector. But he was well out of effective range, and shooting him would not solve the problem. Judgment Day would come, though, in a courtroom where justice would deal with Lord Hector. And if some aristocratic loophole granted to only a few were to set him free, then she would take matters into her own hands.

She put the Walther in her lap, picked up the binoculars, and surveyed the boat again. There was no sign they were intending to leave soon; in fact, one of the men was rowing a dinghy across the harbor toward the shops. But something bothered her; she had a sense of foreboding. *Female intuition again. Listen to it this time.* There were footsteps outside, the broken kitchen door shuddered open, someone entered, and Caitrin reacted automatically. In one fluid movement, she dropped the binoculars, snatched up the Walther, flicked off the safety catch, rolled to her left, and aimed it at the intruder—Duncan, a statue, staring wild-eyed at the pistol.

"Is that real?"

"Very real," Caitrin said and lowered the gun.

He kept staring but at her, not the gun, and only his mouth moved. "I walk in and you're sitting against the wall. Then— *zip!*—you're in a corner with a gun pointed at me, and I never saw you move."

"You must have blinked."

He shook his head.

"You can move now, Duncan. Next time cough or whistle; give me warning you're coming," she said and put the gun away.

"I've never seen anything like that before," he said as he sat next to her, but not close, and replayed the action in his mind. "Will you teach me?"

"Maybe, one day."

"Yes, yes!" Duncan the exuberant puppy returned. He glanced through the window. "Anything happening out there?"

She shook her head.

"I might have something," he said. "There's an Irish freighter off Vatersay. My friend Collin told me a Navy cutter went alongside to investigate. The skipper said they were heading for Oban, had steering problems in the storm, and got blown off course. They are supposedly waiting for parts."

Caitrin straightened and from the corner of her eye saw James and Hector go below. "Anything else?"

"Although Eire is a neutral country, the skipper is terrified of being torpedoed by a U-boat, so he's flying a gigantic Irish flag from the mast and another from the stern."

"I want to see the ship."

"I'll show you." He grinned. "We'll take my boat to Vatersay."

Duncan rowed them across Caolas Bhatarsaigh to the north shore of Vatersay. From there it was a brisk hike over a series of low hills until they reached the west coast. Duncan dropped to the ground, and Caitrin followed him. Below them the island narrowed into an isthmus with long white beaches on either side before widening again into a shallow hammerhead.

Duncan pointed down to the west. "There she is."

Caitrin inspected the freighter through her binoculars. Anchored a half-mile off Traigh Shiar, West Beach, it was at least twenty years old, steam-powered, and about three hundred feet long. The superstructure was amidships, with a tall narrow funnel, and she was dirty, the paintwork heavily rust-stained.

"That is one hard-worked vessel," Duncan said.

"The *Celtic Twilight*," Caitrin said, reading the name on the bridge. "How very William Butler Yeats of them."

"See the flag on the mast? Below the big Irish one," Duncan said. "Delta. Yellow stripes with a blue center means—"

"Stay clear. Maneuvering with difficulty."

Duncan was disappointed she had stolen his thunder. Caitrin saw it on his face, and although she knew the answer, asked him, "What does the blue and white swallowtail one below it mean?"

He brightened. "Alpha. It means I have a diver down. Keep clear at slow speed."

"Well done." Caitrin focused her attention on the stern. "Diver down, huh? I can see the diver's air-supply line, but I also notice something else. Can you see it with those keen young eyes of yours?"

She handed over the binoculars and watched him as he inspected the vessel. Duncan MacNeil was such a charming young man.

"I don't see anything strange."

"Start where the air-supply line goes underwater, and then follow it up to the deck."

"I don't . . . I see it now, I see it!" He lowered the glasses and grinned at her.

She wanted to hug him. Such glee, such open joy. "The end of the line is tied off to an inboard cleat. There's no air compressor and that means there's—"

"No diver."

"Well done, Watson."

"Elementary, Holmes, old sport," Duncan said and sat up. "Do you think the men back there on the *Island Star* have been waiting for her to arrive?"

"We'll soon find out," Caitrin said and pointed to the freighter. "The skipper won't want to be anchored long on the weather side of this island."

"And Collin said they were waiting for parts—maybe from the fishing boat?"

"Or that's their excuse."

"What are we going to do next?" Duncan asked, with myriad visions of heroic deeds, including many gallantly saving Caitrin, flooding his imagination.

"We're going to go talk to your mum."

29

Barbara MacNeil sat in her kitchen, drinking tea as she listened to Caitrin. It was dusk, and they had sent Duncan off to the ruined cottage to keep an eye on the *Island Star*. A glow from the peat fire and an oil lamp burning on the mantelpiece made the room golden and cast satin shadows. Except for a clock ticking in a far corner, it was quiet as Caitrin finished speaking.

Barbara thought for a moment before replying. "So you believe the *Island Star* and the Irish freighter are connected?"

"This is a well-organized operation, but I could not understand why the *Island Star* would come to Castlebay. There was no logical reason, until the *Celtic Twilight* turned up."

"They are going to meet up with the *Celtic Twilight* and transfer the, the . . . ?"

Caitrin shrugged. "I'm sorry. I really cannot tell you."

"Let's call them the important objects."

"Yes. A bigger ship could take the important objects farther. And I don't believe for one second the *Celtic Twilight* was driven here by the storm."

"Why not?"

"Supposedly, it was going to Oban. It's an Irish-registered vessel, so it probably left from Dublin, or maybe Liverpool, and was traveling north up along the west coast, until the storm hit. But the storm came from the northwest. Regardless of the phony steering problem, a northwest wind would have driven the ship *east*, toward the mainland, not *west* out to the Atlantic side of the Hebrides. The nonexistent diver just adds more suspicion."

"So you believe she's here for a definite reason?"

"Yes, but it's too dangerous for her to remain on the weather side of the island. And if she stays too long, the Royal Navy or Coastal Command will get suspicious." Caitrin sat back and sipped at her tea.

"And what is your plan?"

"If the *Island Star* does offload the important objects onto the freighter, which will have to be soon, I need to be on board that ship when she sails."

"How will you manage to do that?"

"I need your help and Duncan's too. But it's all up to the *Island Star*. When it moves, so will I."

They both heard the clatter of Duncan's bicycle outside as he skidded to a halt and raced into the house. The kitchen door flew open, and he charged in, filling the room and blurting out, "The *Island Star*! She's leaving!"

The moon was new and the night black as the *Island Star* slipped its moorings and glided out of the bay. Soon after, another fishing boat, the *Ben Lui*, cleared its moorings and followed. It showed no lights. In its wheelhouse, with Barbara at the helm, Caitrin and Duncan stared hard into the darkness.

"The *Ben Lui* is my brother Andrew's boat," Barbara said. "He's been away in Edinburgh for a while seeing his son, Ian."

"Ian came back from Dunkirk," Duncan said.

"Not all of him," Barbara said and shook her head to erase

the thought. "Caitrin, you haven't said how you intend to get on board the *Celtic Twilight*."

"You stand off some distance, on the ocean side so your silhouette doesn't show against the village. Duncan and I will row to the stern on the opposite side from where they're loading. Their attention will be focused on getting the important objects aboard, and I'll climb up the diver's air-supply line."

"And if the line is not there?"

There was the briefest of pauses. "I know," Duncan said. He went on deck and returned with a coil of rope. He held up one end and tied it to a three-pronged grapnel. "Sometimes, when the lobster pots drift in the spring, I drag for them with this."

"You're a savior, Watson," Caitrin said, and he beamed with pride.

"Naturally, Holmes."

"As soon as I start climbing, Duncan rows back to you," Caitrin said. "Once he's on board, you do not wait around but go back into Castlebay. I don't want to chance them seeing you."

Barbara hove to some distance from the freighter, idled the engine, and handed down Caitrin's knapsack as she settled in the stern of the rowing boat. "I put some haggis slices in there. You never know."

"I've grown to love it," Caitrin said.

"And as soon as the pigeons come back from the mainland, I'll send your message to Mr. Churchill."

"Thank you," Caitrin said. "Thank you for everything, Barbara."

"We all have important objects in our lives." Barbara smiled and squeezed her hand. "Some old, some new. Be careful."

Duncan pushed away from the boat and turned toward the starboard side of the ship, Caitrin whispering guidance as they got closer. There were few lights, but much noise from winches and tackle as the Jewels cases were offloaded from the *Island Star* on the port side of the freighter.

The freighter was some distance off, then loomed over them

as the rowing boat bumped against the hull. Caitrin found the air-supply line and gave it an exploratory tug. It held firm. She slipped on her knapsack.

"There'll be quite a few men up there. Going alone is dangerous. I should come with you," Duncan whispered.

"No." Caitrin took his face in both her hands and kissed his forehead. "You are a wonderful young man, Duncan MacNeil, and the most important of important objects."

She gripped the air line, wrapped her legs around it, and inched her way up the side of the ship. Duncan watched her for a moment before he turned and rowed away.

On the *Ben Lui*, Barbara took binoculars from the wheelhouse and stepped out on deck. Her eyes had grown used to the darkness, and she could now see shapes and edges. Sound carries over water, and she heard voices calling commands. Behind her, Duncan tied off the rowing boat and climbed aboard. She raised a hand to silence him.

The rumble of winches died, bells rang, and the derricks were secured.

"They're leaving soon," Barbara said and swung her binoculars toward the stern to see Caitrin climbing the air line just ten feet below the deck.

"Will she be all right?" Duncan said.

"I think so. They're leaving now. She—" Barbara stopped as commands rang out on the ship to raise the anchor and haul in the air-supply line. Barbara did not hesitate. She switched on all the *Ben Lui*'s navigation and deck lights, pushed the throttle wide open, fired a red flare into the sky, and surged toward the bow of the *Celtic Twilight*.

Hector and James Gordon were sitting on a capstan in the bow of the ship, smoking celebratory cigarettes and watching the hold being closed, when the sky above them glowed red.

James instinctively reached for his pistol, paused as he saw his men race for the starboard rail, and shouted, "No guns!"

They joined the men and looked down at the *Ben Lui*, its lights blazing, running parallel to the freighter. A mad woman, gray hair whipping around her head, was shouting up at them from a wheelhouse window. "My son, have you seen my son? He's not allowed to go fishing by himself."

"Out here at night? Are you mad?" one of the men shouted back and made a "crazy" gesture.

"My son, my son. I've lost him."

The men laughed as Duncan, wearing only his underpants, climbed up from the hold. He rubbed his eyes and stared up at the freighter in dumb amazement.

"There he is, old lady! Behind you!" a man shouted, and they all pointed at Duncan. "Buy your idiot child some clothes," another man yelled and threw a coin at her.

Barbara glanced at Duncan, glared up at the men, and shouted, "*Tha thu cho uilebhstein grànda!*" *You are all monsters!*

"What did you say?" a man said. "You want me? All of me?"

"*Bha do mhàthair na lachan!*" Barbara screamed at him. *Your mother was a duck!*

Duncan disappeared, came back with a blanket wrapped around him, glanced toward the stern, saw Caitrin had reached the rail, and whispered, "*Mhàthair, tha i sabhailte.*" *Mother, she is safe.* "Our pantomime worked."

"I just hope you are wearing clean pants," Barbara said as she slammed the window shut, switched off the deck lights, and swung the helm hard to starboard.

"*Bha do mhàthair na lachan.*" Duncan shook his head and said with a grin, "Your mother was a duck?"

The *Celtic Twilight* picked up speed as they saw Caitrin wave from the stern. She was safely aboard.

As Caitrin swung over the top rail, her knapsack caught on a metal edge and split open. Its contents scattered across the deck, and the Walther pistol bounced off a stanchion to go spinning overboard. She collected the pieces, jammed them into her pockets, picked up the greaseproof-paper-wrapped haggis slices, and peered down at the water. "Damn!"

She waved as the *Ben Lui* motored past, found a lifeboat, climbed inside, and pulled the canvas cover over her. She was safely aboard but unarmed.

Standing at the starboard rail, Hector watched the *Ben Lui* fading into the distance. James nudged him and said, "What a strange event. The wonders of the deep, huh?"

"Yes, indeed."

"You seem a bit distracted, Hector."

"I keep thinking about Caitrin Colline," Hector said. "By now I imagined we might have read a newspaper report or heard something about her on the wireless."

"She chose a bad place to leap off the lorry. That was almost a sheer drop to the river."

"Do you think she survived?"

"No, which is sad for her but good for us," James said. "I doubt we'll ever hear about her again."

30

They were young men with aged faces. Thompson recalled a phrase he once read in an American Civil War book about soldiers facing the horror of battle: *They had seen the elephant.* But unlike soldiers or sailors, who usually had quiet periods between battles, these young RAF fighter pilots faced the elephant daily, sometimes more often. And, as elegant as their Spitfires were, he could not imagine being strapped into that claustrophobic cockpit alone. Death in the air could strike in an instant, if you were lucky, and you never knew or saw who attacked you. But so many young men fell to earth, wounded and trapped in their burning metal coffins, and it could take a while to hit the ground. No wonder they looked old.

Churchill had bluntly refused to remain in London, insisting instead on being seen; he said the nation demanded it of him. He usually traveled to where it might be dangerous and was a magnet to the pilots as soon as he arrived at the fighter station. His speech about the Few, given in August, had given recognition to their struggle. *Never in the field of human conflict was so much owed by so many to so few*. They were the Few, the young men who faced overwhelming odds, survived, although with great losses, and for the time being had kept the Germans at bay.

The airfield had taken severe punishment too. It had been bombed repeatedly, buildings were destroyed and aircraft damaged, and numerous bomb craters needed to be filled. But still the aircraft flew.

A Spitfire roared low overhead, turned, leveled off, and made a perfect three-point landing. Some of the pilots applauded, and they all watched as it taxied up to dispersal and stopped.

"It's a new delivery," a pilot said. "We've lost a couple lately."

Thompson was surprised when the pilot climbed out, whipped off her flying helmet, and shook free a mane of blonde hair.

"ATA, Air Transport Auxiliary," the pilot said. "Those women are damn good too. I hear they might even be getting equal pay soon."

Thompson nodded to the Spitfire. "That is a fine aeroplane."

"Aircraft, not aeroplane," Churchill corrected him. "And it's called an airfield now, not aerodrome." He turned to the pilots. "Are there any complaints about them?"

They shook their heads, but one pilot said, "We did have one a while ago, but it was taken care of."

"What was it?"

The pilot raised his hands, flat, one behind the other, an aircraft chasing another aircraft, and said, "The German 109s have fuel injection, while the Spit has a carburetor. When we'd chase one, they'd push the nose forward and dive." He dropped the forward hand and put it behind his back but left the other one still. "We'd follow, and the carburetor would cut out, just for a second, but it was long enough for him to escape." He dropped the second hand.

"You say it was taken care of. What was the answer?"

"When we thought all was lost, Sir, a certain Miss Shilling saved the day."

"Explain, young man."

"Beatrice Shilling designed this to fit inside the carburetor and prevent fuel cutoff," the pilot said and held up a small brass ring on the tip of his index finger. "Officially it's known as the Royal Aircraft Establishment Restrictor."

Churchill's face softened as he played straight man. "And what is it called unofficially?"

"Ah, it's called Miss Shilling's Orifice, Sir," the pilot said, but not without blushing.

"And what does our clever Miss Shilling think about that? Or have you not asked her?"

An aide hurried up and gave Churchill a note before the pilot could reply. He read it and with a broad smile swung toward Thompson. "At last we have a breakthrough on Operation Cat, Thompson. A Flight Lieutenant Dafydd Colline called from the Scottish wilds to say he knows exactly where his sister is."

Dafydd Colline's morning schedule was supposed to include instructing an especially leaden-brained student pilot in the intricacies of high-speed, low-level flying. He was not looking forward to it with any enthusiasm because in a previous flight the student revealed a marked inability to differentiate sky from ground. Neither did it appear to matter much to him. But it seemed like a heavenly gambol through a host of golden daffodils compared to where he was now standing—in 10 Downing Street, London, facing the prime minister of Great Britain and the entire British Empire: the Right Honorable, and somewhat irascible, cigar-smoke-wreathed Winston Churchill.

"You are Flight Lieutenant Colline?" Churchill growled.

"Yes, Sir."

"You are the brother of Caitrin Colline?"

"Yes, Sir."

"You two are close?"

"Very close. She saved my life when I was born."

"Explain. No, don't; there's no time. You know exactly where she is?"

"More or less."

"More or less. What is that supposed to mean?"

Dafydd raised a hand and, without looking around, pointed behind him. "Prime Minister, would you ask the gentleman in the corner to move so I can see him? I'm unhappy having someone staring at the back of my head."

Churchill held back a smile. This young man was without a doubt Caitrin Colline's brother. He had the same confidence and clarity. This was a family to be reckoned with. A good bloodline. He nodded at Thompson, who shifted his seat so he could be seen.

"Thank you, Sir. It means I know where I last saw her, about a week ago."

"Where?"

"On the island of Barra in the Outer Hebrides."

"Now, explain to me how you and your sister found yourselves on the island of Barra. And why."

"I was on a scarecrow flight. That's—"

"I know what a scarecrow flight is. And a damn silly idea it is too."

"We landed on the beach in Barra, and she cycled off to Castlebay."

"Why?"

"I do not know, Sir."

"She told you nothing about her reason for going to Barra?"

"No, Sir, nothing, only that it was of great importance."

"What did she have with her?"

"Just a bicycle. Oh, and a Walther PPK, twenty feet of parachute cord, and four elastic bands. And some sandwiches."

"*Hmm.*" Churchill released a great cloud of cigar smoke, and his fingertips drummed a nervous tattoo on the desk. "Young man, you are seriously trying to tell me that your sister, with whom you are very close, told you absolutely nothing about what she was doing? Or why she wanted to go there?"

"Only that she insisted the country, *our* country, had been betrayed and intended to catch the men who did it. That's all. No details."

"And you weren't at all curious?"

"I certainly was, but I respect my sister's integrity. And also, I know from experience that pursuing the matter with her would be pointless."

We are going to win this damn war if the country has more people like this young man. "If I remember correctly, I believe your sister is not an enlisted member of the Royal Air Force. Is that correct?"

"No, Sir, she is not."

"No, I thought not." Churchill peered up at him over his glasses. "And taking a civilian in an RAF aircraft on an unauthorized flight, particularly in wartime, is an offense for which I could have you court-martialed. Possibly even shot. Do you understand?"

"Yes, Sir."

"The question is, should I? What say you?"

The telephone rang to save Dafydd from giving an impossible answer. Churchill picked up the receiver, listened, grunted, and hung up. He assessed the young man standing in front of him before saying, "Flight Lieutenant Colline, for the time being, we are going to forget all about this, this silly escapade. You may go back to Scotland. And don't do it again."

"Thank you, Sir," Dafydd said.

Churchill watched him hurry away, settled back in his chair, puffed out another cloud of smoke, and turned to Thompson. "What thinketh you, Thompson, about our young man and his sister?"

"Peas in a pod, Sir."

"An apt description, and I may have misjudged the other pea, who I have just been told is no longer in Castlebay. She is now traveling south on a freighter named, of all things, the *Celtic Twilight*. Lavender shades of Oscar Wilde. We shall have the Royal Navy or Coastal Command find and stop this vessel immediately. That should be quite simple. *Cherchez la femme* and find the Crown Jewels." He laughed and shook his head. "We got the information from a Mrs. Barbara MacNeil, sent by carrier pigeon. To the mainland, I mean, not London. Carrier pigeon. What wonders will they think of next?"

"There's no knowing, Sir. If Miss Colline is innocent, what does that say about Lord Hector's intentions?"

Churchill's head snapped up. "Thompson, Lord Hector is a Neville-Percy whose grandfather went to Harrow, my alma mater."

31

On a wet, sullen morning off the Scilly Isles, the Irish freighter *Celtic Twilight* disappeared from the waves. As the day brightened, she reappeared, now named *Joana,* flying large Portuguese flags on her masts and steaming south for neutral Lisbon.

Caitrin assumed that by now Dafydd and Barbara MacNeil had contacted Churchill, which meant she had to find a way to stop the freighter or at least slow it down enough to attract the attention of a Royal Navy ship or a Coastal Command flying boat.

Staying in the lifeboat was cold, wet, and confining, so she had slipped down into the cargo hold, where there were myriad hiding places. Hector's jacket helped keep her warm, and she looked forward to returning it to him. Caitrin guessed there were about a dozen men on board. A half-dozen were German sailors, who would not be that dangerous, but she would need to be armed with more than the remaining slice of haggis to lessen the odds against James Gordon's men. Her best chance for survival would be to disarm them one at a time. No, on second thoughts, she would start with two, the Pickled Pair.

These two men had almost found her hiding place in the cargo hold the same time they discovered a case of French cognac. Every other night—presumably they needed a day off to recover—the men would creep down into the hold, remove a few bottles, find a corner, and get devoutly drunk until they passed out. No one seemed to notice their absence, so she decided the Pickled Pair would be the first to fall.

They duly entered the hold and got drunk. Caitrin waited through their juvenile antics and, once they had passed out, dragged them into a paint locker. There she sat them up, back to back, tied hands to feet with parachute cord—silently thanking her brother Dafydd for putting it in her knapsack—and finished with a connected loop around each neck so that if one moved, he would choke the other. The paint locker had a steel door and was built against a bulkhead shared with the engine room, so even the most anguished shouts for help would not be heard.

She was now armed with a Luger taken from the more flatulent drunk, but to whittle down her enemies, she would have to leave the security of the hold and go hunting on the open deck.

It was growing dark when she raised her head above the hatch to see the deck deserted and the *Joana* carving her way through a heavy-surfaced sea. It was cold as she cleared the hatch and slipped into the shadows of the superstructure. She edged around a corner and was hurled to the deck when a heavy steel door flew open and knocked her down. The Luger skidded away as a huge man stepped out, overcame his surprise, grasped a handful of her hair, and pulled her upright. He expected resistance, but instead she moved with him. Her right knee drove into his groin, and her heel scraped down his shin to piston onto his instep. He released his grip and staggered away, howling in pain. Caitrin retrieved the Luger and fled back to the hold. Soon they would all know she was on the ship and would come looking for her.

It did not take long for the hunt to begin. The first two men searching for her appeared at the head of the steps. It was dark because Caitrin had broken the light, and they were cautious. Under the steps, she let the first man through and jerked a parachute cord tripwire tight on the second one. He fell, tumbling down the steps to slam into the first man. Caitrin was on them before they could rise. She forced them to lie flat, tied each of their hands in turn, and pushed them into the paint locker. Now for the others.

She stepped back and froze as something hard pressed into the base of her skull. "You can rise from the dead once, Caitrin Colline, but not twice," James Gordon said from directly behind her. "Put down the gun. Don't move except to open your hand, release your grip, and let it fall."

She dropped the Luger and shifted a little, first left and then right. James's gun pressed harder. "Stop. I know what you're doing, sensing if I am right- or left-handed so you know which way to spin and attack. I suggest you stop doing that because I know the routine and have fast reflexes too. Sit down, on the deck, slowly."

Caitrin sat as he bound her hands and released the men. He pulled her upright and searched her pockets. "Four elastic bands, a slice of haggis, and a *sgian dubh*. You are a heavily armed lass." He laughed and returned the elastic bands and haggis. "The knife I'll keep. I doubt even you can cause much mayhem with a haggis. Although, looking at this sorry bunch of men, you've done damn well with what you have got."

The ship's engine rumbling died, and the *Joana* slowed as James and Caitrin reached the deck. Two hundred yards away off the starboard beam, the dark edge of a U-boat conning tower cut up through the waves. The submarine surfaced, the sleek gray shape low in the water as it maintained a parallel course. The hatches opened, and a half-dozen sailors spilled out, ran to the deck gun, and aimed it at the ship. "*Motoren stoppen.* Stop engines," a voice came through a loud hailer.

The *Joana*'s engine stopped, and the ship rolled in the swell.

Caitrin glanced at James. He seemed unperturbed and pointed at a flag breaking open above them at *Joana*'s mid-mast: blue and yellow rectangles.

"*K*," he said.

A second one followed: two blue horizontal stripes separated by a white band.

"And do you know what that letter flag would be?" he said and nudged Caitrin with the muzzle of his pistol.

"*J*."

"Good girl. *KJ*. *Krone Juwelen*. Crown Jewels," he said and waved to the U-boat. The U-boat captain waved back, the gun was cleared and the hatches sealed, and the submarine dived.

"We're quite safe out here, as you can see," James said. "On second thoughts, *I* am quite safe, you not so much. Shall we join the others for tea? I am sure Lord Hector will be dying to see you again."

32

Thompson knew the old man was exhausted, and at sixty-six he *was* old, but he mostly hid it well. The Blitz casualty and damage numbers were horrifying, and the RAF fighters, who fought so heroically by day, were helpless to defend the cities at night. London, Birmingham, and Coventry could only watch as wave after wave of Luftwaffe bombers dropped their lethal loads. Thompson knew this must weigh heavily on Churchill, although he would never let it show. At the head of the usual flock of army officers and local officials scurrying around him like solicitous quail, Churchill strode across the drawbridge and through the massive brick arch of the Citadel to stand on Dover's Western Heights.

"Dover, the Key to England." Churchill moved a few steps ahead of the crowd, gazed down at the city spread at his feet and then out across the water to the French coast and Calais. "The English Channel," he muttered to himself. "It's the *English* Channel."

He glanced to his right at Dover Castle and said, "If I were a little boy and wanted to draw a castle it would look exactly like that one. Towers, arrow slits, and crenellated battlements."

"Yes, Sir," Thompson said. "I agree, it is indeed a splendid castle."

"And I would also add the concrete pillbox they're building and the miles of barbed wire. Bertie Ramsay directed the evacuation of Dunkirk from there. There's been a castle on that hill for a thousand years." He gazed out at the Channel again, pointed his cane toward Calais, and asked, "How far?"

"Twenty-one miles, Sir," an officer said.

"*Hmm*. At three hundred miles an hour an aircraft can cross the water in seven minutes and, in safety, drop bombs from high above. What's the use of a splendid castle now?"

No one had an answer or was brave enough to offer one.

"Geoffrey de Havilland was right in the Great War. He said we need fighter aircraft, of course, but the real defense comes from bombers. Not bombing troops, because they get used to it, but behind the lines, bombing those who manufacture and supply materials for the troops. It destroys morale, unless you're English, of course, as Mr. Hitler will soon find out to his cost." He swung his head to look left and right, up and down the Channel. "Commander Axford."

Naval Commander Axford already had his attaché case open as he approached Churchill. "Sir?"

Churchill waved a hand toward the far coast. "Tell me what they have. What's out there?"

"The latest reconnaissance has spotted two hundred and seventy barges at Ostend, one hundred at Flushing, and there are more arriving every day."

"What is the estimated final total?"

"Sir, we believe eventually as many as one thousand six hundred invasion vessels carrying one hundred thousand German troops. That would be just the first assault wave."

"A little like Dunkirk in an odd way, only they will meet the force of the Royal Air Force and our Navy. Might not be a second wave after that. Thank you, Commander," Churchill said and turned to Thompson. "What's your knowledge of history like, Thompson?"

"I'm afraid it's regrettably spotty and shallow, Sir."

"That's because they teach it badly in school and make it dull and dusty. History is not a line that fades away behind your grandfather. It's alive and all around us, and we are in the middle of it. Remove me or you, and it pokes a hole in the fabric of history."

"I think removing you more than me, Sir."

"No, Thompson, that is not true," Churchill said and gave him one of his impish smiles. "Where should I be without you to protect me?" He pulled a sheet of paper from his overcoat pocket and unfolded it to read. "They tell me our freighter *Celtic Twilight* does not exist, because neither the Royal Navy nor Coastal Command can find her. They assure me they have scoured the Irish Sea, the Western Approaches, and south to the Bay of Biscay, but without luck. However, a lowly clerk in the Admiralty found her."

"Where?"

"The original *Celtic Twilight* was a wooden fishing smack out of Kinsale. The freighter *Celtic Twilight,* which stole the name, has vanished, taking along with it our Welsh warrior Caitrin Colline."

"That's disappointing, Sir."

"It's much more than that. Caitrin Colline is making her own history, but I fear for her life, and I do not want her to be a martyr for her country."

Caitrin's right hand was tied to a steam pipe, and her left foot to the base of a bed on which she was sitting in a junior officer's cabin. It was cramped, with only the bed, a shelf below a mirror for a table, and a chair. James Gordon sat in the chair, facing her—relaxed, legs crossed, and pistol resting on his knee. The muzzle was pointed at her.

"I owe you a debt of gratitude, Caitrin. After encountering you and your fury, two of my men swear they will join the Band of Hope the moment they reach dry land, two more promise to always watch where they're walking and will never go into dark places again without a torch, and then there's Tiny Herman." James shook his head and sighed dramatically. "Tiny recognized you from the cemetery in Greenock, grabbed your hair, and was intending to heave you overboard. It didn't work out quite as Tiny wished, however, because you didn't react as he expected, and it will take months for his voice to settle a few octaves. It seems unlikely he will ever walk again without a limp, or even reproduce."

"Pity, that."

"Yes. Is it really that bad, though, the Tiny not reproducing thing? Did you just make the world a safer place?"

Caitrin stared through him. She had been stopped, but only for the moment. There would be other moments. Her disdain for people like James intensified. With their airless diction and privileged attitude, they were cocooned in their own insular existence. Their lives ran along well-maintained grooves. They looked alike, spoke alike, wore the same clothes, went to the same schools, hunts, and affairs. Nothing changed or challenged them. They mirrored each other in their ignorance of the real world. But a different time was coming, and a new world was being born.

The cabin door opened, and the atmosphere instantly shifted as Hector entered. He saw her restraints and said, "James, do we really need to tie her up like an animal?"

"I should say so. Armed with just four elastic bands, a piece of string, and a slice of haggis, she annihilated five of my men."

"I'm so sorry, Caitrin," Hector said and cut her free. There was nowhere for him to sit, so he stood leaning in a corner with his arms crossed. He did not look at her, but her eyes never left his face, even as James spoke.

"Caitrin, we need to make a few matters clearer," James said. "First, I must say how much I applaud your pluck. It's truly remarkable, especially for a—"

"A woman?"

"I meant for someone working alone. But you are either mistaken or misinformed. We are not the enemy, certainly not *your* enemy. The English and German nations are much alike, we come from the same root stock, which is why *Die Brücke* exists. I will be the first to admit Hitler is an odious little man, but then so is Churchill. Hitler at least wants to raise up and protect his people against the socialists and communists of Russia, while Churchill wants only to be a great hero and maintain the British Empire. He earned the name Butcher of Gallipoli, where his hubris led to three hundred thousand Empire casualties, with over fifty thousand deaths. He would have every English city obliterated and thousands of Englishmen, and women, slaughtered just so he can be glorious. The Germans do not want this carnage."

"They could always prove that by not invading other countries or bombing ours."

"Caitrin, it's actually quite simple. If Churchill agrees to an armistice, the bombing stops immediately, there will be no invasion, and the Crown Jewels go home. Russia with its godless communists, along with the international Jewish bankers, is the enemy. They are *our* enemy too. *Die Brücke* connects two great nations who wish only to live in peace and maintain their way of life."

"And everything goes back to the way it was?" she said, breaking her gaze on Hector to stare at him.

"Of course, why not?"

"Because I am not at all mistaken or misinformed, and your going back is going backwards." Caitrin's chin tilted as she turned away from James and focused on Hector. "Do you also believe this nonsense?"

Hector glanced at the ceiling, looked at her for the first time, and said, "Is that my jacket on the bed?"

"Take it," she spat back.

Hector snatched up his jacket, turned his back on her, and left.

33

Just after sunrise, the *Joana* was steaming five miles off Portugal's Cabo da Roca, Europe's westernmost point, when a main engine-bearing bolt sheared to leave her without power and rolling in a long swell. James Gordon doubled the watch on Caitrin's cabin, because it had no lock and he did not want her taking the slightest opportunity to create mayhem. He met on the bridge with Hector and Dieter Brandt, a taciturn man from Hamburg and the ship's skipper.

"I have radioed for a tug," Brandt said. "It will take them a few hours to get here." His mouth creased into a tight smile. "I told them our position was closer to the coast than it actually is, so they will respond a little faster. Nobody wants to be blamed for a shipwreck."

"Good man," James said.

"I'm also lowering the Portuguese flags. We'll be Swedish until we berth, because I don't want them asking questions about our nonexistent Portuguese registration. Salazar's Estado Novo is neutral, but only as much as it suits him. He does not love Hitler and hates communists but is determined to stay out of the war. Worried about losing the Portuguese colonies if he makes a bad choice and ends up on the wrong side."

"How much longer will this delay extend our journey?"

"Not much. We're close to Lisbon, and assuming the tug gets underway soon, I would say a day at most."

"I should visit our Miss Colline," James said. "To make sure she's not planning to dive over the side and swim to freedom. Although I would not be surprised if she has already walked to shore. Are you coming, Hector?"

"No, I don't think so," Hector said. "Better not."

Caitrin was standing outside her cabin, flanked by two of his men, and gazing out at the coastline. They looked wary, even though she had her hands tied. "Good morning, Caitrin," James said.

"You might want to replace these two sorry gargoyles soon. With the ship wallowing like a drunken pig, they're turning a bit green and wobbly," she said and stage-whispered, "Between you, me, and Admiral Dönitz, they are not exactly Kriegsmarine material."

James could not hold back a smile. This woman was irrepressible. "If I untie your hands, will you promise not to do anything heroic?"

She shook her head. "No promises to traitors. My job is to escape, and that is what I will do."

"All right, have it your way," he said. "Put her back in the cabin, and change guards."

Caitrin retched, pretending to throw up, and her theatrics were rewarded by one of the seasick guards vomiting. "It's the little talents that are often most rewarding," she said with a pert grin, stepped into the cabin, and closed the door behind her.

The tug arrived promptly, took the ship under tow, and brought them up the River Tagus and into the heart of Lisbon. They were assigned a mooring at Cacilhas in Almada, next to the shipyard on the south bank. There they would have to wait until it was their turn to be berthed and repaired. James and Hector went out onto the flying bridge with Brandt.

"I had planned to be moored on the north side of the river," James said. "Now we'll have to get a boat to carry everything across, and that's another unnecessary step."

Hector shrugged. "We have no choice, and we still have plenty of time. It will be all right."

"I'll take care of getting a boat," Brandt said as he gazed out over the river. "This is a fascinating city. Right here in 1588 is where the Spanish Armada started from when it sailed for England."

"Let's hope we have more success than it did," James said with a frown.

34

Miss Edna Warbery was much more nervous than she looked. To begin with, she was not supposed to be in the Cabinet War Rooms, and she didn't like the place one little bit. It was cramped, with steel girders everywhere to protect against air raids, and smelled of damp wool, lavatories, and Churchill's cigars. As assistant to John Cardington she was supposed to stay in the background and only offer information, but he had begged off the meeting, saying he had a tremendous migraine. That, Edna knew from experience, translated as *tremendous hangover*. So here she was, sitting at the end of a table with military officers and politicians on either side, and a glowering Winston Churchill at the other end. He *was* prime minister and the man solely responsible for saving Britain and the Empire from the Nazis, but to Edna he looked daft in that silly blue romper suit.

"Explain, if you will, please, exactly why you are here, Miss?" he growled.

"I am Miss Warbery, Prime Minister," Edna said. "First, Mr. Cardington sends his profuse apologies and—"

"Let's ignore profuse apologies and get to the heart of the matter, shall we?"

"Yes, Prime Minister."

"And there's no need to keep calling me Prime Minister. Everyone knows who I am by now. Sir will suffice."

"Yes, Prime . . . Sir." Edna sat straighter, coughed, and opened the folder on the table in front of her.

To Churchill she looked a little like one of those Hollywood film stars who was supposed to be a mousy creature until she took off her pebble-lensed glasses, unpinned her hair, shook it free, and transformed into the most alluring woman in the world. And for some unfathomable reason, no one had ever noticed her before. He coughed and shook his head to banish the enticing thought and asked, "What have you for us, Miss Warbery?"

"When the Luftwaffe started bombing Britain, their aim was somewhat puzzling. Apart from London, which is a large target with many landmarks and easily identifiable, they scattered their bombs all over the place. We assumed that was because their bomb-aiming skills were rudimentary. But that is all about to change."

"Where are you from, Miss Warbery?"

"Cockfosters, Sir."

"I meant what government department?"

Edna colored. "I'm sorry, but I'm not allowed to say, Sir."

Professor Lindemann, sitting next to Churchill, leaned over and whispered in his ear.

"All right, hush hush, then. Please continue," an irritated Churchill said, his cigar jabbing the air.

"For the Luftwaffe, bombing by day was not successful because the RAF shot down many of their aircraft, and bombing by night is difficult, except when there's a full moon to illuminate the target."

"We already know this."

Edna sat back and squared her shoulders. She was not supposed to be there and did not want to be there, as usual the only woman in the room. But no man—be he prime minister, president, or Grand Poobah—was going to intimidate her, especially a short, fat, bald one in a blue velvet romper suit. "All German aircraft, military and civil, use the Lorenz radio beam system, which allows them to land in bad weather conditions. The Luftwaffe has taken Lorenz and developed it further into something called Knickebein. I believe it means *crooked leg*, or the name of a magical raven in their mythology. Who knows with the ever-annoying Germans?" she said. "Put simply" (she was tempted to add, "because you might not be smart enough to understand," but did not), "there are two radio beams sent out from separate stations some distance apart that intersect over the chosen target. One transmits dots, the other dashes. The pilot flies along one beam, and when he hears a steady tone in his earphones knows he is over the target and releases the bombs. It is very effective."

"And what are we doing about it?"

"Nothing particularly successful at first, until we bought an American Hallicrafters S-27 amateur radio set from a shop in Lisle Street, stuffed it into an RAF Anson, and sent it to fly around until they found the beams. Our next task is to send out spoof beams and/or deflect theirs."

"Is there any other way, more aggressive?"

"Yes, Sir, there is one. We could send one of our bombers along the beam, but going away from the target and toward the transmitter. When the signal stops, they would be directly over the station and could drop their bombs."

"Splendid."

"We have had some difficulties, though," Edna said. What she was about to tell them would set several cats among flocks of pigeons. Or at least she hoped so. "There is a secret Luftwaffe unit known as Kampfgeschwader 100, or KG100. They are a highly trained unit and experts at using Knickebein. Recently one of their bombers, carrying Knickebein radios, went down in the sea off Bridport. It landed more or less intact and close to the shore. We were looking forward to examining the radios and getting valuable information. But." She stopped.

"But what?" Churchill's head shot up. "Go on. What happened?"

"A Royal Navy retrieval squad immediately wanted to dive down and remove the equipment, but unfortunately the army declared it had jurisdiction over the aircraft and refused them access. While the two services were squabbling over who had command, heavy weather broke up the wreck."

Churchill glared at the officers, who had become mute statues. "Thank you for your presentation, Miss Warbery."

"There is one thing more, Sir," Edna said. "From collating various information, we believe that the Luftwaffe, spearheaded by KG100, will increase its bombing raids over the next few months. And, as the radio beam system develops, they are likely to attack other cities and factories with great precision and heavier bomb loads."

"So it is going to get worse, not better?"

"Yes, Sir, we believe it will. For the whole country, not just London." Edna exhaled. It was somber news and she saw the effect it had on Churchill.

"Could your superior, John Cardington, have given as precise and cogent a report as you just did, Miss Warbery?" Churchill asked and she saw the wicked glint in his eye. "I want you to be absolutely candid with me."

"No, he could not," she said. *Because the sod's always drunk and I'm smarter than him anyway.* "Because, as usual, I collected, analyzed, and then compiled the information you just received."

"Then you alone should continue doing so, and Mr. Cardington can become an air-raid warden in Peckham. I look forward to our next meeting, Miss Warbery."

"So do I, Prime Minister."

Churchill rose to his feet and left. More precision bombing meant more deaths and more destruction. And as committed as he was to defeating the Third Reich, he could not completely banish the voices of those who insisted he should negotiate an armistice. It would save the lives of thousands. Of men, women, and children.

35

By early evening, Dieter Brandt had found them a boat to ferry the Crown Jewels across the Tagus to a wharf at St. Apolonia, on the northern bank east of the city center. They unloaded the boat and then reloaded the cases into a lorry while hidden from view by rows of low red-brick warehouses. As they drove away, Hector was in the cab with the driver, while for Caitrin, sitting in the lorry bed, the drive west along Avenida Infante dom Henrique was unreal. The avenue was filled with traffic, the pavements thronged with people, and there was light and color. Everyone was well dressed, children were running unchecked through the crowds, and Lisbon was bright and noisy with outdoor cafés and restaurants. Yellow trolley cars rattled along on narrow rails, while on street corners women sold paper flowers, and the scent of roasting chestnuts caught her unawares. Dour, battered London and the dread and violence of its daily existence belonged to a different world. Seeing the contrast between the two cities evoked a yearning for all the madness to be over. Seeing the difference, it would be easy to go insane.

She unconsciously moved her right hand to brush back an errant curl, but James, sitting across from her with the Crown Jewels cases stacked between them, had tied it to a stanchion. He held his pistol pointed at her.

"The Portuguese are usually a somewhat lugubrious lot," he said as he watched the avenue pass. "But today they're happy because 1940 is the year of the Portuguese World Exhibition or, if you'll excuse my execrable Portuguese, *Exposição do Mundo Português*. The country is celebrating eight hundred years of existence and three hundred years of independence from Spain."

At that moment, Caitrin had no interest in Portuguese history. "Where are we going?"

James deflected the question and gestured to the avenue. "Not the whole world is at war. You see what can happen if we accept Germany's offer and agree to an armistice? You will have cities intact and happy, *alive* people. Like those people out there."

She ignored him.

"All right, I'll tell you. We're going west along the coast, through Estoril and Cascais, and then north to Sintra."

"Why?"

"Why? Because it's the plan, of course."

The lorry passed Cascais, turned away from the coast, and went north, climbing a serpentine road through a forest until it reached Sintra. There the road narrowed and steepened; the lorry turned hard right and stopped. Caitrin heard hinges squeak as heavy iron gates swung open, and gravel crunched when the lorry pulled in and halted. When the tailgate and canvas flap opened, James cut her restraints and led her out to a square, solid three-story house. The grounds were encircled by a high stone wall. With Hector, he guided her up a long flight of stairs into a room, and the door closed behind them. They were standing in the middle of an oak-paneled library. A wood fire burned beneath an ornate marble mantelpiece, oil paintings of long-dead noblemen and their families hung on the walls, and under those was heavy furniture of dark wood and red leather. The floors, worn and polished wood, were covered with Turkish carpets, and the window drapes had been drawn shut.

In front of the fireplace stood a slender, clean-featured man wearing a gray Nazi SS uniform. Caitrin recognized him. He was the third smiling young man in Hector's Kolbensattel skiing photograph.

"*Guten abend.*" He stepped forward and put out his hand as he switched to flawless English. "Welcome to Sintra. Your Lord Byron thought it was a glorious Eden."

"He's not my Lord Anything," Caitrin said.

"You are definitely Caitrin Colline, the woman who James says has caused us so much trouble."

"And you must be used to *kinder, küche und kirche Fräuleins*. But that's not me," Caitrin said and ignored his outstretched hand.

He lowered it, gave a thin smile, and took a step back. "I am SS-Brigadeführer Walter Schellenberg."

Caitrin caught her breath. She had learned about Schellenberg in 512. He was a true Nazi, a lawyer and an intellectual who believed Hitler's edicts were above normal law and should always be obeyed without question. He and Reynard Heydrich were close friends, both rising stars admired by Reichsführer-SS Heinrich Himmler. Schellenberg had been in command of SD and Gestapo commandos when Germany invaded Poland. They were brutal to their captives. Rumor had it that he was in Portugal to offer the duke and duchess of Windsor fifty million Swiss francs to work for Germany. Schellenberg was on record as saying Britain was run by Freemasons, Jews, and the public-school elite. She glanced at James and Hector with the sinking feeling that they were completely out of their depth in dealing with this man.

"We are now close to the end of our journey," Schellenberg

said in measured tones, and Caitrin guessed he was a man who enjoyed the sound of his own voice. "It is a journey that will bring lasting peace between our nations, and I wish to ensure that you are unable to further disrupt our plans."

Caitrin bit back an answer. This man, in his precise gray uniform, was sinister, and she had no wish to antagonize him.

"Sintra has many of these grand houses, few of them now occupied," Schellenberg said and spread his arms to encompass the room. "They were refuge for the rich Lisbon merchants and ancient families from the summer heat. High walls and a secluded property are ideal for our purpose. Let me show you where you will stay until we are finished."

He put up a hand to keep Hector and James in the room and pushed her out. He forced her up to the top floor to a door at the end of a long corridor, where a man in SS uniform was waiting: short, squat, his face saber-scarred.

"Fräulein Colline, allow me to introduce you to Untersturmführer Heiko von Eisen."

Caitrin made no movement. Schellenberg was sinister, but this man von Eisen exuded evil.

"He has been with me through many difficult campaigns. He does not speak English. *Polen war hart, oder, von Eisen?* I said, Poland was hard, no?"

"*Nein*," von Eisen said.

"Show her the room."

Von Eisen opened the door and stood back. The corner room was small, with two windows and a minimum of furniture. Caitrin noticed the windows were barred. Schellenberg saw them too.

"With a room high on the top floor such a barrier would seem unnecessary. But I am told the original owner had an *untermensch* son, a giant of a boy with a malformed brain, and the kind of creature who will no longer exist in modern Germany. He sometimes got quite violent. They were forced to lock him away in here after he was found scampering around the grounds, naked and on all fours, chasing a maid and baying at a full moon. I suppose all families have their secrets and weaknesses."

Caitrin fought back a suggestion that he might be his family's weakness.

"James told me of your abilities in great detail and insisted you should not be underestimated, so there will be a guard outside your room, day and night," Schellenberg said. "They will be von Eisen's men. *Gute nacht, Fräulein.*"

He gave the thinnest of smiles, turned on his heel, and left. Caitrin heard a key turn in the lock and the click of Untersturmführer Heiko von Eisen's jackboots.

36

Bodyguard Thompson liked going by train almost as much as did Churchill, and both enjoyed traveling in Saloon 45000, Winston's luxurious private carriage. Built in 1920 for the chairman of the London Northwestern Railway, the exterior was a gleaming crimson lake with cream edging. Inside, it had bedrooms, a dining room, staff quarters, and, for Churchill, the inevitable bath. Although the journey from London to Birmingham would take only a few hours, it did mean Thompson would not be chasing after Churchill over some perilous bomb site while urging him to wear his tin helmet. And safe in the carriage, Churchill got to wear one of his flamboyant dressing gowns as he worked. At the moment he was dressed in a floral-patterned one and reading the *Times*.

"The Nazis bombed Birmingham Town Hall, the university, and the Spitfire factory in Castle Bromwich. I shall hear all about the last one from Beaverbrook, after he resigns, or tries to, yet again."

"Yes, Sir."

"What do you think about Kennedy?" Churchill asked

Kathleen Hill, his long-suffering and patient secretary sitting behind her silent typewriter.

"Kennedy?" she said, startled by the question.

"Brave Joe Kennedy. As soon as the first bomb dropped, Kennedy raced away from the American embassy and out of town to his house in the country. But the Germans almost got him there." Churchill laughed, or growled—it was hard to tell the difference sometimes. "There's a joke going around the Foreign Office. They say, I always thought my daffodils were yellow until I met Joe Kennedy."

Kathleen laughed, but it was a polite and inoffensive English laugh.

"Americans and their love for the showy," Churchill said. "Lindbergh's attacking Roosevelt again, and with what qualifications, may I ask? Roosevelt comes from a fine family of good pedigree used to command, while Lindbergh's lineage is what? His sole claim to fame is that he sat on his bottom for hours staring at an aircraft control panel and then managed to miss England altogether and land in France, of all places."

He paused to light a cigar but was obviously not finished. "They are an easily distracted people, the Americans, and prefer style over substance, comfort over command. Thinking does not come easily to them; they believe it hurts. Worse, they're convinced it's not manly."

"They are a different lot, Sir," Thompson said.

"They are men who look like us and speak somewhat the same language, but there the similarity ends. We need them, though. We need their weapons."

Kathleen got up from behind her typewriter to pour Churchill more tea as he scanned the newspaper. "A bomb hit Virginia Woolf's home in Bloomsbury and exploded a week later. Destroyed the place. Woolf wasn't there, fortunately for her, but it might mean an end, or at least a temporary cessation, to all the fluttering-hands-woe-is-me-for-being-a-woman writing."

Bristling in response to his, "woe-is-me-for-being-a-woman

writing," Kathleen made as much fuss as she could rattling the teapot and rolling a fresh sheet of paper into the typewriter. She was even tempted to whistle, knowing how much Churchill hated it, but that might have been passive resistance taken a step too far.

Churchill frowned. "The latest Blitz numbers: thirteen thousand killed, twenty thousand wounded, and still I am pressured to negotiate with the Germans."

"Surely not, Sir?"

"Surely, yes, Thompson. Even within my own party, there is frequent mention of my so-called capricious ego and its love of glory. They say if I agree to an armistice, Hitler will instantly make some grand emollient speech to smooth the troubled waters, while mentioning that sadly, family feuds are often the most intense. He will excoriate the cowardly, surrendering French and put most of the blame on them, while noting our similar German and English backgrounds. Praise for our Anglo-Saxon heritage, a mention of England and Germany fighting together, Wellington and von Blücher against Napoleon at Waterloo, and probably chuck in Victoria's Prince Albert to season the pudding."

Thompson stayed silent as Churchill put down his newspaper and picked up a folder marked MOST SECRET. He opened it and read aloud: "'*Die Brücke*. All of the following persons should be considered as fervent Nazi sympathizers and likely members of *Die Brücke*: Harold Sidney Harmsworth, Viscount Rothermere; Archibald Ramsay, MP; Ronald Nall-Cain, Second Baron Brocket; David Bertram Ogilvy Freeman-Mitford, Second Baron Redesdale; Joslyn Victor Hay, Twenty-second Earl of Erroll; Arthur Charles Wellesley, Fifth Duke of Wellington; Walter Francis John Montagu Douglas Scott, Ninth Duke of Buccleuch; and Charles Vane-Tempest-Stewart, Seventh Marquis of Londonderry.'"

He paused and exhaled a deep breath. "As I read these

names, I hear the clarion call of Caitrin Colline's voice when she eviscerated Lord Hector for the length of his name. I cannot imagine what she would do to these fine gentlemen."

"No, Sir," Thompson said, and he too could hear that insinuating Welsh voice.

Churchill grinned. "And can you imagine what she would do with Dr. Leigh Francis Howell Wynne Sackville de Montmorency Vaughan-Henry?"

"He'd end up as Franky."

"Mrs. Hill, would you leave the room for a moment?" Churchill said, and Kathleen exited as he turned to Thompson. "I need the innermost thoughts and counsel of an Englishman, unadulterated by title or politics."

"Sir?"

"What would you think if I were to announce publicly that the Crown Jewels had been stolen?"

Thompson fought for a reply. Churchill filled in the empty space. "It would be a terrible shock at first," he said and waved a finger as his voice rose. "But if later the Germans did admit to having them it would most likely stoke English fury, rather than bring about collapse. Perhaps arouse world sympathy too. How would you feel about that, as the common man?"

"Shocked, Sir," Thompson said.

"Or what if, at the moment of triumph, the Nazeez were to discover they had been thwarted, hoodwinked even, in some unexpected way. Imagine then the pride in our plucky men and women. Would that not be an amazing episode in this sorry war?"

"I suppose so, Sir." Thompson wrestled with what to say next because he was more than a little puzzled.

"This is no time for prevarication, Thompson. This is a moment for honesty."

"Yes, Sir, I understand. And in all honesty, it's somewhat confusing, and I would give it a little more time."

"Why?"

"Because Caitrin Colline is still out there somewhere and where there is—"

"Where there is Colline, there is hope?"

"Yes, Sir. A very slender hope, but it's all we've got."

"I'm not exactly sure how she can save the day now. She disappeared into thin air aboard our Flying Dutchman freighter, the *Celtic Twilight*."

"Perhaps I'm grasping at straws, and perhaps it's a peculiar Welsh talent, Sir, or a woman's thing, but she does seem to reappear out of thin air, just when you're quite sure she's gone forever."

37

Decades of paint had layered the windows shut, while the steel security bars, although rusty, were close together and still strong enough that Caitrin would not be making an escape that way. There was little else in the room that might help her, but at least she knew her captors. She could not see them but instead listened, concentrated, and learned who they were. To begin with, although Untersturmführer Heiko von Eisen was not the kind of officer to enlist inadequate men, and escaping would not be simple, no one was perfect. If you knew how to observe, and she had been well trained, there were always weaknesses. Being a methodical German, von Eisen had assigned three men to guard her. They were the same three men, and each stood the same eight-hour shift, twenty-four hours a day.

Caitrin listened to them, especially when they changed over, and made her assessment. She gave them names, alphabetically, and the first one was called Adolf, a precise heel-clicker of a man, much given to speaking in clipped sentences. Throughout his shift he rarely stayed still, and Caitrin heard his jackboots squeaking up and down the hallway. He also constantly muttered to himself, although what he said was a mystery to her because she spoke only a little German. Adolf would be an obedient soldier who would follow orders, a suspicious man and not easily overcome.

Boris was next, a big, shambling man with a heavy foot and an asthmatic wheeze. He sat with a great thump and did not move until his shift was relieved. By pressing an ear to the door, she could sometimes hear him snoring. Boris would be easier to fool, but fighting a big man in a small room could cause both of them damage. Big men were often deceptively fast, could absorb punishment, and there was no guarantee of success.

Curt she named the last one, and he worked from afternoon until midnight. He was not a big man—Caitrin guessed he was about her height and size—and walked with a light scuffing of one foot, which meant he had a limp. Like Boris, he did not move much, and she sometimes heard the sound of pages turning. Perhaps Curt was a reader, which might be a problem because it suggested he was intelligent. There was a squabble outside the door when Boris was relieved by Curt.

"*Was kostet liebe?*" she heard Boris say with groans and a loud lip smacking, as though he was pretending to kiss someone. "*Es is Jüdischer müll.*"

"*Zumindest lese ich!*" Curt shouted. She heard Boris shambling away, Curt's chair scraping on the floor, and then silence. She had decided. Curt was the one.

During her 512 training, Caitrin had been taught to use every weapon in her arsenal, but there was one she was reluctant to deploy. Until today.

Curt was halfway through reading *Was Kostet Liebe?* (What Price Love?). It was a book of which his wife Gartrude would not have approved, and perhaps it *was* lascivious Jewish garbage, but he had not seen her in such a long time and a man had needs that demanded satisfaction. Caitrin's scream startled him. He dropped the book, pulled out his Luger, and opened the door.

The woman was agitated, hopping from one foot to the other, tearing at her shirt as she screamed, "Spider! Spider!"

He had no idea what that meant, but he did know that she looked terrified, and the front of her shirt was almost completely open to expose such lovely breasts. If Curt had been a dispassionate observer watching at some remove, he would have seen himself staring at her breasts and then, distracted, crumpling in pain as a foot hammered into his side. And almost before the pain of broken ribs registered, he would have watched as the woman's right hand caught his jaw and rendered him unconscious as her left closed over the pistol. It was all performed in one fluid and deadly movement.

But unfortunately for Curt he was not a dispassionate observer, he was a participant, albeit a passive one. All he remembered later was seeing her breasts, hearing his ribs fracture, and feeling something explode against his jaw. When he regained consciousness, it hurt to breathe, his fellow soldiers were standing over him, the woman was gone, and so too was his Luger. *Was Kostet Liebe?*

38

From her hiding place, Caitrin watched as SS-Brigadeführer Walter Schellenberg commandeered the conservatory at the north side of the house. A long, glass-walled room with a parquet floor, it was the only space large enough to accommodate all of the Crown Jewels and display them properly. He had the furniture removed and replaced with a long table set up down the center with a riser at one end to form a T. Blackout curtains shrouded the windows, and they had found red damask drapes somewhere in the house and used them to cover the tables. Hector stood with Schellenberg and James at his side, as the soldiers, supervised by Heiko von Eisen, carried in the cases.

"You have the inventory with you?" Schellenberg asked James.

"Here," James said and took a list from his pocket.

"The most important crown should be placed at the head of the *T*, with the others to the left and right. Less important things, such as swords, orbs, and scepters will be set up along the long table. I will depend upon your knowledge. First one?"

"There are crowns dating back to the 1600s," James said as he scanned the list. "But I would say the Imperial State Crown is probably the most important one."

"Why?"

"It is worn as the monarch leaves Westminster Abbey, after the coronation. It has St. Edward's Sapphire, belonging to Edward the Confessor in 1163, the Stuart Sapphire, the Black Prince's Ruby, and the Cullinan II Diamond."

Von Eisen read the case labels until he came to the right one. He placed the box on the table, unlatched it, and brought out the crown. It glittered with diamonds, and a murmur of admiration swept through the room. Von Eisen put it at the head of the *T*.

"Then the modern crowns, I think," James said. "Queen Alexandra's Crown, Queen Mary's and the Queen Mother's Crowns."

As the crowns were placed on the tables, and there were so many, followed by the swords, scepters, and orbs, the atmosphere changed in the room. These were remarkable objects in their own right, but much more than that. They were also the history of a country, a record of a nation's life and endurance. Its heart. Its soul.

Schellenberg picked up a sword and unsheathed it. "Beautiful craftsmanship."

"That is the Sword of Spiritual Justice, 1626," James said, and there was a quiver to his voice.

A door opened, and a tall, blonde woman entered. She stopped, surveyed the table, and turned to Schellenberg. "A majestic display. Walter, I am here, ready to make history again."

They embraced. "That you are, Leni, and that you will. Let me introduce you to our British *Die Brücke* friends. This is James Gordon, and Hector Neville-Percy, Lord Marlton. Gentlemen, this is the renowned Leni Riefenstahl."

Hector and James were impressed. Riefenstahl, a devout Hitler disciple, was a legendary filmmaker, with *Triumph of the*

Will and *Olympia* to her credit. She was also a beautiful woman with open features and shrewd, confident eyes that missed nothing.

She spread her hands to encompass the Jewels. "We will start with close-ups of all of these, and then I will place two cameras"—she turned and pointed at the corners of the room—"there and there to film the people who come to see the display."

"Today is Thursday. The first invitation goes out tomorrow morning, and all of this will be shown to the world on Monday," Schellenberg said. "That gives you three days to shoot whatever you wish."

"Good, that is good. I will have my cameraman Albert Bentiz and his lighting crew—"

Adolf hurried in and whispered to von Eisen, who whispered to Schellenberg.

"There is a problem?" Riefenstahl asked, irritated at being interrupted.

"A small one," Schellenberg said. "It seems our Welsh Houdini has again pulled one of her amazing disappearing acts. She has vanished."

"No, I haven't," Caitrin said as she stepped into the room and to one side of Riefenstahl, her Luger pointed squarely at Schellenberg. "If any of your men even blinks, I will shoot you."

"Tales of your ability did not underestimate you." Schellenberg rubbed the length of his jaw and tapped a fingertip on his chin. "*Hmm.* I would not like that."

"No."

His hand moved deliberately toward his pistol.

"I wouldn't do that."

"Oh, but I will," he said and unclipped the holster flap.

Caitrin lowered the pistol, aimed at Schellenberg's leg, and fired. The shot echoed in the room, but he was unhurt. She fired again, with the same result. He raised his Luger and pointed it at her face.

"*Leerzeichen,*" von Eisen sneered. "*Keine kugeln.*"

"Blanks," Schellenberg translated. "No bullets. Your reputation is deserved, Fräulein Colline, and I knew you would eventually outwit the guards and escape from that room, although I had no idea how."

He paused as von Eisen took the Luger from her and held his own gun to her temple. "I do know that you are much smarter than all three of the guards put together and would find your way out, so I didn't want you to escape with one of their weapons. I had them loaded with blanks, the *Leerzeichen.*"

Caitrin felt Riefenstahl's eyes on her. She looked amused, and perhaps a little impressed.

"Von Eisen, take our escape artist down to the cellar and lock her up. Remove all the light bulbs first, and let no one in. Perhaps sitting in total darkness will blunt her abilities."

"*Warum nicht einfach auf sie schießen?*" von Eisen said.

"No." Schellenberg gave him a tired smile. "Because we are trying to build a bridge with our English brethren. Shooting Fräulein Colline would not help that. Take her away."

Von Eisen grabbed her arm, and Adolf took the other. She glanced at Riefenstahl as they crossed. "Don't like your pictures much, Leni. Too much oompah and no sense of humor. Then again, you are German."

Von Eisen directed her down spiral stone stairs, opened the cellar door, and shoved her inside. He held his gun to her head while Adolf scurried around unscrewing light bulbs. Caitrin stayed still; she was not scared but wanted to commit her surroundings to memory before it all went black. There was a row of large barrels against the far wall, another wall filled with wine bottles, and assorted furniture covered in dustcovers. A hard push sent her staggering to the floor, the door slammed shut, and she was alone. It was completely dark.

39

Caitrin sat on the top of the four steps that led down to the cellar floor and leaned back against the door. She had closed her eyes for five minutes, mentally counting off the seconds, until her pupils fully dilated. When she opened them, the cellar was not quite so dark. The faintest of lights bled through the gap at the bottom of the door, and a thin green stripe glimmered at the far end. Tiny curves revealed the location of the row of barrels on the far wall, and minuscule glints of glass showed the racks of wine bottles to the left. An edge or two marked the furniture in the center. So far, though, there was nothing she could use to combat a couple of SS soldiers armed with Mausers guarding the door. But she had to find an asset.

First, a careful assessment of her surroundings. Heel to toe, she measured the cellar: sixty-eight paces deep and forty-nine wide. The barrels were too big to have come down the spiral staircase, and that meant somewhere there must be a larger · opening, a delivery trapdoor. Which perhaps explained the green stripe. She moved toward it and tripped on the bottom of a ramp. So there *was* another entrance. This is where the barrels were lowered down into the cellar.

She edged up the ramp until her head bumped on a surface that flexed: the door. Closer now, she could see a thin line of green light, the gap between two delivery doors no doubt covered over with moss and vegetation. She pushed, and it moved. Here was the asset, the way out. In the center of the stripe was a dark horizontal line, which her fingers discovered was a bolt. It was padlocked, but the wood around it was rotten, and if she pushed hard, it might well break away. She could escape. That would be a start.

She stiffened her fingers and rammed them into the wood. It dented, and she rammed them again and again until the soft wood separated. Her fingers wriggled through the gap to grip the wood, and she screamed in pain as a jackboot slammed onto her fingers and a voice outside shouted, "*Nein!*"

She fell back into the darkness, eyes tear-filled, wringing her hand to ease the pain. It was not a start.

There was still some light left in the sky when Hector entered the conservatory to find James sitting in shadow at the Jewels table. He ignored the guards standing around the room perimeter and sat next to him. "You look unhappy, James."

In reply, James picked out a golden orb and held it up. The diamonds flared in the failing light. "The Sovereign's Orb. It was made in 1661 and has been used in every coronation since. And that little beauty there," he gestured to a small crown, "is Victoria's Small Diamond Crown. Small it may well be, but it's covered with a thousand diamonds."

Hector had never seen James look so sad. "You are having second thoughts?"

"I do sometimes and think I'm being a traitor to England, but then I imagine what will happen if Churchill is too proud to sign an armistice. I saw the Wehrmacht in action in France,

Hector. The SS are cruel men. And you know what the last war did to your family. If the drunken old fool just signs the agreement, they will leave England alone."

"Do you really think so?"

"Yes, I do." The light was gone now, and James was a silhouette as he continued, "If the Germans are not allowed to turn away from us and then lose to the Russians, we will have socialists and communists taking over England. Every man will be wanting his little acre from our estates. They shot the tsar and all his family, and they will come for us. This antic with the Crown Jewels may not be the most . . . most tasteful way to do things, but it needs to be done. I cannot see any other way."

Hector patted James's knee. "Cheer up. I'm walking down to the village to see if they have decent cigarettes. Want to come with me?"

"No, I'll stay. Thank you, Hector."

"For what?" Hector said as he stood.

"For being a good friend."

"It's not difficult. Chin up. We'll get through this debacle together." He patted James's arm and left.

Two soldiers guarded the closed front gates, and one stepped forward to block Hector as he approached, saying, "Not to go."

Hector released an irritated sigh. "I speak German."

"No one is allowed to leave," the soldier said in German.

"Why not?"

"Because I said so." Schellenberg's voice turned Hector's attention away from the gate. As he approached, Schellenberg smiled, shrugged, and spread his hands. "I'm afraid it applies to all of us, old boy."

Hector would readily admit Schellenberg's English was far better than his own German, but using the vernacular—old boy, chum, beastly, darling—always seemed odd, as though he didn't quite understand what they meant but said them anyway. "I was thinking of wandering down to the village to see if they had any decent cigarettes."

"You don't like Trommler?"

Trommler were the cheapest, and nastiest, of German cigarettes. And the most popular. "I think they make them out of Göring's old underwear."

Schellenberg grimaced. "That is the most unpleasant image, and I think if Göring's underwear were to help the war effort, they would be best used as parachutes."

Hector laughed. Schellenberg was one of the few Germans he had met who could laugh at the corpulent Herman Göring, at least outside Germany.

"Trommler only cost three and a half pfennigs, so what do you expect? I have Neue Front if you want. They're a little better."

"I was rather hoping for Craven A or Senior Service."

"Sorry, chum. After Monday I promise you can have all the Craven A you like." Schellenberg had turned to leave when Hector stopped him and pointed to the hill above them.

"What's that up there?"

"That's the Palace of Pena. Part Gothic, part Manueline, part Islamic, part Renaissance, and all put together by someone who still believes in fairy princesses and unicorns."

Hector stared hard at the intricate silhouette gracing the hilltop. It was the most eclectic of buildings.

"You should see it in daylight. Every wall, turret, and column is painted a different color. Quite remarkable. Southern European romantic taste, I suppose. You must go visit. After—"

"Monday."

"Yes, Monday."

"Walter, would you mind if I looked in on Caitrin Colline? I'm sure by now sitting in the dark has cooled off her enthusiasm."

Schellenberg gazed up at the castle for a moment and spoke without looking away. "I doubt that. Look in if you must, but take von Eisen with you." Schellenberg nodded and strode away. Hector watched him leave, waited a moment, and walked toward the house, toward Caitrin Colline in her dark prison.

*   *   *

Caitrin spun away and covered her eyes as the cellar door opened and closed. There were men outside, and someone was in the cellar, she could tell. She heard the door lock. "If you have a torch, leave it turned off."

"I'll point it down and cover the lens with my hand," Hector said. "I need to talk with you, Caitrin."

"Feel free to chatter away, I'm going nowhere. For now."

Hector fumbled his way toward her voice, and the faint light from the torch edged her face. "There isn't much time left. Tomorrow, the British ambassador to Portugal will be invited to view the Crown Jewels as a beginning to initiate an armistice. By Monday, if Churchill still refuses to sign an agreement, the Jewels go to Germany and Leni Riefenstahl's film is sent to British cinemas."

"Who won't show it."

"There will be photographers and newspaper reporters too, including Americans, who will show it."

"Congratulations, Hector. It's not every man who can successfully betray his country. I'm sure your dear leader Hitler will give you and Lord Haw Haw matching medals."

He noticed her bloodied right hand. "What happened?"

"Does it matter?"

"You are cold?" His question startled her. He flashed the torch into her face, dazzling her, and bellowed in German, "It's not my fault you're cold! It's your fault. You're stupid! Here, take this jacket!" He peeled off his jacket and threw it at her.

"I don't want your—" Caitrin stopped because there was an odd weight to the jacket.

"It's the last thing I do for you. The hell with you!" Hector pounded on the cellar door. "Herr von Eisen, unlock the door and get me away from this ungrateful bitch!"

The door opened, he slipped away, and it slammed shut, leaving Caitrin in the darkness again. She *was* cold and put on the jacket. Her right hand went into a pocket, felt the weight there, and her fingertips traced a familiar, forgotten pattern: the distinctive zigzag grooves on the cylinder of her Webley-Fosbery revolver. She broke the action to check if it was loaded; it was—and not with blanks. A note was tucked into the trigger guard, and she read it by the light filtering beneath the cellar door: *Please do not burn the place down. I'm coming back for you.*

40

Not every man is given the opportunity to see his prime minister naked, especially with a handful of papers and a cigar clamped in his jaws. Bodyguard Thompson rolled his eyes and wondered yet again what grievous horror he had committed in a previous life to have gotten so lucky. To be fair to Winston Churchill, he had begun the morning dressed, or at least partly covered with a towel, having just left his bathtub. But that had long since fallen away as he marched up and down the bedroom, puffing great clouds of cigar smoke and waving his arms while he worked aloud on his latest speech. "I must explain that a fire has been started that will burn brightly and increase daily until it scorches and consumes every last vestige of Nazi tyranny from Europe. And having done so, the Old World and the New can then work together building the foundations of an honorable and new freedom for all men that this time will not so readily be overthrown." He stopped and swung to face Thompson. "What say you to that, Thompson?"

"That would be very stirring stuff, Sir," Thompson said,

which he believed was true, even if it was delivered by a naked old man who looked rather like a large, pink, cigar-puffing baby.

"Yes, it is, and it should, God willing, finally get the Americans involved," Churchill muttered and shuffled through the papers. "And listen to this bit. 'Countries that are still, at this moment, free of war, are astonished and humbled at the courage and tenacity of the citizens of London as they daily face the most terrible of ordeals. And which have yet to end. But from that suffering our people will draw strength to carry on. And not only endure, but grow stronger, until that day when they forge victory from adversity. It will be a glistening triumph, not only for today, but for generations to come. Their struggle to overcome the most horrific tribulations will ever be remembered.' I still have to edit this part."

"Yes, Sir."

"Mrs. Hill, come in here."

"If you don't mind I'd rather not, Sir." Kathleen Hill's voice carried from the sitting room. She had long since grown used to encountering Churchill's occasional nakedness but had also recently eaten breakfast.

"What? Why not?" Churchill growled.

"Because of this, Sir?" Thompson pointed to the towel at Churchill's feet. He looked down at it, seemed to become aware of his nakedness for the first time, and grumbled something inaudible before saying, "All right, I shall get dressed."

Once dressed in his blue siren suit, Churchill accepted a phone call, listened with great concentration, hung up, and strode into the living room. "I just spoke to Sir Charles Harmwood Montague Bilby, our ambassador to Portugal."

"Yes, Sir."

"He has gotten a most unusual message from a German SS officer, telling him he has in his possession certain objects taken from a horse box." Churchill grinned. "The Crown Jewels are in Portugal, of all places. Where exactly remains a mystery, but Bilby is soon to find out because they requested that he see them, and I have given him permission. *Softly softly catchee monkey*, Thompson. Damn the Germans with their ham-fisted plans. We shall slay the Nazee monster yet."

41

Sir Charles Harmwood Montague Bilby, KCMG, CB, VO, British ambassador to Portugal since 1937 and an elegant man with a well-groomed mustache and thick wavy hair, had celebrated his sixtieth birthday by buying himself an Aston Martin Lagonda Rapide convertible, in gunmetal gray with a red interior. The afternoon was cool but clear as, warmly wrapped and with the top lowered, he drove the winding road from Lisbon up to Sintra. He usually would have brought an assistant or a bodyguard with him, but the German was insistent he come alone, a condition to which Churchill agreed. It was all a bit of a Bulldog Drummond mystery, which he was rather enjoying. It made a change from always being polite to everyone, and the Lagonda, even though it was right-hand drive, was built for this kind of sinuous road motoring. At times, he felt a little guilty driving around Portugal in his Aston Martin while England was being bombed and use of a private vehicle there was forbidden. Fortunately, the guilt usually passed after his first *meia de leite* and *pastel de natas*. Sir Charles had developed a taste for Portuguese coffee and pastries.

He slowed as he drove uphill and turned into the town square. He had been instructed to park on Praça da República outside the Palácio da Vila. It was an odd building, white fussy Manueline architecture with two immense conical chimneys out of all proportion to the palace. This late in the year, the square was almost deserted. He checked his watch—a few minutes early. The sun would be setting soon.

A Citroën Traction Avant pulled up behind him, and a slender young man got out and walked toward him. "Sir Charles?"

"Yes."

"Hello, Sir. I'm James."

"An Englishman."

"Yes, Sir."

"You are an Englishman working for the Germans?"

"I would prefer to say liaising."

"Would you now?" Sir Charles got out of his car to face James. He was a few inches taller than the young man. "While you are *liaising*, to which country are you loyal, James?"

"I am, and will always be, English, Sir. Could never be anything else. Would you please come with me?"

Sir Charles glanced at his Aston Martin.

"It will be quite safe there, I assure you. You'll be back within the hour."

Sir Charles got into the Citroën. It was foreign and shoddy compared to his Lagonda.

"I have to ask you to wear this until we get there, Sir. My apologies," James said and offered him a pillowcase.

"Is this silliness really necessary, just so I can examine some objects found in a horse box?"

"I'm afraid so, and they are rather extraordinary objects, so the Germans do not want their location known. Understandably."

"*Hmm.*" Sir Charles made a sour face and slipped the pillowcase over his head.

"It's just for a few minutes," James said, started the motor, and pulled away.

Billy the Brick, Caitrin's weapons instructor, had consistently emphasized to his trainees that taking a life would forever change their own, and so it was not to be done hastily. Having decided to fire a weapon, it was essential not to stop until your assailant was no longer a threat. Always fire more than once, because in the adrenaline heat of action often a person would not know they had been shot. And even after being shot, there was still enough blood circulating to keep a man, or woman, active for several seconds. That could be a lifetime and long enough for them to end yours. First shot in the body, to the heart if possible, and the second to the head. Shoot until convinced all danger was gone, but remember, after, you will have been permanently changed.

Caitrin was one of the few women who passed her shooting test the first time. If ever Billy had to walk down a dark alley in unfriendly territory, he would want her at his side. Now she was sitting in the dark cellar with her Webley-Fosbery revolver in hand, waiting. Hector would need to tell her a story when he returned—a true story, one that she could believe, if he wanted to live.

"Caitrin." Hector's voice came from behind the cellar door.

She moved to the steps. "Yes?"

"Schellenberg's got all his men in the conservatory, but this door's locked and there's no key."

"There's a delivery trapdoor at the back of the building, but I'll need a crowbar or something to free the bolt."

"All right, I'll go around there."

"Wait. If I'm to trust you, tell me why you've switched sides again."

"I didn't. I was supposed to work with *Die Brücke* so we could expose them at the right time."

"Might have helped if I knew that when we started. Keeping the invisible little woman in the dark again, huh? That worked out well for us both, didn't it?" She held back her anger and wondered yet again when she, and all women, would be as valued and accepted as men. There was a touch of guilt there too that she had so quickly assumed Hector was a traitor, and perhaps their different backgrounds, along with indignation at being considered a second-class person, had unfairly colored her opinion of him. She had much to learn.

"I would have told you more but didn't expect you to jump out of a moving lorry," Hector said, although that was not necessarily true. He might not have told her anything more but did not know why. Perhaps it was because his training emphasized his life depended on secrecy, or it might have been because no matter how remarkable, brave, and intelligent she was, Caitrin was still a woman, untried in battle.

"I leaped out of the lorry because when captured, escape," she said. "They never taught you that? We'll fight about it later. Go."

Caitrin heard him hurry up the steps. Waiting in the dark for someone else to take action before she could do anything was grating on her nerves. But it did give her time to correct an oversight. Pleased at discovering the delivery doors as a likely exit, she had stopped exploring what remained of the cellar, especially the right-hand corner. Bethany Goodman's instruction came to mind: *Do not be afraid to act alone and always, always finish the job.* She was not going to wait long for Hector to return but would find her own way out by finishing the job.

42

The sun was behind the Palácio Nacional da Pena, making it look even more like a fairy-tale castle, as James pulled up to the house. The gates swung shut behind them.

"Please leave it on, Sir," he said to Sir Charles, who was peeling off the pillowcase. "It will be just a minute more, I promise you. I'll guide you safely inside."

Sir Charles let himself be led into the house and stripped the pillowcase away the instant he heard the front door close. He blinked to clear his vision and saw he was facing a man and a woman. The woman he knew; the man, an SS officer, was a stranger.

"Thank you for coming, Sir Charles," the officer said as he stepped forward. "I am SS-Brigadeführer Walter Schellenberg."

To Charles's relief, Schellenberg did not click his heels or thrust out his arm in that silly Heil Hitler salute. Instead he put out his hand. Charles ignored it.

The woman, elegantly dressed in a long silver gown, stepped

forward, kissed both his cheeks, and murmured, "Charles, how wonderful to see you again. You do remember me, don't you?"

"Yes, of course I remember you," Charles said. He remembered Leni Riefenstahl well as being both a shameless self-promoter and an ardent Nazi. He had met her a few years ago in Vienna, at some pointless banquet celebrating "eternal friendship" between Germany and Austria. The *Anschluss* came a little later and changed everything. She had recently finished *Olympia*, her film about the 1936 Berlin Olympics, to great acclaim. After the banquet, Leni had cornered him to gush about her first meeting with Hitler. It was such an outlandish statement he scribbled it into a notebook as soon as she left. *I had an almost apocalyptic vision that I was never able to forget. It seemed as if the Earth's surface were spreading out in front of me, like a hemisphere that suddenly splits apart in the middle, spewing out an enormous jet of water, so powerful that it touched the sky and shook the earth.*

Charles was well aware that the Nazis were much inclined to cockeyed myths and legends to support their odious Aryan beliefs, but this bizarre imagery baffled him utterly. No doubt the good Doctor Freud, given enough time, could have explained what the woman was babbling about. Leni Riefenstahl was beautiful, talented, and poised, but with her devotion to broadcasting these ludicrous ideas he thought her the most repulsive woman he had ever met.

"I promise you this will not take long, and the journey will be well worth your while," Schellenberg said as he led them to a set of double doors and made a theatrical gesture. "Are you ready?"

Before anyone could reply, he pulled open the conservatory doors, and the brilliant light from a dozen film lamps blinded them. At the same time, Heiko von Eisen and his twelve SS soldiers snapped to attention with a synchronized clicking of heels. As bright as the lights were, more startling were the jewels strewn along the center table. They absorbed the light and reflected it back in a million blade-sharp stars. Schellenberg urged them into the room.

Sir Charles was dazed. It was almost too much to take in, and for long moments he did not understand what he was looking at, and then, to his horror, he did. "The Crown Jewels."

"Yes," Schellenberg said. "More precisely, the *British* Crown Jewels." He caught a movement as Hector hurried through the hallway. "Hector, come in here."

Hector, startled at being seen, stopped, hesitated for a moment, and reluctantly entered the conservatory.

"Lord Neville-Percy? Hector," an incredulous Sir Charles said.

"Sir Charles."

Sir Charles's expression shifted from surprise to anger. He waved a hand at the jeweled table. "You are involved in this . . . this outrage?"

Hector looked away.

"I knew your father, and I thought I knew you. He was a good man, a true Englishman." He was suddenly aware of the film cameras running. "Turn those damn things off."

"But Charles, we are recording history," Leni said with a pout. She waved for the cameras to continue turning.

He ignored her and spun to face Schellenberg. "What do you expect to achieve with this vulgar display?"

"Do?" Schellenberg gave him a world-weary smile. "Sir Charles, I have already done what needed to be done. I have the Crown Jewels in my possession. The next step is completely up to you and your country."

"Explain yourself, Sir."

"Gladly. You are free to leave whenever you wish. James will take you back to your car. When you do return to the embassy, I suggest immediately telephoning Mr. Churchill to tell him what you have just witnessed. Please tell him he has until

Monday at noon to publicly announce that England and Germany have reached an armistice agreement. If he does so, I shall have every single diamond delivered safely to your embassy in Lisbon by the following morning."

"You do not know England, or Winston Churchill," Charles said, his face tight. "He will never agree to being coerced by Nazis."

"Then one minute after noon on Monday newspaper reporters will be allowed to view them, and Leni's film will be in all the cinemas." Schellenberg shrugged as though it was all inevitable. "After that the Jewels will be shipped to Germany, where I am sure Reichsmarschall des Grossdeutschen Reiches Herman Göring will be beside himself deciding what pieces to take back to his Carinhall lair. What's left, if anything is after *Der Dicke* has pawed through them, will be melted down or sold to aid the Third Reich. Leni will film every moment for the world to see. Tell your Mr. Churchill that, and it might well change his mind."

Sir Charles angled toward Hector and James. "You have both disgraced your country and your families. You will never be forgiven."

"It's for the best," James said, but with no great conviction. "People are dying, innocent civilians in London. This will bring it to an end." He took a step back, as though concerned Sir Charles might strike him.

"Your carriage home, Sir Charles," Schellenberg said, the pillowcase raised, hanging from his finger. "Monday, before noon, or you will make Göring a very happy man."

Schellenberg, Leni, and Hector stood at the conservatory door as James slipped the pillowcase over Sir Charles's head and led him to the car.

"Poor man. I thought he was going to expire from apoplexy," Schellenberg said.

Leni tilted her chin and shook her head. "The stupid English can be so—"

She stopped as all the lights failed.

Heiko von Eisen joined them. "I knew this would happen. The film lights were too much for an old electrical system. They have probably blown every fuse in the building."

"Then repair them," Leni said.

"Where are they?" Schellenberg said.

"In the cellar," Heiko said, and paused, his expression changing. "It's not the film lights that blew the fuses. The Englishwoman's down there. She did it."

"She's Welsh, actually," Hector said. "And I wouldn't make matters worse by upsetting her and calling her English if I were you."

Heiko shouted for soldiers to follow him as he fumbled toward the cellar. In the frantic darkness, Hector slipped away, went out the front door, and ran around the house toward the cellar delivery doors.

43

Billy the Brick was foremost in Caitrin's mind. If he was right that killing a man forever changed who you were, then she was prepared to be changed. It was better than being killed. That was a permanent change. She sat in the dark cellar beneath the delivery doors, hidden behind a wall of wine cases, and at such an angle the cellar door ahead opened away from her. There would be no protection for any man once he entered. Her right hand was still swollen, but adrenaline would take care of that. And if not, she would shoot just as well with her left.

A stab of light showed at the bottom of the door, followed by another flash, mutterings in German, and a boot scrape. Metal on metal. They were outside. Caitrin listened and guessed there were three, four at most. The spiral stone steps down to the cellar were steep and narrow, the door low, and there was little room for them to maneuver. She exhaled, inhaled a calming breath, raised her revolver, and waited.

A key turned in the lock, the door squeaked open, and light

beams cut through the darkness. If she had been one of the Germans, Caitrin would have sprinted through the doorway, low, without the torch, and rolled for cover. They did not enter that way. Instead, two of the men came in cautiously, aimed their torches into the cellar, and Caitrin killed them. The first shot shattered the left torch, the second went to the heart, the third to the head. The second man died the same way, and they fell to the floor almost together. A beam of light edged her for a moment, and a third man shouted, "*Sie hat einen sechs schützen!*"

Caitrin fired her remaining two shots; one to destroy the torch, the second a head shot to kill the man. "Wrong, not *sechs*, eight," she murmured to herself. The gunshots echoed and died into silence. The cellar was dark again, and she heard boots scuffing the stone steps as a man retreated up them. She was safe for the moment, but they would be back, with more men, and now, having used all her ammunition, she was unarmed.

A pounding on the cellar doors overhead startled her. The blade of a garden spade cut through the soft wood and tore away the bolt. "Caitrin!" Hector hissed from outside.

"Here."

She pushed while he tugged open the doors and helped her out. "The stables!"

"No, over there," Caitrin said and ran toward thick undergrowth at a corner of the boundary wall. A full moon made the night clear.

Hector dropped down next to her. "Why not the stables?"

"Because they'd expect us to go there, and we'd be trapped." She pointed to a group of soldiers who had crept across the grass to surround the stables. "Our first thought is their first thought. Our second thought is ours."

"Take this." He handed her his Browning automatic. "You're a far better shot."

"Thanks, but no," she said, her expression softening. Hector was swallowing great pride to offer her his gun. "It would feel wrong somehow. I'll find one inside."

"Inside?"

He saw the gleam of her smile in the moonlight.

"While they are busily looking for us out here, the one place they won't think of is *inside* the house." Caitrin pulled the electrical fuses from her pocket and threw them aside. "And without these, in there it will be equally dark for everyone."

"Why don't I watch them while you go over the wall and raise the alarm?"

"No. Let's just imagine that for a moment, shall we? I go over the wall, run down to the village, and find the one person who is awake and who miraculously also happens to speak English. If I can convince them about what's happening—battling Welsh/Portuguese accents—they'll ring up the mayor, who'll ring up, oh, I don't know who, his mistress, or his mum?" She gave a Portuguese shrug, eyebrows mimicking her shoulders. "And by the time they sign the right triplicate forms, work out who's paying for the overtime, and get their pitchforks out to assault the castle, the Germans will be gone, over the hills and far away with the Crown Jewels tucked in their lederhosen. And this time they won't take you with them."

"Then what do you suggest we do?"

"We find *le* SS-Brigadeführer Walter Schellenberg and show him the error of his ways. And if we have to run over swashbuckling Heiko von Eisen and the irritating mountain-climbing *Jungfrau* Leni Riefenstahl in the process, so be it. I would actually enjoy that bit."

He laughed, but she was not finished.

"Then we pack up the Crown Jewels and head for Blighty. For performing such heroic deeds in service to the empire,

they'll give me the morning off and probably make you a lord—
oh, I forgot, you already are one."

"And you are irrepressible."

"Perhaps they could make you Groom of the King's Stool,
and you'd get the great honor of wiping the king's bum."

"Stop it."

"Now we actually have to go and sort these Nazeez out."

"How do we get in?"

"The way they won't expect. The way we left, through the
cellar. And Billy the Brick was wrong."

"Who?"

"I'm not changed, I still want to defeat these men, and I'll
shoot every one of them to do it."

Headlights swept across the wall above them as a car pulled in.

"That will be James returning," Hector said. "What do we
do about him?"

Caitrin shook her head. "No idea. Yet."

Inside the house Schellenberg's men had found an oil lamp
and a few candles to cast pools of light in the darkness as James
entered. He pushed past several soldiers and found Schellenberg, Riefenstahl, and von Eisen in the conservatory. "What
happened to the lights?"

"We had an intrusion," Schellenberg said.

"From the Englishwoman and your friend Lord Marlton,"
von Eisen said. "He freed her from the cellar after she killed
three of my men."

Schellenberg stared hard at James and said, "You have something to tell me, don't you, James? Something you think is important."

The question surprised James, and he stumbled over an answer before managing to say, "Yes, I do. I told Sir Charles
where you are."

"Where *we* are."

"No, not me, not anymore," James said and gained courage from his admission. "I should never have done this. I betrayed my country." He pointed to the array of jewels. "Those should not be here, they belong to Britain. And that is where I should be, not here."

"A little late in the day for that sort of self-revelation, no?"

"They're sending up guards from the embassy."

"Oh dear," Schellenberg said. "How disappointing."

Schellenberg's serenity disturbed James. He had expected anger. Heiko von Eisen was angry, though, the saber scar on his cheek livid, while Leni Riefenstahl simply gazed at him in disgust, as though he were some odd, foreign creature. And he had no idea what to do next.

"Well, here we are, then," Schellenberg said. "What do you think we should do now, James?"

"It's . . . it's finished. Just surrender and be done with it."

"Surrender?" Schellenberg leaned closer, and there was something frightening in his placid demeanor as he answered in a soft voice. "James, I am SS-Brigadeführer Walter Schellenberg of the Third Reich. The Führer personally gave me my commission. I planned, organized, and carried out this operation to steal the British Crown Jewels." He waved a hand toward the table. "And there they are, in my, in the Third Reich's possession. This success will propel me higher, and you suggest I should just throw my hands in the air and surrender?"

James Gordon, son of William Gordon, and survivor of Dunkirk, looked into SS-Brigadeführer Walter Schellenberg's eyes, saw the simmering rage behind the calm, and knew at that moment he was about to die. But Schellenberg surprised him.

"It upsets me that we are no longer friends, James, because I trusted you and thought we agreed on our task. But, after all is said and done, a man's fate is a man's fate, and that being so, I suggest you leave us to go find your own," Schellenberg said and gestured to the front door.

For what seemed an eternity, James could not move, and the word *leave* echoed in his mind. *Leave. Leave. Leave, now.* He nodded in relief that he was not about to die and said, "Thank you, Walter."

Schellenberg put out his hand, and James gratefully shook it before walking away. He had taken three steps toward the front door when Schellenberg whispered one word: *Gleiwitz.*

"Gleiwitz," von Eisen repeated with relish. He remembered Gleiwitz. In 1939, Schellenberg had helped create a plan to initiate the Nazi invasion of Poland by staging an attack on a German border radio station in Gleiwitz. Prisoners from the Dachau concentration camp were dressed in Polish military uniforms, killed, and left as "proof" of Polish aggression. They were shot in the head. By von Eisen. His Luger swung up as he stretched out his arm, aimed, and fired twice into the back of James's head.

In the shadows at the top of the stairs, Caitrin and Hector witnessed the execution. Caitrin's hand clamped onto Hector's wrist and forced the Browning pistol down. "No, Hector," she hissed. "Not yet. We're still outnumbered."

They saw Schellenberg and Leni Riefenstahl hurrying to their rooms, while two men dragged James's body outside. Von Eisen barked orders and moved the oil lamp onto a high shelf in the hallway to cast a broader light for his men to work.

"Now all we have to do is stop them from leaving with the loot until the cavalry arrives," Caitrin said. And to Hector, as he watched the soldiers enter the conservatory to pack up the Jewels, she made it sound like the simplest task in the world. But he knew it would not be. As she pointed out, they were greatly outnumbered in a confined battle place, the Germans were not stupid, and Caitrin was right. If they managed to escape, which was not guaranteed, and ran to the village for help, Schellenberg, his men, and the Crown Jewels would be long gone before such help ever arrived. They had no choice but to put her plan into action, even if he had doubts it would be successful. But although he did not want to admit it, her plan, ambitious though it might be, was much better than anything he could conjure up.

44

Hector crept up to the top floor and slipped silently down a corridor to a window at the back of the house. From there he could look down at several of von Eisen's men searching the garden. He waited a few minutes, hoped that would be long enough, and opened fire. Caitrin had told him the windows were painted shut, so he fired three rapid shots through the glass and stepped back. The men below would have no idea where the shots came from, just that they were under fire. He resisted the temptation to look and waited another minute, silently counting off the seconds.

Downstairs, Caitrin watched the soldiers who were packing the Jewels run out as they heard the three shots. She broke cover, crossed the entrance hallway to the conservatory, snatched a crown, and ducked under the table, where she would be hidden by the damask covers. She waited for the next volley.

Hector leaned forward. The men were hiding, and none of them had seen him. He fired another quick volley. That would keep them in place longer.

When Caitrin left Castlebay, which seemed a lifetime ago, her brother Dafydd had stuffed things into her knapsack. The haggis she had long since eaten, the parachute cord had tripped and tied up several bad men, and all that remained were the four elastic bands. She could hear her brother's voice: *You'll be surprised how handy elastic bands and parachute cord can be.*

"We're about to find out, my dear brother Dafydd," she whispered, took the elastic bands out of her pocket, and linked them together. Removing the large diamond from the front of the crown was not easy, but she finally managed and crept toward the end of the table, where there was a gap in the covers. Two soldiers entered, grumbling about something, and stood with their backs to the conservatory. She watched their boots to make sure they were turned away from her.

Caitrin stretched her right thumb and index finger wide and looped the elastic band over them to make a catapult, nestled the diamond in the center, pulled back, closed one eye to aim, and fired. The diamond shot out from under the table, flew across the room, and shattered the lamp. Oil poured down the wall and across the floor. In moments the hallway was ablaze.

Up on the top floor, Hector fired another volley.

Heiko von Eisen appeared in the hallway, waving his arms and shouting, "Close the doors! Keep the fire away from the Jewels!"

They shut the conservatory doors. Hidden from sight, Caitrin came out from under the table, listening to the panic outside as they attempted to quell the fire. She picked up two of the swords, pried open a window with the tip of one, and dropped to the ground. She and Hector had created confusion; now it was time to prevent the Germans from leaving. To keep them pinned down a little longer, she needed just one final—

Hector fired the last volley.

In front of the house, cases were scattered around the tail of the lorry, dropped there when the soldiers reacted to the shots and went searching for her and Hector. She slipped around to the front of the lorry and swung a sword at a tire. Air hissed as it collapsed. She moved to the radiator. The metal was hard to puncture, and she had to stab repeatedly until it was pierced. The last thrust jammed the sword fast in the metal, and she left it there. The lorry would be useless.

Crack! A shot hummed over her head and another ricocheted off the lorry as she ducked and rolled for cover. The Citroën raced past with Schellenberg driving, a grim-faced Leni Riefenstahl next to him and her terrified cameraman cowering in the rear.

"Open the gates!" Schellenberg roared at a guard. The guard pulled them open and ran for cover as the Citroën sped through and was gone. In the distance rose the sound of emergency sirens.

"Stop, stop! Wait for me!" Von Eisen ran out the front door as the Citroën cleared the gates. Angry at being abandoned, he fired his pistol after them until it was empty.

Caitrin stepped out of the shadows behind him, the sword in her hand glinting in the moonlight as she called out, "Von Eisen."

Von Eisen spun on his heel to face her and did not move, did not blink. He seemed dazed, unaware of what was happening. Caitrin took a step toward him, and it broke the spell. He threw his empty Luger at her and ran for the open gate, but not downhill toward the village. Instead, he ran uphill, toward the castle.

Caitrin ran after him.

45

As Caitrin ran uphill through the moonlight, the world became reduced, elemental: impenetrable black shadows, cold blue surfaces, and bright shards of silver. Her mind registered that she was running up a steep hill. It noted that the road was narrow and undulating; that it rose and plunged through woods and manicured gardens; that it veered sharply left and then right, but always continued uphill. Her mind was aware of all this, and so was her body, but it did not care. The sword was heavy in her hand, but it meant nothing; the steep gradient was punishing on lungs and muscles, but that did not matter. Caitrin Colline's body was indifferent to pain or fatigue or time, and it would run to the ends of the earth to avenge the death of James Gordon.

Heiko von Eisen, a frightened animal, sprinted for his life, but no matter how hard he ran, the woman with the glittering sword was behind him. The castle loomed above. He raced up the steepest part of the road that curved around to the main doors, twin monoliths of carved oak. They were locked. He stumbled to another, smaller door. It too was locked, and he could hear the woman getting closer. Frantic, he kicked hard at a window, felt the glass crack, and threw his whole weight against it. The frame collapsed, the glass shattered, and he was inside, stumbling down a dark corridor. Behind him he heard the crunch of glass underfoot as Caitrin followed.

Von Eisen pushed open a door into a black void. Moonlit windows revealed a few edges and gave him some reference. It was a large room with a long table in the center. He put out a hand to touch a wall and felt his way into the room. A suit of armor toppled with a metallic crash as he tripped over it and fell to the floor.

Lights flared on, dazzling him, and he turned to face Caitrin standing at a panel of light switches. They were in a great hall, wood-paneled, with grand arrays of armor, and above them hung ranks of regimental banners. On a wall close to him was a circular display of swords. A plaque beneath the sword display stated they were sabers from the Second Cavalry of the King's Lancers. *Sabers.* A saber would change everything. He got to his feet, tugged a saber from the wall, and faced her, this little woman with her ridiculous, jeweled ceremonial sword. Now he was armed, Untersturmführer Heiko von Eisen was no longer afraid.

He straightened, ran a finger down the saber blade, tapped his chest, and hissed, "*Deutsche Experte.*"

Caitrin cocked her head to one side, placed a finger on the tip of her nose, tapped it, and said, "British Woman."

She was quite calm because she would not be fighting this man; her certainty would. Caitrin knew in every fiber of her body that Heiko von Eisen would not defeat her, no matter what. Her training and the principle of certainty would carry her through.

Heiko moved toward her, the saber ready, searching for flesh to cut. He swung, and the blade shuddered against her sword. He feinted, swung backhanded, and felt the tip gouge into her left shoulder. In response, she made the tiniest of sounds and moved away. He circled her; this would be easy. He had never killed a woman before but would gladly slaughter this one. First, though, would come pain and punishment. He attacked.

Caitrin stepped back, shifted to her left, and saw a tall door. She jerked it open, and a cold night air swept in as she stepped outside. There was a half-glimpse of a tower hard to one side, a low crenellated wall on the other, and beyond that nothing. In the great hall, von Eisen, with his dueling experience, could easily defeat her by attacking from various angles, but on this narrow, cramped battlement, with the courtyard below to their left and a dark abyss to the right, the fight would be more restricted. He came after her.

He struck—left, right, high, low—and each time she parried the blow, blade against blade. Another feint, and this time the edge of the saber cut into her upper arm. She winced. She was getting tired, and he had her. *Time to kill.*

Caitrin parried his next cut, wrapped her fingers around the saber blade, and held it tight. Surprised, von Eisen tried to pull it free. He felt the blade move, saw pain flood her features as the edge bit into her hand, tugging at her flesh, and knew he had won. Until she swung the saber aside, lunged forward, and drove the pommel of her sword into his face. Von Eisen staggered back in pain, eyes tear-blinded, and dropped the saber.

Caitrin held her sword with both hands, raised it level with her shoulders, rotated, and swung with all her might. The blade howled through the air, the edge eager to cleave flesh and gouge bone, until at the last moment she twisted her wrists. The flat of the blade hammered against von Eisen's cheek, he shrieked in agony, stumbled back, caught his foot, and fell spinning over the edge into the abyss.

*   *   *

Emergency vehicles blocked the road, and outside the house surrendered German soldiers lay in a row, face-down, arms bound behind their backs, with a Portuguese soldier standing guard over them. Hector was talking to some military officers, but all activity ceased as Caitrin walked through the gates. Her left sleeve was blood-drenched and the sword heavy in her hand, the tip scraping a furrow through the gravel.

Hector went to her, saw the deep cut in her hand, and wrapped a handkerchief around it. He tried to make her sit down, but she refused and walked past him into the house. The fire had been extinguished, and several men were packing away the remaining Jewels. They stopped as she dropped the sword on the table and said, "Pack this away too. There's another one stuck in that lorry's radiator out there."

She sank to one knee, hand reaching down, fingers splayed on the burnt carpet to steady herself, and rose unsteadily to her feet as Hector caught up with her. "That's a lot of blood you've lost. You need medical attention right away, Caitrin."

She ignored him and stared at the men. "Who are they?"

"The Policia de Vigilância e do Defesa Estado, Salazar's security men. He doesn't want an international incident, which means getting us and the Jewels out of here fast."

"That's fine by me. It will be good to go home," she said.

"What, um, what happened—"

"To von Eisen?" she said.

"Yes, von Eisen." Hector looked into her eyes and saw something he knew he would never have. Behind the pain and fatigue, he saw a profound confidence.

"He stumbled," she said with a weary smile as the blood drained from her face, "and fell from grace."

He caught her as she fainted.

46

In safer and warmer times, an invitation to spend the weekend at Chequers Court, the prime minister's country retreat, was to be much coveted. Forty miles northwest of London, the sixteenth-century Elizabethan red-brick manor house sat in a hollow on extensive grounds. Guests could walk or ride across endless pasture and wander ancient woodlands or immaculate walled gardens. There was also a croquet lawn on which, guests were warned, Churchill's wife, Clementine, was a cold-blooded assassin.

Lady Mary Grey, sister of the tragic Lady Jane Grey, had once been confined to Chequers by Queen Elizabeth. Portraits show Lady Mary was a tiny, unattractive, crook-backed woman, while her secret husband, Elizabeth's serjeant porter, Thomas Keyes, was a mountain of a man at six feet eight inches tall. He was also of minor Kentish gentry and over twice Mary's age. Ignoring the unspeakable horror of such an age-warped and morganatic relationship, the physical disparity alone so appalled Elizabeth she banished Mary from court to permanent immuration at Chequers. Mary and Thomas never saw each other again. As a repository of so much of England's history, her bedroom was kept exactly as it was when she left it in 1567.

But these were not safer or warmer times, and invitations to visit were viewed with some understandable alarm because Chequers was a security nightmare. After passing through immense wrought-iron gates and between twin brick lodges, the visitors would drive along Victory Way, an arrow-straight road that led directly to the south side of the house. An RAF aerial reconnaissance photograph showed how detrimental that road was to security. On a landscape of open fields, it was a glaring direction marker for a Luftwaffe bomber, which had only to follow Victory Way to the end, drop its bombs, and leave. And if no bomber deigned to attack, with such vast grounds it was agreed that scores of bloodthirsty German paratroopers would have no difficulty descending unnoticed to earth, to then slaughter all the occupants in their beds before they could wake.

Added to all that was the near-impossibility of adequately patrolling the estate, although recently a detachment of the Coldstream Guards had set up camp in a wood behind the house. Churchill understood all of this but was not to be deterred from using it as refuge from the pressures of London. And this weekend was to be a very special one, which no zealous Luftwaffe bomber or murderous paratrooper would dare spoil.

The tall leaded-glass windows of the Great Hall were covered with blackout curtains, but the light oak paneling and oil paintings of ancestors past glowed with candlelight. A fire burned in the marble fireplace, and the invited guests sat at a table in the center of an immense red Turkish carpet.

They were all dressed for the occasion, and Churchill had even put on his pinstripe siren suit. Hector sat to his right,

Caitrin to his left. Farther down the table SOE Brigadier Alasdair Gryffe-Reynolds, splendidly filling his uniform, sat across from Bethany Goodman, with Clementine Churchill's gracious presence anchoring the far end.

Caitrin glanced at Clementine and wondered what kind of woman would be married to Winston Churchill. What it took to stay married to him.

"I'm told most of our food came from local Victory gardens, so we're not transgressing rationing laws, much." Churchill's eyes twinkled as he gestured to a bowl of fruit in the center of the table. "Lloyd George kindly sent us apples from the orchard on his Surrey estate. No doubt the fair hand of Frances picked them."

There were muffled laughs and giggles in response. Lloyd George's thirty-year-long relationship with his mistress, Frances Stevenson, was an open secret in Westminster.

"Tell me, Miss Colline. You are fully recovered from your combat?"

"Yes, Sir," Caitrin said and flexed her bandaged left hand. "A little sore is all, and the right hand is just about healed."

"But we did get the Jewels back," Hector said.

"More or less," Churchill said. "The Sword of Spiritual Justice is bent from being thrust into a lorry's radiator and the Sword of Temporal Justice is somewhat serrated from Caitrin's fight with Heiko von Eisen."

"But the hilt and all the jewels are intact," Caitrin said. "Just replace the blade."

"They were made by Andrea and Giandonato Ferrara—in Italy."

"Oh, yes, Axis Powers, Mussolini. Pity, that. The Italians won't last long, though, and then the Ferrara boys can get to work again."

"In 1580."

Caitrin thought for a moment. "A good bashing with a hammer won't straighten them out?"

Churchill winced at the thought. "No."

"Then it's time to replace them with good English Sheffield steel."

Churchill laughed. "There is a larger deficit. The Crown of Queen Elizabeth, which is incidentally the only crown made of platinum, lost its, dare I say, its crowning glory. The Koh-i-nūr Diamond."

"Forgot." Caitrin shot upright, snapped her fingers, and said, "Got it!" She dug into her pocket, retrieved the diamond, balanced it on her thumbnail, and flicked it in a high parabola toward him. To his credit, Churchill caught it in midair as she said, "I used it to start a fire and create a diversion."

"Which worked rather well," Hector said.

Caitrin leaned toward Churchill, and with an impish grin said, "I will confess to larcenous ideas. I thought of selling it and using the proceeds to buy every home in Abertillery their own swimming pool. Although I'm sure they'd be just as happy with running hot water and an indoor lavatory."

"Miss Colline, I have only just gotten used to the New Woman, and now it seems there is the New New Woman to contend with."

Caitrin nodded in happy agreement. "We're on our way."

"Overall, I thought our plan worked quite well," Gryffe-Reynolds said.

"Our?" Bethany Goodman said. "Our? Unless my memory fails me, when we first met, you insisted you knew nothing about the planned operation."

Gryffe-Reynolds colored. Churchill saved him. "The error is all mine, Miss Goodman. When we began, I mistakenly thought that Miss Colline would not be up to the complex demands the operation might put on her."

"Why? Because she is a woman?"

"I was completely, utterly wrong, and I beg your, and Miss Colline's, forgiveness. Both of you and your 512 organization deserve our gratitude. You may count on us to turn to you for help in the difficult years to come. And you did deflect us a bit by saying Miss Colline was only a police constable."

"Not entirely. If my women are not in training or involved in an operation, I encourage them to return to their previous occupation. It keeps them in touch with the real world and authenticates their background story if ever they are caught."

"What exactly was the plan?" Caitrin asked.

"To get the Crown Jewels to Canada, and for you and Hector, working as a partnership, to thwart *Die Brücke*'s attempt if they tried to steal them, of course," Churchill said.

"In that we failed, because the *partnership* did not exist," Bethany said. "We saved the Crown Jewels, but *Die Brücke* is still alive."

"How did *Die Brücke* know we were carrying the Jewels in the first place?" Caitrin asked. "Someone must have told them. Someone with access to secret government information."

"That we do not yet know," Churchill said. "But we will search them out."

Clementine interrupted to change the subject. "Now we have the Jewels back, what is going to happen to them?"

"They are going to be well hidden, I assure you," Churchill said.

"In England?" Hector asked.

"Yes."

"But wasn't the whole idea of the operation that they should go overseas so if we were invaded, the SS or Gestapo could not torture people to learn their location?"

"Agreed. The Jewels will be hidden somewhere in England, and we will send the men who hid them, on separate ships, to Canada."

"Ingenious," Hector said.

"My idea," Churchill answered.

"What happened to Walter Schellenberg and Leni Riefenstahl after they escaped?" Bethany asked.

"They hared away from Sintra to the German embassy in Lisbon. He is back to being a scourge throughout Europe, while I hear Riefenstahl was given millions of deutsche marks by Hitler to make a grand film about a German opera. No doubt some overblown Aryan fantasy. On to better things." Churchill picked up his champagne glass. "It's not Pol Roger, I'm afraid, but a Pommery et Greno '26 and a fine vintage, though. I propose a toast to Lord Marlton, Hector Neville-Percy."

They all raised their glasses in salute. "Lord Marlton, Hector Neville-Percy."

"And our Welsh sword master," Churchill caught Caitrin's admonishing eye. "I mean sword mistress, Caitrin Colline."

Again, they toasted. "Caitrin Colline."

Caitrin raised her glass. "And I propose a toast in honor of Captain James Gordon." She quieted the room.

"But he betrayed the country," Gryffe-Reynolds said. "Lord Marlton's report—"

"Is wrong," she said. "Lord Marlton was under great strain and was mistaken in the identity of the men who stole the Jewels."

"But he says quite clearly that Captain Murray—"

"The actual Captain Murray was Heiko von Eisen, who happened to look remarkably like James Gordon," Caitrin said, gazing directly at Hector, daring him to dispute her flagrant lie; the two men did not look at all alike. He was wise and did not contradict her.

"Lord Marlton reported he believed James Gordon was overwhelmed by the deaths in Dunkirk, captured, and in such a weakened mental condition his good friend Walter Schellenberg was able to persuade him to help them steal the Jewels," Gryffe-Reynolds continued doggedly on. "Although terribly misguided, I accept that at the time he believed he was doing the right thing."

"That is absolute nonsense," Caitrin said and rose to her feet.

"In France, Captain James Gordon, with his men, fought a desperate and glorious rearguard action against overwhelming odds so that other British soldiers might escape from Dunkirk. The action cost him his life, and I believe he should be remembered. His body has been recovered and deserves a military funeral at his family's cemetery at Mauchline Hall. If I may be allowed, I would be honored to attend."

She sat to a silent room.

"Lord Marlton?" Churchill said.

"Caitrin is right," Hector said, as his mind raced for a plausible explanation. "I hadn't seen James for a few years and likely mistook von Eisen for him. That was my error. My apologies."

"No apology needed. Then I suggest tearing up the report and writing a new one," Churchill said. "What say you, Brigadier?"

"Yes, Sir. Splendid idea," Gryffe-Reynolds diplomatically replied.

"Sir, I have a request to make," Caitrin said.

"No independence for Wales, young lady."

"That will come in good time," she said. "It is about Barbara MacNeil in Castlebay."

"The Scottish pigeon-post lady."

"Yes. She is a widow and has one son, Duncan. He is all she has."

"A fisherman, I should imagine?"

"Yes."

"We need a fisherman more than another soldier. It's an essential occupation, and so a fisherman he will stay throughout the war."

"Thank you, Sir."

"Bodyguard Thompson is assured we will win solely because of my official title versus Mr. Hitler's," Churchill said with a mischievous smile. "He says the Germans concentrate their effort on the wrong things. In England the leader of the country is known, insults and profanities aside, simply as the prime minister, or PM if you like. But in Germany, Mr. Hitler is referred to as *Der Führer und Oberste Befehlshaber der Wehrmacht des Grossdeutschen Reichs.*"

"I won't be sending him a postcard," Caitrin said.

Churchill got to his feet, champagne glass in hand. "I have one more toast. Every day that passes brings us closer to winter, which makes a German invasion harder and more unlikely. A toast to winter."

"To winter," they all raised their glasses and toasted.

"A wicked one!"

"A wicked one!"

47

Caitrin wrapped her overcoat tighter and wished she had brought gloves. The early morning air was damp and cold, her breath became vapor, and frost had diminished the landscape's colors. A weak sun barely lightened the southern face of Chequers behind her.

"Good morning. You are up early." Hector's voice caused her to turn as he approached.

"You are too, m'lud Hecky."

"It's a chilly breeze."

"It is that."

"In the north, we call it a lazy wind because it can't be bothered to go around so it goes right through you."

"Right enough. I needed to stretch my legs and get some fresh air. Plenty of that to go around out here."

"Are you going to look at the garden?" Hector said and pointed to the walled enclosure in front of them.

"No, I have never liked obedient plants," she said and gestured at a rise some distance away to their right. "I'm going up there. Mrs. Churchill said there's a grand view from Beacon Hill."

"Mind company?"

"Who?" she said, straight-faced, then laughed. "Of course not, come on. Think you can make it?"

They left a dark trail behind as they crunched through the frosted grass.

"I wanted to tell you that what you did at dinner last night was impressive," Hector said.

"The way I covered my grievous etiquette error of using the rice knife instead of the soup fork by twirling the pickle prod?"

"By standing up for James. I should have done that too; he was my friend. I'm afraid I let him and the side down badly."

"There are no sides in this, Hector, just survivors, and you did as you were trained and ordered. But I remember his father when he spoke about James and the pain when he mentioned his wife being in a sanitarium because of her son's absence."

"You saw things I didn't."

"No. We all see things differently. We each have our own kind of seeing. James's death will not come as a surprise, and I'm sure William half-expects it by now, but being told he was a traitor would ruin him. And that doesn't need to happen. The least we can do is let him keep his pride in his son. There will be so many empty houses and lives by the time this war is over."

"I have asked to go up there and tell them what happened in person."

"William will appreciate that. Perhaps I might come too."

"His father would like that."

They reached the top of Beacon Hill, where the sun offered the slightest warmth. Mist tendrils were withdrawing from the fields below.

"I am curious about something. How did you end up with the Koh-i-nūr?"

"I used the diamond to start the fire," she said, imitating

drawing a catapult, "and saw it on the carpet when I came back to the house. I dropped to one knee and picked it up."

"Remarkable. I never noticed." Hector shielded his eyes against the hazy light. "It was not an easy operation, and it didn't turn out at all the way I imagined, but we did do a good job, eventually."

"Did we?"

"Yes. The Crown Jewels are safe."

"And what about *Die Brücke*? Viscount Rothermere will still have his estate and his newspaper empire. The duke of Buccleuch gets to hide away in his two hundred and forty thousand acres of land, and nothing will happen to him, or to the duke of Wellington. The establishment will close ranks around them and all the other Nazi sympathizers. They are the true traitors, not misguided men like James Gordon."

"Caitrin, even if you stripped the land away from them and distributed it to the people, in a few generations they would get it all back."

"Not all of it, and not necessarily back to them, and just the redistribution would be beneficial. More than that, it is the breakup of power that matters most. A fresh start. There will always be men who want everything." She put her arm through his. "Damn, they even want all the names! Do you know there are towns in England and Wales with inhabitants who are nameless? They walk around, trying to get to know each other, but it's impossible because the aristocracy has taken them all. Ponder that, Lord Marlton, Hector Bobby Neville-Percy."

He laughed and said, "Caitrin, you are truly an original."

"My dad always said that to me, sometimes with a frown. Power has always resided in the country estates, and for centuries Parliament was just a rubber stamp for a king and his cronies to raise taxes on the people. Not anymore, Hector. The people deserve better now, times are changing, and I'm going to push the clock hands to make it move a bit faster."

"I surrender. Consider me defeated aristocracy." Hector raised his hands. He took a half-step back, turned to face her, and brought a small box from his pocket. He opened it, took out the wedding rings they had used on the journey, and held them up to the light. "It didn't last long, but I enjoyed being married to you. Perhaps enjoyed is not quite the word I'm searching for, but I thought — "

"No."

"No? You don't know what I was going to — "

"No."

"Yes, you do know what I was about to say."

"Hector, one day soon you will find a lovely woman, make a fine husband and a wonderful father to keep the Neville-Percy line going, which will delight your mum no end. But it won't be me."

"Oh."

"I would like an invitation to the wedding, though. I promise to be on my best behavior, speak only English, and you know I can be trusted to use the right knife and fork."

He nodded, disappointed.

"I'll be seeing your mum as soon as the war's over anyway. I told her I would go visit, and I'll be taking my mum up to meet her. She's never been out of the valley, and we will go on a grand mum odyssey. First, to see yours, then to visit Barbara MacNeil in Castlebay, and finally back to Glen Coe to say hello to Big Maggie. And while I'm there, I intend to ask her where I can get a dog of my own like Fiona."

"That sounds like a pleasant journey."

"It does, doesn't it? And I am looking forward to it." Caitrin half-turned away, closed her eyes, and tilted her face toward the light. "But there is just one important thing I need to know before I set off."

"And that is?"

"Why you and Winston Churchill are such stone-cold liars."

48

Caitrin was motionless, face raised to the light. Gazing at her, Hector was at a loss for words. She turned toward him, opened her eyes, and again he was struck by her simple beauty. Her serene expression and steady blue eyes unnerved him, and always would.

"I beg your pardon?"

"Hector, you're not a beagle, so don't beg. Let's start with the grand teller of whoppers, Winnie-the-Prime-Fibber. I took the so-called Koh-i-Nūr Diamond to a jeweler for an appraisal. He said it was a very good copy and offered me a fiver. Said he'd make it an even tenner if I had dinner with him. I told her I wasn't hungry, but my husband was famished and I'd send him down. Surprise, huh? I mean the jewel, not the hungry hubby."

He nodded. It seemed the safest thing to do.

"If I were a betting woman, I'd wager the Fifteenth Farquharson of Invercauld's one hundred and thirty thousand acres that months ago Winston took a huge gamble and sent the authentic Crown Jewels across the Atlantic along with the gold. I'd bet this very moment they are nestled securely in a Montreal bank vault."

A cloud bank drifted across the sun, the air grew colder, and they both shivered.

"Now, fibber number two—you. When we were staying at your mum's place, you rushed in early one morning and said the submarine *Talisman* had already arrived in Greenock and was leaving early. Before I came here, I had my nautical chums at 512 check that out. Seems it docked and departed on schedule. First big fib."

Hector shuffled his feet, stared out at the horizon, and said, "Plans suddenly changed."

"Not true. You were trying to keep me in the dark, and to my shame I helped. Next big fib. We arrived in Greenock, and you went to a telephone, supposedly for instructions on how to get to the ship. You returned, having written them down. To the dismay of some, and that's about to include you, one of my talents is an exceedingly good memory. Reading what was supposedly written in the notebook, you said: 'Go through green gate entrance and travel uphill. It gets steep, and about three hundred yards in and on the left is Highland Mary's grave. It is a tall monument surrounded by a low black fence.'"

Hector looked stricken.

"I found the notebook in your jacket—every page a blank one." She spread her hands and pretended to look surprised. "Fibbers, both of you. The prosecution rests, m'lud."

Hector straightened and squared his shoulders. "You must learn to separate your class enemies from the political and national ones. Much of the aristocracy is brain-addled or married off to some wealthy American heiress because they're broke. They will rage about Jews, Freemasons, and socialists because they're frightened by the future steaming at them. And so they should be. But that's all most of them will ever do. However, we believe there are other men buried deep inside the country who are far more dangerous." He stamped his feet. "It's cold."

"And this is no time for you to get cold feet."

"We were trying to find a way to expose the whole *Die Brücke* network, and someone in my organization suggested dangling the Crown Jewels as bait to bring them to the surface. Naturally we would use copies."

"Naturally."

"Then I got a message from James. His unit was slaughtered outside Cherbourg, and only he survived. He was a mental ruin when the Germans captured him, and they were not kind. Our old skiing schoolfriend Walter Schellenberg came to the rescue and convinced him an armistice would save England. Because he was so beaten, it was a simple step to implant the idea that there would be no more wasted lives and no harm would befall anyone if they used the Crown Jewels as a bargaining chip. And after it was done, Schellenberg promised to send him home. Poor James."

"Yes, poor James. It must have been a terrible time. Why didn't you include me in the plans?"

"You were in the room when I told Churchill I was trained to work alone, but he insisted on his silly married couple idea. Later he told me he thought you would be a distracting presence for the Germans. Which you were, but certainly not the way he imagined."

Caitrin allowed herself a smile.

"To be honest, I still didn't want you, but I consoled myself with the thought that at least you were pleasant to look at."

"Thank you."

"And, as I soon discovered, quite amusing."

"Thank you."

"And so damn bright."

"Thank you. You left out the crack-shot bit."

"And a crack shot."

"Oh, you remembered."

"But just as I was working out how to get you involved, you took a massive swan dive off the back of the lorry and vanished into the wilds of Glen Coe."

"You waited too long."

"For which I will always be truly sorry."

"Me too. It's not finished yet, though, is it, Hector? *Die Brücke* still exists, and this war, like the last one, will not be over by Christmas, or the next one, or even the one after that. There's a lot of work to do, and perhaps in future we should find a way to ferret them out together."

"Yes, I'd like that, unless you're going back to being a flat-footed lady copper."

"And assuming your wonky ticker doesn't fail. Does this mean I'm still invited to your wedding?"

"Yes." Hector paused and improvised being horrified. "But, Caitrin, what if the woman I marry is as smart as you?"

"You should be so lucky," Caitrin said and laughed. "Hector, m'lud, let me explain something to you about women."

49

It was a dark room, save for a thin light that seeped in through a break in the blackout drapes, and Winston, wearing his favorite dressing gown decorated with golden dragons, sat facing the window, alone. Almost. At his side was the black dog of depression. It went away for long periods of time but always came back. Depression. An upset stomach, perhaps a touch of food poisoning, meant Winston had eaten little that day, and neither had he drunk anything, certainly not his usual brandies and champagne.

The endless year was not over. It still had almost two long months to run, and it had been a grievous one: the thin miracle of Dunkirk, the shambles of Norway, the Battle of Britain only now tapering off, and the constant Blitz, which was increasing daily. Émon de Valera, Irish Taoiseach, had refused Britain the use of Eire's ports and airfields, which, considering Irish/British history, was no great surprise. The convoys bringing essential supplies to Britain would have been greatly helped by the military use of those facilities, but they were instead being decimated by German U-boats. The Happy Time, the U-boat commanders called it, when they had a choice of easy targets.

A presence appeared. His father, Lord Randolph, who thought Winston was a simpleton as a child and made it clear he never cared for him. In Randolph's eyes, his son would never amount to anything, perhaps at best be a junior subaltern in a minor cavalry regiment. Winston would go to his grave knowing his father disliked him.

A sound from outside erased his father; waves of Luftwaffe bombers heading for London. The bombers came nearly every night. The inevitable wail of the air-raid sirens, the Wibble Wobbles, were next, and scattered shouts from the street below. Soon fire-engine and ambulance bells would chime into the chorus. In retaliation, the RAF had bombed Hamburg and Berlin. They were at best token strikes but still a warning to Germany and vital for British morale.

The anti-aircraft guns opened fire in a wave of harsh barking. An Air Ministry report stated they were egregiously ineffective; at best, only one shell in five thousand struck an enemy aircraft. Winston did not care if they fired blanks or dead chickens, because their noise and presence were so essential to keeping up civilian morale.

A different appearance replaced his father: his mother—Jennie Jerome Churchill, the girl from Brooklyn, the "exotic" American woman who was one-quarter Iroquois and had a tattoo of a snake around her left wrist. Winston could not see her face, just her presence, and he saw little of that when she was alive—only when he was brought downstairs during the daily children's hour. He was a child, not much more than a baby, when they sent him away to boarding school, to be seen only at Christmas and Easter. He would remember only that Mummy was never near and always moving away from him. Her sparkling gray eyes were the last things to disappear.

The drone of Luftwaffe aircraft engines grew louder, and the first bomb explosions rattled the window panes. The building trembled at a near miss.

By now, Londoners would be hurrying into bomb shelters, some of which were tragically ineffective, while others, like the deepest tunnels of the London Tube, were much safer. But not healthier. His wife, Clementine, had visited some of the tunnels and returned appalled at the conditions.

His mother had gone. She fell downstairs at a friend's country house and broke her ankle. She seemed to be recovering, but gangrene set in, and the foot was amputated. His vivacious, wonderful mother bore the pain without complaint, until a sudden hemorrhage struck her. Wearing only his dressing gown, Winston ran through the streets to be at her side but was too late. He thought the agony of the loss would kill him.

And now there was Marigold smiling at him, his precious daughter Marigold. She had left him twenty years ago. Their fourth child, third daughter, she was born a few days after the last war ended. Winston had thought her given to him as a bright promise for the future after the horrors of the war. He adored Marigold, and he was the father to her his father had never been to him. He sang to her. Marigold loved "I'm Forever Blowing Bubbles," and they would sing it together, as best as she could remember the words, her chubby arms stretching up, fingers wriggling to make bubbles. She was almost three when she died, less than a month after his mother's death. Winston had wanted to be someone hot-blooded who would rend their garments, tear at their hair, and shriek and moan at a child's death. But he was English and could not. The grief lay inside him, sometimes deep and hidden but never forgotten, and he and Clemmie could hardly ever speak of their daughter again.

Clemmie had told him the people were living in squalor down in the Tube. Bunks were jammed in three high, were too short, with hardly space to breathe, and it was cold, wet, and dark. Sanitation facilities were nonexistent, and the tunnels stank. Children were getting lice, and lice would bring typhus. And they were scared of what might befall them.

The bombers were overhead now, a monotonous vibrating drone that rattled the mind, and explosions were becoming more frequent and louder. An orange glow cut through the blackout gap as incendiaries ignited. From the rooftop at night the scattered incendiaries, burning like so many large glow-worms, were eerily pretty. Even now, there were men in government who urged negotiation with Hitler. *At least*, they pleaded, *give it some serious thought. Let us have no more deaths.* As if negotiation with evil was ever successful.

Marigold was gone, fading away in memory like his father and mother. Now only the black dog remained. The dog would always return when the weight of his existence got too heavy to bear. When it seemed better to surrender than to fight the overwhelming loneliness.

As a defense, Winston sang to himself, in a low hesitant whisper at first, hardly recognizable as a tune, but gradually growing stronger. And as he sang, he wept for the men, women, and children who would die tonight, some horribly, painfully; for the young men, just boys really, who daily climbed into their aircraft to face the Luftwaffe armada; and for the sailors who died cold, lonely deaths in the Western Approaches so the U-boats could celebrate their Happy Time. And for the intimacy he had not gotten and now would never get from his parents, and most of all, for the loss of his beloved Marigold.

I'm forever blowing bubbles,
Pretty bubbles in the air,
They fly so high,
Nearly reach the sky.
Then like my dreams,
They fade and die.

> *Fortune's always hiding,*
> *I've looked everywhere,*
> *I'm forever blowing bubbles,*
> *Pretty bubbles in the air.*

Winston Spencer Churchill, Prime Minister of the United Kingdom and the British Empire, also wept for himself. "Oh, my poor little Marigold."

Notes

Winston Churchill, his wife Clementine, and the bodyguard Walter Thompson were real characters, as were Leni Riefenstahl and SS-Brigadeführer Walter Schellenberg. All other characters are fictitious. The Crown Jewels were not sent to Canada. Instead, the precious stones were removed from their settings and buried in a biscuit (cookie) tin sixty feet under Windsor Castle.

Caitrin Colline is based on the strong women in my life, especially my mother, who was the middle child in a family of fourteen raised in a tough Welsh coal-mining town.

I grew up in Wales; lived for some time in Scotland, Germany, and Portugal; and, as a motion-picture director of photography, traveled extensively throughout the world. The locations are real, although I changed the names of the country estates.

I enjoy writing about women, because inevitably, behind every great man is a greater woman.